And the
House Lights
Dim

Tim Major

First published by Luna Press Publishing, Edinburgh, 2019

O Cul-de-Sac! (original to this collection)
Read/Write Head. *First published in Garbled Transmissions, 2013.*
Eqalussuaq. *First published in Not One of Us #58, 2017. Selected by Ellen Datlow for The Best Horror of the Year Volume Ten, 2018.*
Finding Waltzer-Three. *First published in Interzone #255, 2014.*
St Erth. *First published in Into the Woods, Hic Dragones, 2017.*
Tunnel Vision. *First published in Kitchen Sink Gothic, Parallel Universe Publications, 2015.*
The Eyes Have It. *First published in The Third Spectral Book of Horror Stories, Spectral Press, 2016.*
The Forge (original to this collection)
All I Can See Are Sad Eyes. *First published in The Literary Hatchet #13, 2015.*
Winter in the Vivarium. *First published in Winter Tales (Fox Spirit), 2016.*
Lines of Fire. *First published in Game Over, Snowbooks, 2015.*
Honey Spurge (original to this collection)
By the Numbers. *First published in Voluted Tales Vol. 14 Issue 10, 2013.*
The House Lights Dim. *First published in Sanitarium Issue 11, 2013.*
Carus & Mitch. *First published as a standalone novella, Omnium Gatherum, 2015.*

www.lunapresspublishing.com
ISBN-13: 978-1-911143-57-4

For my family.

Contents

O Cul-de-Sac!

O neighbours! If only we might speak!

Do you feel as I feel? Do you think as I think? Here we are, all crouching in our circle, so close to one another. It is maddening.

I see your people come and go. I hear snippets of their conversations. They are happy, your people, are they not? It is healthy, all this coming and going. But we remain rooted, facing one another implacably.

We are so young: sixteen this coming year. How many people have we had between us?

Recently I have paid less attention to your people than to mine, I confess. But in those early days, in those first glimmerings of consciousness, I was empty and I watched you all with intense fascination. There seemed so much to learn, and the opportunities for my education so few. Your people hurried to and fro—on what errands I had no way of imagining—and when they returned they appeared so grateful to see you. I came to distinguish between adults—more direct in their routes across our cul-de-sac, bustling into the cars on your driveways—and children, who dallied and bickered, whose movements were a joy to me. The children belonged to the adults and the adults belonged to you. When your people were nestled within you I gazed at the sky and the fields. I tested the radius of my attention, peering as far beyond my walls as possible. I perceived the disturbances of animals in the long grasses and swooping above me, I saw trees bending with the force of an unseen hand, I saw the rust-coloured roofs of the village that is tied to our cul-de-sac by an umbilical lane. I called out to you. I beckoned to your people. I was alone.

I was unoccupied.

My first people came a year later, following a smattering

of visitors who declared me too large or too expensive or characterless. Their names were Anton and Beverly Grieg. They joked about show homes and the plastic fruit that still filled the wooden bowl beside the sink in my kitchen, but they were happy to have arrived and I was happy to receive them. More than happy! I embraced them from the moment they removed their shoes and padded inside me. Perhaps you remember the too-large white lorry with its rear end awkwardly jutting into our cul-de-sac, blocking three of your five driveways. Anton and Beverly Grieg set to filling my rooms with their furniture, their friends, their conversation. How they talked! Beverly was a lecturer at the university in York. Anton had once been her student and was, if anything, more passionate about learning than his wife. They talked of books and Francis Bacon and the governance of Britain and jazz music and the preparation of food and desire. These were the elements of their world, but they taught me about mine, too. They described the stars in the night sky, patterns hitherto unnoticed by me but suddenly, spectacularly, clear. They named the plants that encircle the lawn of my garden; they defined the willow, ash and pine trees. They lifted tiny creatures in their cupped hands so that I might better see them.

It wasn't only their teachings that provided my education. Two radios—one in my sitting room, one tickling and buzzing in my kitchen—were rarely turned off. Anton and Beverly Grieg watched documentary films and news reports. Through them I was given the ability to see far beyond our cul-de-sac and I came to appreciate the enormity of the world.

Anton and Beverly Grieg occupied me for four years, four happy years. When they announced their intention to leave I struggled to hide my disappointment, my window frames creaking with the ache of mourning. However, I allowed myself to dream. I watched your people come and go, the great numbers of them within each one of you. I dreamed of a family of my own.

I was disappointed. Evie Rattle was a solitary figure, content to spend her time alone. That might not have been a disaster, I told myself at the time. Mightn't we become all the closer, she and I, for the lack of other company? But she confided in me no more than in any human. She was absent for long hours each day, returning only in darkness and retiring quickly to bed. Worse still, she rarely watched television or listened to the radio, so my absorption of information was dramatically curtailed. Her work was as a laboratory technician—of what nature I still do not know, though the spines of the books on my shelves spoke of chemicals and pharmaceuticals. For a time, with my youthful lack of context that might allow me to distinguish between real and make-believe, I suspected her a witch.

Evie Rattle stayed with me for only a little over a year, thank goodness. Did you hear me when she left, o neighbours? It was with only the merest trace of guilt that I called out to you, hooting with triumph.

Then there were the many years spent with my most recent occupants, Piotr Brzezicki and Tom Grace. Though you may have thought me unchanged, judging solely from my exterior, inside I became a riot of colour, filled with mismatching furniture, colourful artworks and plastic trophies of their favourite television programmes. How I loved Piotr Brzezicki and Tom Grace! And I know that you loved them too, all of you—how could it be otherwise? Their joy in the pursuits they loved and in having found one another was infectious. Every day I awoke with renewed delight in seeing them happy. And they spent so much of their time with me, both pursuing their careers whilst burrowed inside me; Tom playing recordings of music as he tapped at his computer keyboard, Piotr listening to radio news broadcasts as he illustrated children's books, bent forward over a tilted board. I spent the days lazily shifting my attention from one of my bedroom offices to the other and back again, constantly unearthing new details to be savoured. At night I watched them sleep until I myself slumbered.

And yet your people felt differently, did they not? I noticed it from the start. Your people watched from their windows, the adults ushering the young indoors when my people appeared together at my doorway. For so long I understood nothing about sexuality and the limitations and rules that your people perceived about it, and when I did I wished I did not. I only knew that Piotr Brzezicki and Tom Grace were happy—so happy!—when they were safe together within my embrace.

I was despondent when they began discussing their plans to leave me. When they yanked their trinkets and trophies from my shelves, their banners and posters from my walls, I felt myself sag. I felt myself no longer a youth. I felt myself settle into my foundations and, worse, beginning to show my age. I watched from each window in turn, trying to keep my people in sight as the two lorries backed noisily from the cul-de-sac, followed by the tiny car containing my Piotr Brzezicki and my Tom Grace.

I sat alone for months.

I cried out, but none of you paid me attention, full as you all were with life of your own.

*

It is wrong to be presumptuous. One does not need to be human to understand that wonderful things will never occur to those who expect wonder. I learned this not from the television or the radio or the spines and tiny print of books; I learned this from my experiences with those that I have loved.

I did not presume, and yet they came.

Carly and Marie and Oliver Scaife.

A family.

Marie Scaife is the oldest. Her hair is white at the crown and that white will creep inexorably down, I am certain. There are lines on her face that converge into arrowheads that point to her eyes, which are full of sadness and pride.

Carly Scaife celebrated her twenty-eighth birthday the day the family arrived. Marie—her mother, though Carly has never referred to her as such—set a cake on a plate on a pile of packing cases that first evening, and Carly struggled to blow out candles embedded in it, and it was all I could do to stop myself from flinging open my windows to let in the wind to help her and to demonstrate my delight at having them within me.

Oliver Scaife is an infant.

He is all I have ever wanted.

He is small and incapable of much. He arrived strapped to Carly's chest and wailed. I whistled through my chimney in conversation. He is hairless and rarely opens his eyes. Marie says he is three months old.

Have you seen them, o neighbours? Have you seen them? I would send them to be witnessed by you, if I were not so reluctant to let them out from within me. Send your people instead and they will provide their reports. There has never been anything so wonderful in our cul-de-sac as Oliver Scaife and his mother and her mother.

*

I am watching you. For now I am content to let my people stroke at my insides and murmur at one another. I am hesitant of intruding upon them in these early days.

A change within oneself prompts other ways of seeing the world, does it not?

O neighbours, are your people as happy as I thought? They come and go often, but my ability to scrutinise, from my position here at the mouth of our cul-de-sac, is limited. They squint at the sky as they emerge from you. Their cars and bicycles buzz noisily from your driveways. When they return they hurry in.

Number four, your people have attracted my attention for so long. Five people, including three children! And yet the eldest only scowls as she stares around at our cul-de-sac, her hands upon her hips. The other two squabble and hit each other as they are pushed into their car seats by one or another of your adults. They are all tired.

Number two, are you as alone as I was with Evie Rattle? You have only one person. He wears a black suit and walks briskly out of our cul-de-sac and briskly back in. There are so many long hours in between.

Number five, I know there are people within you; I have seen your lights turn on and off and I have seen black shapes at your windows. But who they are is unknown to me. They do not look out at our cul-de-sac. Do they speak? Is it wonderful having your people with you constantly? Or is it agony?

Number three, I see that you have new people too, a man and a woman. Their overalls are spotted with paint. It must be a delight to receive so much attention. I am certain that your hopes are high of their loving you. Send them to meet my people, won't you? Perhaps, vicariously, we may be friends. From the little I can see of your rear garden, it requires their attention.

Number six, have your people remained with you too long? That infant who was once so adorable is now almost an adult. His parents are wrong to leave him alone with you for such long periods. He has the face of somebody one should not trust.

*

Carly Scaife is learning, just as I am learning. She is not yet confident with Oliver Scaife. She struggles to feed him from her breasts and he struggles to get what he wants out of them. She listens to broadcasts on a mobile telephone wired up to a speaker in my master bedroom; the broadcasts instruct her to sleep when the baby sleeps. She tries but she does not sleep when Oliver Scaife sleeps; when he sleeps she kneels in her bed, leaning over the wall of his adjoining crib to watch him breathe. He is content when he is like that, but the only time I have seen Carly close to contentment is when her child is sleeping upon her chest while she sits on the wide sofa in my sitting room and she is watching comedies on the television and never once laughing.

The family have been with me for over a week and yet it is only now that I realise that we are alike, she and I. Carly Scaife is a mother and so am I. The infant began life within her, just as this family are within me. She holds him tight.

Carly's hair is cut short. Marie remarks on it often; it seems that the hair was longer until very recently. To Marie this is significant. Carly wears floral print dresses and black leggings. She says she can no longer wear contact lenses, which means she must wear glasses in order to see. I sympathise. My attention sometimes wavers and often I wish I had more clarity of vision.

Within my walls it is often dark and, while I do not yearn for my days spent with Evie Rattle, it is difficult to focus on more than one person in more than one room at a time. When Oliver is asleep I feel compelled to watch him.

O neighbours! I know what I said, but they are drawing me into myself. I have barely looked beyond my walls these last few days. You might all have disappeared and I would not know it.

Carly sometimes cries herself to sleep. Marie does not seem to understand her fully. She offers to help placate the infant, but Carly rebuffs her and keeps the bedroom door tight shut. What Carly needs is an embrace. If her real mother will not provide it, then I will.

Oliver Scaife likes to look at patterns on the wall. I angle my windows just so, to catch the sunlight and make shadow patterns of leaves above his crib. He thanks me for it, I am certain he does.

*

Marie Scaife is also a mother. But she cannot remember what it is to hold somebody within oneself.

One week after they arrived, Marie left the house on foot and was absent for an entire day. Carly and Oliver crept downstairs. Carly shifted the coffee table aside and stood in its space and whirled Oliver around and around above her head. Oliver did not laugh or smile, but he stared at her and then he twisted his body as she held him. It was difficult at first to know whether the contortion spelled delight or disgust, but then he looked up and around him—at *me*—and he spread his arms as if to say, "Is this not magnificent?"

When Marie returned she was driving a car. She parked it on my driveway, crunching its handbrake to prevent it from sliding back down the incline and into the turning circle of our cul-de-sac. She entered me and then backtracked, coaxing Carly to stand beneath the overhang of my porch. Carly held the infant and gazed at the car.

"I'm not getting into that," she said. "Oliver's not getting into that."

"I've had it checked over," Marie replied.

Carly glared at Marie until she closed the door, hiding the car from her. I shifted my attention outside: was the vehicle so bad? I glanced at the cars belonging to your people, the cars perched on your driveways, humming and cooling in the evening air. They all look alike to me.

"We might need it if we want to get away," Marie said as they ate pasta at the kitchen table, hours later.

Carly glanced at my door, at the invisible car beyond.

"We need money," Marie said. "I'll get a job."

Carly bent to fuss over Oliver in the basket on the floor beside the table. Then she rose, ate a mouthful of food, and nodded.

*

I do not know what employment Marie has found for herself, and I find that I do not care. Only occasionally does she take the car from the driveway. She is gone for long parts of each day and I am better able to relish spending time with Carly and Oliver.

*

My doorbell rings. It startles me—I have been watching Oliver in his crib and so has Carly. She is humming a melody that I find very beautiful.

I struggle to tear myself away, but then I shift my attention downstairs and outside before Carly's feet have touched the carpet of my master bedroom.

I watch the boy standing on the doorstep warily. It take several moments before I recognise him; people look altogether different up close. Number six, he is yours, is he not? His wild, long hair pushed under his cap is unmistakable. On the front of the cap is written in blue text *SO WHAT?*, which is a reference to a composition by the jazz musician Miles Davis.

He scowls and pushes my doorbell again. I try to smother the sound. There is a child in here, asleep.

Carly edges toward the door slowly, slowly. She glances several times at the staircase and the trailing, invisible rope that connects her to Oliver in his crib. I am capable of metaphor, o neighbours.

I consider jamming the door, holding it fast.

Carly is quicker than me. Even as it appears she is having second thoughts, she yanks at the lock and pulls open the door. It stings like a wound.

"Yes?" she says in a voice that is not quite level.

The boy pushes back the peak of his cap. When I last paid him any attention he suffered from acne; now I see that it has cleared. He reeks of confidence.

"Kieran," he says. That is his name. "From across the way."

He gestures over his shoulder with his thumb. Carly tilts to see past him and so do I. I was right: number six. Number six, you sent him and I will hold you accountable.

"What do you want?" Carly says. She sounds very tired.

"My dad said we should say hi sometime."

"Where's your dad?"

"Work. Summer holidays, but not for him."

"Your mother?"

"Same."

"You're on your own?"

"I'm sixteen."

"All right then."

"Yeah."

Carly and I are so close that my anxiety transfers to her.

"So you've done it," she says. "You've said hi. And hi back at you."

"So do you know anyone round here?"

"No." Abruptly, Carly shudders. I see it and Kieran does too.

"If you want I could—"

"No."

Kieran stares at her and Carly reaches out a hand. She holds the brass knocker that is fixed to the centre of my door. Her grip is tighter than I would expect; it hurts.

"Want me to wash your car?" Kieran says.

Carly looks at the car as if she has never seen it before. "No."

"I wash everyone's car. Everyone in the cul-de-sac, I mean."

"It's new. It doesn't need a wash."

"It's grubby. There's sand in the air came from the Middle East on the wind."

"In Yorkshire?"

Kieran shrugs. "That's what my dad said. Middle Eastern sand. Gets your windscreen proper filthy."

"Seriously. Kieran, was that your name? I don't want my car washed." I see something in Carly I have never seen before. A hardness inside.

"Twenty quid."

Carly splutters. "For a car wash? You've got to be kidding."

"It's what everyone pays." He waves an arm to gesture at you all, o neighbours, as if it proves something.

"No. Off you go now."

Kieran grins and I do not know what it means. His eyes leave Carly's face. He is looking at her body and now I know what the grin means.

Carly presses my door closed and Kieran's head tilts, trying to keep her in sight through the narrowing gap.

Carly stands looking at the door. She shakes her head and then pads upstairs, following the rope back to Oliver, bundling it in her fists as she climbs.

I see her safely up, then I turn my attention back to the boy outside. He slinks back to you, number six, but within moments he returns. He is carrying a bucket and a sponge.

*

I raise myself from the sag of my foundations to see as far from my walls as possible.

That village at the end of the lane. How many roofs can I see—twenty? Thirty? The sunlight multiplies the number of surfaces that are visible to me. How many people do they shelter in total? A dizzying amount.

The people of our cul-de-sac so rarely encounter one another, but I understand now that this is not usual. People are not relegated to their family units. Any of them might speak to any other. Once free of their wombs, they are capable of travelling anywhere, and perhaps they do, every day. I look at you all; I consider the six of us sitting in our tight circle. We are so close and yet we do not speak. Perhaps our indifference has affected our people.

Beyond the village there is more life and movement, more and more. An aeroplane is a distant speck.

*

On the mantelpiece in my sitting room is a painted wooden doll. Carly shows it to her infant and then pulls its upper half free of its lower half. Inside is another doll, and inside that another and another.

I dream of a life free from my lumpenness and my rootedness. But I am a mother and I understand my responsibilities.

*

The boy was right about the sand on the car. Now that he has dragged his dirty sponge across its bonnet the copper-coloured streaks are clear to see. But the dust has been disturbed and nothing more. The car looks far worse than it did before.

Even after finishing with the car Kieran must have been watching and waiting. The moment that Marie appears at the mouth of the cul-de-sac he emerges from you, number six. He follows Marie along my driveway. She notices him only as she is struggling to locate her keys whilst grappling with a holdall that threatens to slip from her forearm.

"Is your daughter in?" Kieran says.

"I hope so." I think Marie is trying to hide her being startled by him.

Kieran moistens his lips with his tongue; a grotesque action. He opens his mouth to speak, then closes it. After a pause he says, "She owes me twenty pounds."

Marie turns to face him fully. She folds her arms and her holdall knocks heavily against my doorframe. "Don't be so silly.

What for?"

"Is she all right?" Kieran says, quickly, as though he has spoken before he is ready. He tries to look past Marie.

"She just needs peace and quiet. She's a mother now. We don't want visitors."

Kieran gives up. He nods at the car. "I'm all finished. Twenty quid. We agreed."

Marie's expression is unchanging as she surveys the mess on the windscreen and bonnet. "Wait there."

She plods inside and groans as she deposits the bag in my hallway. She calls out for Carly, who I know is upstairs in the nursery that Oliver uses only for play and not for sleep. I do not follow her. Instead I wait, watching Kieran, making sure that he does not step over my threshold. Number six, what have you inflicted upon us?

I sense raised voices—o neighbours, do you suffer from these same uncomfortable vibrations, even when your attention is elsewhere?—and then Marie is clopping down my stairs again. She strides to the door brandishing a twenty pound note.

"We both know it's extortion," she says.

Number six, you should be ashamed. Kieran smiles and takes the money. He demonstrates no remorse. He tries again to see inside. He is looking for Carly.

"Go home now," Marie says. She closes the door and I sigh at the healed wound. My attention rises to my upper floor. Carly is standing in the nursery at my window. She is gazing down at Kieran as he lollops away. Oliver rolls ineffectively on a playmat behind her, unable to turn himself onto his front. Carly lifts both her hands and her fingertips graze my glass.

*

Oliver Scaife keeps us all awake. He squeals and snorts and rattles the bars of his crib. Even when he sleeps his breathing is as loud and abrasive as the pipes that lead from my boiler, which have been maintained inexpertly and shudder when anybody showers.

Carly's attention to the task of placating Oliver wavers.

Sometimes she hushes and soothes him, leaning over his crib in her nightdress or, more often, hefting him to lie like a sack upon her while she is cradled by pillows in an awkward half-sitting position. Sometimes she remains lying in her bed and pulls one of the pillows over her head. I understand this impulse. We all love Oliver, but why won't he quieten? When will this stop?

At this moment she is walking up and down in the darkness of her bedroom, bouncing Oliver Scaife in her arms. She tells him that she will do anything for him, but he grumbles whenever she pauses and then his grumbles swell into splutters and then piercing howls. It is too dark to determine whether his eyes are closed, or whether hers are.

I think Carly may be weeping. The holdall that Marie was carrying is now in the bedroom. It bulges with its contents and I fear that Carly may be intending to slip away from me. My wish that there were some way for me to help reminds me that there is somebody else in the house, after all. Where is Marie right at this moment? I shift my attention across to her bedroom and peer at the bed. The covers have been thrown off. There is nobody here or in my bathroom.

It is with a sense of excitement rather than anxiety that I scour my other rooms. She is not upstairs. A thought occurs to me and I am not ashamed of it: perhaps I am more a mother to Carly than Marie is.

I find Marie in the dark at the foot of my stairs, an area that some of my previous occupants designated an entrance hall but which the Scaifes have made a dining area by means of putting a mahogany table here. They seldom use it; they almost always eat sitting at the pine table in my kitchen, almost always one at a time, one of them washing dishes or cradling Oliver while the other chews food.

Marie is walking slowly alongside the dining table, up and down its length and then up and down again. She is wearing a dressing gown but I can see her day clothes underneath. Occasionally she glances at my staircase. She can hear Oliver's shrieks, I am positive. Can she also hear Carly's sobbing?

O neighbours, I do not want to say that I hate Marie.

Something happens. It is Marie's sudden spasm that alerts me, rather than the sound itself. She freezes and cocks her head.

I am upstairs in an instant.

Carly shouts, "Stop!" And again: "Stop!"

She means Oliver and his howling, but Oliver does not stop it. Even in the dark I can see the black O of his mouth, a hole wider than his head ought to allow. The sound he emits is more than mere sound. I am blinded by it.

Marie clatters upstairs. She pauses outside the door to Carly's bedroom.

"I'm here," she says, so quiet that I wonder whether she really wants Carly to hear.

I am inside watching Carly. In the darkness I see her head snap up. She faces the door but does not speak.

Oliver continues his shrieking.

"Can I do anything?" Marie says outside the room, shifting her weight from foot to foot, an itch upon my floor.

Carly's head drops again. She speaks to Oliver in a softer, kinder voice: "Stop, now."

Oliver stops, now.

After that squall of sound the silence seems like deafness. Carly comes to a halt at the foot of her bed, beside the holdall. I cannot see her expression, whether there is triumph or only relief.

Outside, Marie watches the door. Her face, I can see. Her eyes gleam with wetness. She rubs her cheek again and again, as if she has been slapped. She turns and creeps away to her bedroom. She leaves the door ajar and climbs into bed. As soon as I see that she has fallen asleep I swing the door closed slowly and she flinches only slightly at its click.

*

It is after ten o'clock when I rouse myself. Do you wake early, o neighbours? Do you even sleep? When I am unoccupied I am capable of sustaining myself with infrequent naps or a constant doze. But a family of three is exhausting and I find more and more that when they are sleeping I must sleep also.

Marie must already have left for work and Oliver is snoring in his cot. For a moment I panic at not finding Carly close by. She is not in my bathroom or my sitting room or my kitchen. I spread my attention wider. I peer into my garden that, so far, the Scaifes have not explored, then, in desperation, beyond. Then Carly shuffles somewhere and I find her.

She is in my smallest bedroom. There has been a desk and a chair and nothing more in here since the day the family arrived. Now there is a computer with a folding screen upon the desk and Carly is sitting before it, circling her index finger on its black surface. Her feet are tucked beneath her on the chair, which rotates slightly with each of her movements. She is humming that same song as before. I think of Tom Grace and his joy at hearing music. Perhaps later I will send a surge of electrical power to the rarely-used stereo in my sitting room, and perhaps that will operate it, and perhaps Carly will take to listening to music too. There is little that I desire nowadays, but I desire music.

I look at the computer screen and see images of bright-coloured things. These are pictures of toys, like the ones that litter Oliver's playmat in his nursery. He shows little interest in them. He prefers clutching at Carly's necklaces or watching the play of light on the grey bars of my radiators. On the computer screen I see dolls and animals and cubes and twisted wires strung with beads. Carly is deliberating over these pictures, clicking on one and then another as she hums her song.

When Oliver wakes Carly goes to him. She lifts him and then holds him under his armpits and pretends that he is walking downstairs, tickling me as she scuffs his feet on each of my steps.

She feeds him at her breast while she sits on the sofa and— joy!—she turns on the television and together we three watch a documentary programme about ceramic artists. Then she assembles a lunch for herself; it occurs to me only now that it is rare for her to eat during the daytime, when Marie is absent. She eats a little of the salad leaves and tomatoes, but afterwards she retches into the sink.

Then she carries Oliver to my back door and she throws it open and it is not so much like a wound as a cleansing. I pull the breeze inside, tousling the hair of the two of them, tugging the air along my walls and ceiling and floors. I gasp at first and then I sigh in contentment.

They leave. It is not so terrible; I can see all parts of the garden. Although I cannot feel any sensations it is almost a part of me, in the same way that Carly's short hair is part of her—do you feel the same, o neighbours? The discomfort is only in my mind, a fear that having gone this far they might stray further. But Carly deposits Oliver on his back under the shade of the willow at the garden's eastern edge, and then she lies upon the grass herself. I watch from my windows, first at ground level, then above.

I think of Carly watching Oliver asleep in his crib and I am terribly tired and I feel that if I could I would cry.

In my swoon it is difficult to tell how much time has passed. Carly and Oliver reenter and I welcome them back with all the warmth I can muster. When Marie returns I snarl at her, but she does not react. Her attention is fixated on Carly, who descends my staircase dressed entirely in black.

"Are you okay to watch him?" Carly says. She means Oliver.

Marie watches Carly with her eyes narrowed.

Carly laughs. "You look like you're going to say, 'You can't go out looking like that'."

She goes to the utility room beside my porch and fumbles until she produces a pair of shoes. She has not worn shoes since she arrived, and these are not the pair she was wearing that day. They are bright orange, sickeningly vivid against the black of her leggings and her long-sleeved top.

"Where are you going?" Marie says.

Carly stands and looks down at her outfit. "To the opera, obviously." I clench with anxiety before I recognise that it is a joke. "I'll be twenty minutes. Thirty, tops."

She pushes her way past Marie and through my front door and she sets off at a sprint.

*

Carly is absent for forty-seven minutes. Marie frets as much as

I do. She moves from window to window, watching as the sun drops behind you, o neighbours, and then when Oliver wakes she is occupied with pushing toys towards him where he lies on the playmat and pleads with him not to cry. He squeals each time she tries to come close. Who can blame him?

She and I both rush downstairs the second my front door slams.

Carly is soaking wet. I did not realise that it has been raining. She is panting heavily and she is grinning. When Marie stumbles into the dining room carrying Oliver, I notice her expression of revulsion. Is she so old that she cannot remember the delight in physicality? For an awful flash of a moment I feel that Marie and I are alike—static—but I push the thought away.

Carly wipes a hand across her mouth. There is a sheen of sweat on her face. She is unimaginably beautiful.

She reaches out for Oliver. Marie seems reluctant, but Carly tugs the infant free. He settles upon her neatly like a sheet upon a bed.

When Marie speaks her voice cracks. "Were you safe?"

"Of course."

"Did anybody see you?"

"Nobody."

Carly hefts Oliver onto her shoulder and carries him back upstairs. He is asleep even before she lays him in his crib. She tiptoes to the bathroom, a mere shadow in those clothes. She hums as she peels the outfit from her body. I hum the same melody to myself as she showers and I watch her, wondering what it must be like to be so alive.

*

Oliver Scaife cries throughout the night.

*

I edge my window open to let the breeze stroke Carly's cheek. I miss her terribly when she is asleep. O neighbours, do you feel the same about your people, your favourites among them? Perhaps mothers are only ever complete when they are with their children.

All the pleasure of yesterday has gone. Oliver's nighttime mewling has left Carly desolate again. Is it any wonder that when he wakes—my breeze has inadvertently roused him too—she scurries out of the bedroom and downstairs?

"You go to him," she snaps at Marie. Marie has the sense to obey.

Later, after breakfast, Carly says to Marie, "Don't go out."

"I have to work."

"Don't leave me here with him."

"You're his mother."

Carly leans upon the kitchen table. She gazes down at Oliver in his wicker basket. "I would never hurt him," she says.

Marie hesitates, then rises and stands before her. Carly tries to look past her at my garden.

"Why did you say that?" Marie says.

Carly doesn't answer.

"Carly."

"Go to work. We'll be fine."

"First tell me why you said that. Why you said, 'I would never hurt him'."

Carly scoops up the basket from my linoleum floor. "I'm just tired. Go on. Go."

Marie checks all of my doors and windows before she leaves the house.

An hour later my doorbell rings. Oliver is strapped to Carly's chest and for thirty minutes she has been walking in circles in the front room. At first she told Oliver again and again that she loved him but her voice lowered and lowered in volume until it became only a shush. I have been trying to distract myself by watching documentary footage of an auction on the television, but Carly's circles have been drawing my attention and I do not know what to do. I am happy about my doorbell ringing because it rouses Carly from what almost seems like sleep. She goes quickly to my front door. Perhaps she is grateful too.

"Who is it?" Carly whispers, without opening the door.

"Delivery for Mrs Scaife?"

Carly scowls. "Miss. Or mizz."

"Sorry. Miss."

They wait, Carly inside and—I check—an obese man in dungarees outside.

"I'll need a signature, miss."

Oliver shifts on Carly's chest. He is asleep. "I'm feeding my child. Put the signature thing through the letterbox?"

The delivery man lifts the letterbox. He is holding a bulky electronic device. "It won't fit, miss."

Carly's jaw clenches. She yanks the door open and I wince. She holds out a hand for the device. The delivery man glances at Oliver, who is beginning to stir, and then relinquishes it. Carly scribbles upon the screen of the device with a pen attached to it with a cord, then hands it back so quickly the man almost drops it.

"Right," he says. "Back in two shakes, then I'll pop them wherever you want them. There's a whole lot of them, isn't there?"

Carly looks the obese delivery man up and down. Then she moistens her lips, which makes me think of you and your odious Kieran, number six.

"Just leave them outside," she says.

"Can't, miss. Not with the value of them. I have to show they're in their right place and take a photo."

"You're not coming inside," she says, and I could not love her more.

Oliver emits a tiny cry. The delivery man looks at the infant and then at Carly and he takes a step backwards. "All right, miss. All right."

Carly presses the door closed and takes a deep, ragged breath while the man returns to his absurd red lorry parked on the kerb of our cul-de-sac. I watch as he heaves each bulky box from the tailgate and into the lee of my porch.

Across our turning circle I see you, number six, and I see Kieran at your kitchen window. He watches me with undisguised interest, but I am watching him right back.

*

I had not even noticed that I had a phone. When it rings I scratch around, trying to locate the itch.

Carly answers it. The phone is in the cubbyhole beneath my staircase, where Anton and Beverly Grieg placed a drinks cabinet they opened only when entertaining guests which contained only bottles of gin.

She listens attentively. I strain to decipher the hum in the telephone wire: nothing. I watch Carly's face.

"Come," she says. "Please come."

Marie is making her way downstairs, showered and dressed after her day at work. I force each step to emit a loud creak as she descends.

Carly replaces the handset carefully and turns to face Marie.

*

The suspicion comes upon me slowly.

I am a mother. I care for all of my children. But one of them in particular requires my careful supervision. Carly is at risk. From what, I do not know.

But what I do know is this: Marie is not capable of protecting her.

Carly is protecting Oliver and I am protecting Carly. Marie is protecting nobody. Marie does not belong here.

I have another suspicion. A question.

Is Marie really Carly's mother?

They share the same surname, but that could be a ruse. It is only visitors to the house—removal and delivery men, an obnoxious estate agent—that have spoken the name Scaife. I spend many hours examining one woman's face and then the other. They share no physical characteristics that I can see. Marie's face is a lattice of creases; in another context I might describe it as kindly. Those arrowhead lines that point to the corners of her eyes suggest a life of laughter, but she has never laughed that I have seen. It is another ruse.

Carly's face is a wide, pale circle. She has no creases despite the torture that Oliver puts her through each night. She might never grow old. Her front teeth are bent inwards slightly, as though she has bumped them on something hard.

*

Take him away, number six. We have no time for your people.

Kieran knocks again, louder.

Upstairs, Carly crosses my landing to look out of the window and down at my porch.

She covers her mouth with a hand. She watches your Kieran, number six, as unflinchingly as I watch him. Then, hurriedly, she turns away and goes to my bathroom and vomits into the toilet bowl.

Kieran finally stops his knocking. He turns and runs a finger across the bonnet of the car.

*

After dinner Carly excuses herself. Marie coos at Oliver in the sitting room but he is happier without her intervention, stretching his little arms toward my fireplace where the painted wooden doll sits on its mantelpiece. Perhaps he is imagining himself free of her. I watch Marie intently, ready to shriek if she tries anything untoward.

When Carly returns she is wearing her black clothes again. She has already put on her shoes, which are an even more nauseating colour than they were yesterday. They are filthy with mud as red as copper.

"No," Marie says.

"I need to," Carly replies. She grips my doorframe at the entrance to the sitting room. She rolls her neck and it clicks.

"You mustn't. Please. There must be something else."

Marie has risen to her haunches. Oliver rolls onto his side but I will not let him injure himself on the hearth. Carly glances at the infant but she does not move from the doorway.

"If you cared, you wouldn't stand in my way," Carly says.

Marie presses both her palms to her face. I imagine touching that crenellated surface and it is all I can do not to shudder.

"I care," she says in a voice full of fatigue.

"I'll be quick, I promise. I know where I'm going."

Marie scoops up the infant, ignoring his squeals. She holds him before her, presenting him to his mother. But it is only to allow Carly to kiss the boy on his forehead.

Slowly, Marie shakes her head. "No. Don't be quick. Take your time, do it properly. Go as far away as you need to and be careful."

*

Marie sleeps downstairs in a wing-backed armchair that she shifted from my sitting room and into my dining room.

When Carly returned Marie and I scrutinised her: was her mood improved? She was exhausted and covered with copper-coloured mud and bark. I followed her upstairs and watched her undress and shower and feed Oliver and slip into bed, cooing at her infant asleep in his crib. When I turned my attention back to Marie she was already in the dining room with the lights so dim and her body so slight that the large chair might as well have been empty.

Piotr Brzezicki loved to watch fiction on television. Before that time I had been accustomed to documentary films and at first I was startled by these visions of the world outside, of outlandish creatures, dizzying animated illustrations and arguments upon arguments. Tom Grace did not enjoy crime fiction, so Piotr and I watched these types of television programmes together when Tom was busy working or sleeping. In these television programmes everybody has a secret and one can only look away once the most important secret has been revealed.

Television has taught me one thing: the ways in which humans can create obstacles to other humans' happiness are too numerous to count.

I have dwelt upon the themes of these crime stories. I believe

I have an idea about what may be happening here, within me, right at this moment.

I believe that I am a sanctuary. That Carly is here to hide from something outside, something from which only I can protect her, and of which Marie is aware and afraid. I have seen stories on television about people who hide away from their enemies or even their lovers. They change their names and they hide for days or months or years.

Here is my reason for believing this: even in the dark of the dining room I can see the thin black pole that is propped against Marie's chair. I am convinced that it is a rifle.

*

I watch Carly pick her way carefully past Marie sleeping in her chair.

Upstairs, Oliver stirs softly.

It is just before dawn and it is raining outside, heavier than it has rained in weeks. The water slops against my roof and it is funnelled through my guttering, an almost unbearable prickling.

Carly searches the room beside my porch and retrieves an indigo waterproof coat and waterproof trousers that crinkle as she pulls them on. Marie turns her head toward the sound but does not wake. Carly hops from foot to foot as she squeezes into lime-green Wellington boots.

Oliver splutters. Carly looks to my staircase but does not approach it.

She pulls open my back door and she is in the garden.

I beg her not to go any further. There is something out there and she must not go out alone, not without warning Marie, much as I dislike the old woman.

She cannot leave me with Marie and Oliver.

It is difficult to make Carly out through my windows smeared with rain. Her silhouette twists unnaturally as she makes her way away from me across my lawn. She stops at the picket fence that marks my boundary. I sigh with relief: surely she will turn back.

With some difficulty, she clambers onto the fence and then

drops down onto the other side.

The wind grows stronger, tossing rain at me, and I howl through my chimney.

I watch as the spindly speck that is Carly crosses the lane and pushes through a hedgerow, beginning to plod through the cornfield opposite. I watch until she passes the point where the trees obscure my view.

I have two contradictory thoughts. One is that she must be kept safe. The other is that she must not escape.

I know it is the rain, but I feel that I am weeping.

Perhaps Oliver hears me. He bellows and rattles his crib.

Marie—stupid, careless Marie—finally wakes. She looks at my window, at the rising sun and the rain, and she grabs for the gun. She blinks and finally recognises the sounds that Oliver is making and she staggers upstairs. She bursts into the bedroom still holding the rifle and I hammer my windows against the frames—*watch what you're doing, you oaf!* Then she runs from room to room, searching for Carly, but Carly is gone and perhaps she will never come back and it is all Marie's fault.

When Marie has finally convinced herself that we are alone, she returns to the infant. She hovers with uncertainty, looking from Oliver to the rifle and back. Finally she props the weapon against the bars of his crib. She carries Oliver downstairs—he kicks and shouts—and attempts to warm a bottle of milk in the microwave whilst holding him, then attempts to feed him. He yells and casts around and looks up at me, pleading for my help.

An hour passes before Oliver falls into sullen silence. In my sitting room Marie wrestles him into a hammock chair made of cushioned fabric and wire. She presses the chair down to set it bouncing and then she joins me in looking out of my window into the garden.

We watch, both worried mothers. At this moment I do not hate her at all.

We are so absorbed we do not hear my front door opening. When I hear a sniffling sound from outside the sitting room, I hurtle away to find Carly bent on the doormat, waterfalls streaming from the shell of her coat. She picks something up from the mat. It is a piece of notepaper, folded once. She unfolds it and reads it—I strain to see past her, but her coat makes her bulky and obscures my view—and then folds it again.

She glances out of the window at our cul-de-sac.

Marie catches up with me. She comes to a stop in the dining room, horrified at the vision of Carly in her gleaming wet shroud.

"I don't want to talk about it," Carly says. Then, "I need your help."

Marie tries to speak, fails, then clears her throat. "Anything."

Carly points at my front door, which hangs slightly ajar. Outside, barely protected by the porch overhang, the boxes that the delivery man put there are disintegrating in the rain. Some of the cardboard has ripped and fallen away entirely.

"Help me bring these inside," Carly says.

*

The boxes contain toys and books and clothes. The largest cardboard box, the one that was ripped even when it was outside, is the size of a coffin and contains another box that is so heavy that Marie and Carly struggle to bump it up my stairs. It is a toy chest with a heavy, padded seat that is also a hinged lid. Its sides are decorated with colourful illustrations of dinosaurs and trees.

For most of the night Oliver is inconsolable. Carly sings to him and pleads with him and strokes his bald head and his back and his stomach.

"I'm doing all this for you," she says softly, again and again.

For the rest of the night, for hours until just before the sun is due to peep above your rooftops, o neighbours, Carly is in my third bedroom, the nursery. It is black dark. There is a cot in here, larger than the bedside crib, but Oliver has never slept in it. In the darkness Carly kneels before the toy box. I cannot see her face but I can hear her stop-start sobbing and I can make out her hands wiping at her face again and again. I do not know why, but I find it revolting.

Before she returns to my master bedroom she carefully places all of the new toys into the toy chest.

*

"Perhaps it would be best for all of us if he were dead," Carly says at breakfast.

She is gazing down at Oliver in his basket.

Marie stares at her and Carly says nothing more.

In the silence I replay Carly's enunciation of the phrase as best I can. Her tone was almost neutral, but was there a slight emphasis on 'he'?

*

I wake in a panic.

Carly reaches my staircase in the dark before I have collected myself and before I am ready to help. One of the steps halfway down has long caused me problems and I fear that without attention it will only get worse. Its loud creak echoes from my walls and I curse my age.

In my dining room Marie springs up from her chair.

Carly continues her descent.

"Stop," Marie says hoarsely.

"Or what?" Carly replies. Her voice sounds slurred. She is dressed in her black clothes again, which have not been cleaned since yesterday. I notice that her face is already smeared and dirty. How has that happened? The last I saw her before I fell asleep, she was kneeling again before the toy box.

Slowly, uncertainly, Marie raises the rifle to point at Carly. I am transfixed and unable to do anything to intervene.

"You've got to be kidding."

Marie shakes her head. "I'm not kidding. You can't do it this way."

"Because?"

"Because you'll be found out."

"There is no other way. You don't understand."

Marie shifts the arm holding the rifle to wipe at her eye with a dressing-gowned shoulder. Like me, she is half asleep. Perhaps this is only a nightmare.

Both women turn their heads. They are looking upstairs.

"He'll grow up," Marie says. "And then he'll be able to look after himself. It won't be as long as you think. You'll see."

"I hate him."

"No, you don't."

"No."

After a few moments of silence Marie says, "I do understand, though."

Until now Carly's attention has been only on the weapon, as though she has been judging her moment to escape. Now she looks at Marie's face.

"I was just the same as you," Marie says in a weary tone that makes her sound even older than she is. "I guess it's a family thing."

*

In the morning Marie says, "I won't go to work today."

"You don't need to hang around here."

Marie is thinking what I am thinking. Carly wants Marie gone so that she can leave the house again, and when she does she will leave Oliver alone. I am afraid. I cannot care for Oliver on my own.

Marie shakes her head. "I'll go out. I'll get more for the toy box."

Carly's foot stops its rocking of Oliver's chair. She and Marie watch each other and I do not know what to make of it. Is it a secret, Carly's nighttime crying at the toy box? After their encounter last night Carly went directly to my unused nursery. Marie remained in her chair downstairs, the rifle on her lap. If she went into the nursery it must have been when I finally fell asleep myself.

"You will?" Carly says. Her eyes shine.

"If that's what you need."

Abruptly, Carly is crying.

When Marie returns in the afternoon she goes directly upstairs and places two orange plastic carrier bags beside the toy box.

They remain there until night when Carly enters the nursery in darkness. I cannot see into the bags, but Carly coughs and cries and swallows noisily as she rifles through their contents. She does not open the toy box until just before she leaves, an hour later.

*

Marie does not dress for work. She stays downstairs in her dressing gown and casts glances at my staircase.

The phone rings and she answers it. She waits only a moment— barely enough time for the caller to make an introduction— before she speaks.

"Don't you *fucking* dare," she says.

*

Carly is singing to Oliver. I recognise the song, which was one of Anton Grieg's favourites: 'Doctor, Lawyer, Indian Chief' by Hoagy Carmichael.

I prefer Carly's rendition. Her voice is very beautiful.

I sway to her singing and I let my attention spread beyond myself. Today it is wonderfully sunny outside. O neighbours, you look like palaces sparkling golden! The village at the end of the lane is an island in its cornfield sea, its spires the tallest trees. It is possible to be content with so very little.

I am enjoying looking directly upwards at the sky. At first it appears steel-coloured, but the more I look the more I am able to see the speckles of stars and even the pale apparition of the moon. Every so often I shift my attention back to Carly, to her lips forming the words, to Oliver pressed tight against her chest as she dances. She is holding him too tight.

She is pressing Oliver tighter and tighter to herself as she spins towards my window. Oliver lets out a muffled cry.

She will harm him like this.

I remember Carly's words. Was that yesterday, or longer ago? *Perhaps it would be best for all of us if he were dead.*

The threat is not out there in the golden sunlight.

O cul-de-sac! Send help!

*

We all wait nervously for the day to end. We all fear the night.

Marie and Carly speak only to arrange their meal and to soothe Oliver.

Carly goes to bed early. She kneels in her bed, watching Oliver in his crib. I beg her to be kind.

Downstairs, Marie does not sleep or even sit in her chair. She holds the rifle in both hands and paces up and down the length of my dining room. She looks out of my front window, peering into the blackness, and then my window that faces the void of the garden.

I do not understand why she is looking outside. Is Marie wrong about the nature of the threat, or am I? Whose maternal instincts are the stronger?

Marie checks her gun and presses her nose to the glass.

She sees something out there, before I sense it myself. O neighbours, what is it?

I pray that it is an animal, a fox. But it is not.

It is a human. It is standing at the picket fence in my garden.

Marie turns from the window to look up at my staircase, but she does not move from her position at the window. If she will not warn Carly then I will. In a flurry I race upstairs.

Carly's bed is empty.

I search for any sign of her. She is not in the nursery. The toy box is open and toys are strewn on the playmat and spilling under the wooden cot. Inside the toy box I see a collection of long struts that gleam white in the moonlight. They are bones. Hanging from them are ragged scraps of meat that are copper-coloured like the soil on Carly's clothes. I realise now that it is not soil but dry blood.

Carly must be here somewhere.

I dart from room to room, struggling and failing to turn on my lights.

All I can think about are bones and flesh and blood.

Carly brought in that toy box. She filled it with something unspeakable and she forced Marie to help her carry it inside me.

Back downstairs Marie moves from window to window, watching and clutching the rifle.

I cast my attention outside. Whoever is out there has moved closer and has almost reached my walls.

"Carly!" Marie cries suddenly. She spins and clatters upstairs. She and I scour my rooms.

Where is Carly?

I push downstairs into my kitchen, my sitting room. I am certain Carly is here somewhere. She is moving somewhere, her bare feet tapping at my carpeted floors. But if she is here she is a shadow among shadows.

I realise that Marie has stopped moving and I fear for Oliver. But Marie is not standing beside his crib; she is at the other side of Carly's bed. She is reaching for a piece of paper that sits upon Carly's pillow.

It is not folded now.

If we peer closely Marie and I can make out the words handwritten upon it.

I know it's crazy, the note says, but I think you're in trouble and I want to help.

And: *I'll come after dark on Sunday night.*

And strangest of all: *Kieran.*

It is Sunday night and Kieran is in the garden.

With a start I realise that Oliver's crib is empty.

Marie and I move in synchronicity. We career downstairs, my boards creaking to match Marie's strangled cries.

There is another sound: something snapping.

And another: that same stop-start sobbing I heard when Carly knelt before the toy box. Or perhaps it is not sobbing but something wet and awful.

I think of those times that she left me and I realise now that she was not seeking escape.

I roar with the horror of it.

Marie hears me. She jerks and the rotten middle step of my staircase cracks and gives way and she slips. I try to catch her but she bounces and then her neck twists and her head strikes my bannister and then she bumps down my stairs, turning and turning and coming to a halt in a heap on my carpet.

I was wrong.

My rear door, the door to my garden, is closed, but a chill tells me that it has been recently open. Outside I can see nothing.

I try to push my awareness beyond my walls, twisting, like Marie's neck twisted, to see back towards myself. It is agony.

But I do see something.

It is crumpled on the paved area outside my rear door. At first I perceive it as a heap of fabric. But there are limbs, too. Bones and flesh and blood. I see a forearm and the meat has been picked clean off. I see your Kieran's face, number six, and he is never coming home.

Carly is a hunter.

She must be here somewhere.

With a jolt I realise that I am empty for the first time in weeks.

I flail around and find Carly at the foot of my driveway.

Even from behind her I can see, from the way her arms are angled, that she is carrying Oliver strapped to her chest. I hear his faint gurgle and I know that he is unharmed.

"I'm doing all this for you," I hear her say.

He is under no threat.

And neither is Carly.

I was wrong.

I tell myself that this is not my doing. Carly and I are both mothers and we are responsible only for ourselves.

But I also know this: while we have our children, we will protect them as best we can.

Barefoot, Carly strides away from me without looking back. Her head swings from side to side as she looks around our cul-de-sac, gazing at each of you in turn.

O neighbours!

Read/Write Head

"Mr Major?"

Timothy John Major blinks rapidly.

"I can come back a little later if you'd prefer?" She must be an intern: other than the name 'E. Tooley', her badge is plain. The nametags on the others' labcoats featured a logo, three trapezia interlocking to create a triangle of red, green and gold. A clipboard rests in her lap.

"It's all the same," Timothy John Major says, "To me."

"You've been given a drink already?"

Timothy John Major glances down at the mug in his hands. The tea ripples. A lake within the crater rim of a sunken volcano.

"Here it is," he says.

E. Tooley smiles. Crooked, teeth just visible. Nicola Bradshaw, Year 6.

"And you're okay to begin?"

He raises the cup. Begin drinking, or begin something else?

She smiles again, the edges of her mouth more pinched than before. Begin something else.

"I'm sorry," she says, "I should explain. I'm an intern—"

Internal bleeding. International dateline. Man of mystery. Velvet.

"—and I'm here temporarily, working with the team. I'll not be involved after this stage. I just need to collect some preliminary details."

Timothy John Major copies her smile. "Yes. Thank you." He extends the word 'you' to show that he has encountered an obstacle.

E. Tooley glances down at her badge. It is precisely the same size, with the same rounded corners, as a bourbon cream biscuit.

Matlock, with a first-ever weak cup of tea. "Oh, sorry. I should have said. I'm Elaine."

Timothy John Major grits his teeth. Pelles, Lancelot, Galahad. *The Once and Future King*. Paige, Marley, Ingham, Robinson. *Seinfeld*. 2nd and East 88th, *Manhattan*. Manhattan. B-side of *The Winner Takes It All*. An eel I, Ani Lee.

He nods stiffly.

"Just a few questions, then. Your procedure wasn't conducted in the UK, is that correct?"

"No. Reykjavik, Fifteen Straumur. Sixteenth of April, twenty-ten. Early. Eight-oh-seven until nine-seventeen."

Words push at the inside of his lips. The temperature. The wallpaper.

"Wasn't that when—"

"Eyjafjallajökull." He pronounces it carefully. AY-uh-fyat-luh-YOE-kuutl-uh.

Elaine Tooley, intern, smiles again. A fraction more tooth. Mrs Lindquist, Geography, second period, Tuesdays. "I suppose that makes it easy to…"

"Remember."

She coughs and looks at her lap. She makes marks on the clipboard form. "Sorry. Look, I have to ask this. Was there a particular reason?"

Forgetful Timothy John Major. Absent-minded. Why can't you just think more carefully when you put something down? Say it out loud as you're doing it. It's Tuesday morning and I am putting my keys in the bowl beside the stereo. It's Friday lunchtime and my sandwiches are in the fridge because the brie will smell. Hey, don't worry about it. That's what the internet is for.

"Lots of reasons."

"And the company? What was it called?"

"MemorIce."

"Funny."

Funny Games. Michael Haneke. Palme D'Or. *The Lost Cities of Gold*. Spandau Ballet. Hawn.

"Yes, funny."

"Seems that they're long gone. Was there any paperwork?"

Forgetful Timothy John Major. Keep receipts and important documents in one place, the inner suitcase pocket. Hardly worth going, but you know how it is. Just have to show up, in and out in forty-eight hours, maybe see the geysers in between conference sessions. A drink with the dullards. 1120 Krona for a weak lager. The Blue Lagoon's shut. Ash cloud like a bursting cauliflower.

"No."

"And what did they offer, exactly?"

'Exactly' blooms in his mind. "Do you suffer from short-term memory loss? Momentary or longer-term confusion? Wish you could recall facts and figures at the drop of a hat? Freeze your memory problems today. Call MemorIce Rekyjavik five-five-four-eight-oh-four-four for a free consultation."

Elaine Tooley, intern, lays down her pen. She tilts her head, neck exposed, Grace Kelly, *To Catch a Thief*. "How did it feel? At first. This isn't one of the questions."

Timothy John Major gathers his wits. "Do you wear contact lenses? Remember when you first wore them, or glasses, when you left the optician? The individual leaves on the trees, the small print on signs in shop windows?"

"No. I don't wear them, I mean."

But Timothy John Major is on a roll. Timothy John Major brakes for nobody.

"So imagine that sensation, but applied to the inside of your mind. Thoughts, images and concepts in absolute clarity. Memories of people, memories of facts, memories of thoughts. Twenty-twenty. Associations. Memories of memories."

His voice remains level but words come thick and fast, jostling him, racing each other to leave his mouth. *Wacky Races*. Dastardly and Muttley. *Stop the Pigeon*. Stop that pigeon now. Stop.

He sees gleams of silver in the eyes of Elaine Tooley, intern. "It's okay, it doesn't matter," she says.

"The first PC my dad brought home, eighth of February nineteen-ninety-four. He wasn't technically-minded, but I was. Tended it better than I did the guinea pigs, left those to my sister. Once a week, on Sunday morning, I set the defragmentation tool running. Sat for hours facing the monitor. A church pew. Rapturous. Watched it ticking away, block by block. Scanning the hard drive. Related fragments, picking up and moving, drawing together. Associations, access points. Green for used, red for fragments, grey for free. Grey matter." Oh dear. "What can the matter be? Sorry. Afterwards, time the difference, load up *Cannon Fodder*, whole seconds quicker. The quick and the dead. To the quick. *Don Quixote*."

Elaine Tooley, intern, stands up. "I have everything I need. They'll call for you in just a moment."

She backs away, Grace Kelly again, *Rear Window* in reverse. Timothy John Major is left alone in the empty waiting room. It is plain with pale green walls, Kemplah Primary bathroom, and the only furniture is the row of crimson seats, Danby Lodge visitors centre, December 1993, before the fire, and a table with a rack holding copies of *National Geographic*, *Cosmopolitan* and *Men's Health*. Above the magazines someone has bluetacked a postcard to the wall. What did the fish say when it swam into a wall? An orange fish, face pressed against the mud. A speech bubble, thick spot-varnish black. Comic Sans within. Dam.

The image abstracts. Holy Island Easter 1995 GCSE revision sky-blue, Nemo, Netherlands, Firefox snout orange. Post-its on the fridge, I'm sorry, it's just become too much, N x, not Comic Sans but as close as handwriting could be. Walls, walls, walls, sausages.

Timothy John Major is floating. He extends in all directions, forward, backwards and side-to-side, everywhere except here, in this waiting room. His face is pressed against the mud.

Dam.

Eqalussuaq

As Lea had predicted, Peter threw a tantrum the instant he threw open the front door to find her standing on the step. She bent and scooped him into her arms, he shuddered against her. She had imagined that he would be taller, visibly older, in the twelve weeks that had passed. If anything, he seemed to have become lighter.

"Don't fret, now," she said. "Mum's back."

Peter buried his face into her shoulder, depositing mucus onto her cardigan. More like a newborn than a six-year-old. His blonde hair had begun to sneak over the tips of his ears.

With her usual tact, Lea's friend Karen had already stepped soundlessly into the lounge, leaving mother and son to their reunion. Lea closed the front door with her hip and entered Karen's house. Peter regained his calm but still said nothing. He wriggled free of Lea's embrace to sit close beside Karen on the sofa. Anyone might have assumed she was his mother, not Lea.

"So. Tell me," Lea said.

Karen wrinkled her nose. "I won't lie. It was tougher this time. But we had our fair share of fun. Didn't we?" She rubbed Peter's head but he shrugged her away in order to glare at Lea.

"And at school?"

"Worse. More biting. Poor Daphne's parents said they'll call."

Lea winced. Stains marked Peter's cheeks, though he wasn't crying. Old tears.

"Peter, listen," she said, "What did we agree, before I left? About how you treat other children?"

Peter only shook his head. Based on past experience, it would take days for him to thaw. Until then, he would be impenetrable. An iceberg.

"That's not all," Karen said. "I couldn't think how to tell you by email. Last week, Thursday, he ran away. I was frantic." Her hands began to tremble. Lea glanced down and saw that her own hands shook a little, too. "The whole island helped me search for him. We found him in one of the refuge huts out on the causeway. He'd been trapped there for hours, Lea."

A shudder ran through Lea's body. She felt chill sting her skin, then seem to penetrate to her bones in an instant. "Thursday? The fourteenth?" she said, her jaw tight to stop her teeth chattering. "You're sure?"

Karen shrugged. "Pretty sure."

Lea examined her friend's expression. There was concern there, but it was directed at Peter, rather than Lea herself. The news mustn't have reached Britain yet. Or maybe the media didn't judge the story as dramatic as it had seemed first-hand.

She glanced at Peter. What was the appropriate parental response to the news about his attempted escape from Lindisfarne? A mother ought to know, instinctively.

On the fourteenth of September, when she had slipped beneath the water—perhaps for the last time ever, she reflected now—the cold had seemed more absolute than it ought. She had felt a sudden shock of fear then, during that solo dive, easily comparable to the fear she experienced during the incident later that day. Perhaps it had been a response to danger back at home. Perhaps she had a maternal instinct, after all.

"You understand, don't you?" Karen said. She was choosing her words carefully, too. Forcing herself not to scold Lea in front of her son. "He wasn't trying to get away, so much as he was trying to get closer to what he wanted. He was trying to follow you."

Lea made her excuses to Karen, with vague arrangements to meet later in the week. As she stepped over the threshold, Karen gripped her arm.

"I know it was an important trip for you," she said. "I understand why you went. And it's not that I mind having him here. You're closer to me than my sister, and Peter's like a son. But three whole months, Lea, and not a single phone call from you…

I can't do that again, okay? Not for a while."

Lea nodded and shuffled into the street with her shivering child.

*

It was only when Peter had finally fallen asleep that Lea had the chance to check the contents of her duffel bag. She pushed aside the thick parka and dirty laundry to retrieve the hard black case beneath. Inside, six portable hard drives made a neat row. Throughout the journey she had suffered from paranoia; all those weeks of work contained within something so easily lost. On the bumpy flight from Ilulissat she had woken shouting from a doze, certain that some atmospheric phenomenon had wiped the drives.

She booted her computer, slipped out the first drive, and ran a backup. She exhaled fully for the first time in days. Safe and sound.

When all of the backups had finished, she glanced towards the staircase. No sounds from Peter. Guiltily, she slipped on her headphones. If he yelled now, she wouldn't hear it.

She selected a file at random and clicked play. A waveform appeared onscreen, reassuring in its dark fluidity. Her eyes narrowed as she concentrated on the skittering sound. Onscreen, a dark peak broke up and away, matching a corresponding sound in the headphones. She smiled. The call of a black-legged kittiwake. Her thighs had ached terribly after she had crouched for hours with her rifle mic pointed at the nest.

She chose another track. Instantly, her headphones filled with a burping, chuckling noise. She checked the filename against the handwritten description in her notebook. Earless harp seals, slithering on the ice as they huddled together.

She settled into the swivel chair, sipping wine as she browsed through the tracks. Her hands shook only a little now, the lingering fear subsiding. The tracks were all pristine. A month of good work.

The most recently-used drive was easily identifiable, as its surface was scuffed and scratched. When she had awoken in the hut on the fifteenth, she had insisted that it be found and brought to her immediately. When she had finally made herself understood to the Inuit guides who watched over her, and they had relayed the message to her colleagues, and the hard drive had been located, she had cursed at Nils for allowing it to be handled so roughly. The look on her producer's face as he handed it over was easy to read. *After what's happened,* his expression said, *you're worried about the work?*

She had earned her reputation as a killjoy early on in the expedition. Of the seven-man team, she was the only one who refused to play along with the in-jokes about the island where they had been based for the first fortnight, insisting on using its Greenlandic title, Qeqertarsuaq, rather than the anglicised Disko Island. She had asked for the Earth, Wind and Fire to be turned down during the jeep ride from the airport. She had complained to Nils when someone had scrawled DISKO SUCKS in Tippex on one arm of her wetsuit. And when, on the first day of work proper, her first hard drive of sound recordings had been replaced with another containing only one track, a repeated twenty-second loop of the Bee Gees singing 'Staying Alive', she had thrown a tantrum that would have awed her six-year-old son.

She didn't care then and she didn't care now. She had the files.

She hooked up the most recent hard drive and selected the first track, labelled *14Sep16_001*. Her two glasses of wine had left her a little drunk. She raised her hands like a conductor as the track played.

It began with a gulp. The sound of her own body slipping into the water, probably. She shivered now. Hadn't the thought passed through her mind, at that moment, of Peter's fate if she were to freeze there in Baffin Bay? Even at the time she had recognised the thought as uncharacteristic. If she was being honest, she hadn't thought about Peter a great deal, up to that point in the expedition. But being alone in icy water, far from assistance, might make anyone behave oddly. From underwater she had looked up at the towering iceberg above, its edges knife-sharp from its recent calving from the Jakobshavn glacier. Refraction had made it bend towards her. She had felt impossibly fragile.

Bubbling sounds followed. Her last exhalation before she had settled herself into position. As the bubbles ceased, the background sounds became more easily audible. Lea leant forward to turn up the amp.

The creaking sound reminded her of her grandmother's rocking chair against wooden floorboards. Except there were layers beneath, too. A sighing, a throb of life. The quiet belch of bubbles released from somewhere in the depths and pushing along the underside of the iceberg before finding freedom at the water's surface. The rumble and snap of the iceberg itself as its regions thawed or refroze. An embrace of womblike warmth that eclipsed the physical memory of the water's icy chill.

It was good. A beautiful, living sound in its own right, as well as fulfilling producer Nils' brief of demonstrating the rate of thaw for the TV documentary. Lea sipped wine and conducted the orchestra of creaks and burbles. It was good.

Even back then, floating twenty feet down, she had had the distinct thought, *This is the best yet*. Then, as she had stifled her shivers in order to hold the microphone tight and to track the fast-moving iceberg, *This is the best work I might ever do*.

At the time.

*

By lunchtime, during the team meeting at the tiny base situated north of Ilulissat, a new opportunity had presented itself. An achievement that might easily surpass the glacier groans.

The second camerawoman, Reeta, was first to notice the change in the Inuit guide, Sighna. She interrupted Nils' summary of footage gathered that morning to rush over to Sighna and steady him, preventing him from toppling into the open brazier in the centre of the hut. Lea and the others watched on in silence as Reeta tried to grasp Sighna's hands. He wrenched them away and pressed them to either side of his head. He shook as though he were trying to squeeze his skull. He hissed a word, again and again and again. *Eqalussuaq*.

Nils tried to speak to Reeta, but she waved him away. He returned to stand next to Lea, his arms folded. He had never been good at inaction. Some other members of the team moved away from Sighna and Reeta, too, similarly embarrassed.

"Eqalussuaq," Nils whispered.

"What does it mean?" Lea asked.

"It's a name," Nils said. "Or two names, depending how you think about it."

They watched as Reeta helped Sighna to sit and gathered rucksacks to make a cushioned throne.

Nils continued, "I read the name first in a book of Greenlandic legends. Kind of a cute one. Some old woman washed her hair in urine—I know, go figure—then dried it with a cloth, which then sailed away on the wind, into the ocean. It became Ekalugsuak, and its descendants, Eqalussuaq."

The first-unit director, Terence, was listening. He stuck out his tongue. "So what's the significance of this progeny of a piss-cloth, then?"

"It'll be of interest to you, Terry, professionally speaking," Nis replied. "Eqalussuaq is an animal. The Greenland shark."

Lea saw Terence's eyes widen. He turned to Reeta, still kneeling beside the Inuit guide, whose lips were moving even though his voice had quietened. "Hey. Hey. Ask him why he's saying that word."

Sighna looked up blearily as Reeta asked the question in Greenlandic. He lifted his hands from his ears, only for a moment. He spoke in a voice too low for Lea to hear.

Reeta turned. "He says it's close. No, that's not quite the word. I don't know. Exalted? High up."

"Shitting hell," Terence said. "Meaning the Greenland shark is close? Does he know that for a fact?"

The guide was still speaking to Reeta, his lips trembling as he spoke. Reeta frowned and nodded, her palm raised to the man, perhaps as a signal for him to remain calm.

"What's the deal?" Lea whispered to Nils. "What's so exciting?"

Nils pressed his hand on his face, drawing it downwards until his jowls bounced. "It's the biggest bastard out there. Twenty-plus feet and with the oldest living to two hundred years. It's notorious, but partly that's just because of the toxicity of the flesh—remember in the port bar last night, I told you the natives use the phrase 'shark-sick' to mean drunk?"

Reeta stood up. She glanced at Sighna, who had slumped back into the pile of rucksacks. "It's all a bit of a jumble. My translation skills—" She blinked, perhaps registering the expressions of her team members. "Sighna says the shark coming close always affects him in this way. Says his head hurts, it's hard to concentrate. I'm not sure I'm getting this right, but he's complaining about something loud. Shouting. Maybe screaming."

Terence held her by the shoulders. "And the shark? He thinks it's nearby?"

"He's positive. Although I don't know why you'd treat that as—"

"Where?" Terence was already packing gear into a bag. He whistled to get the attention of the assistant director and another of the cameramen, who were deep in conversation at the far side of the hut.

"All the way back where Lea was this morning," Reeta said. "Right at the foot of the Jakobshavn glacier."

Terence and Nils exchanged glances. After a few moments, Nils shrugged his approval. "I'll buzz the boat crew. We'll meet them as close as we can get."

Lea started gathering her kit, too. "I'll show you the way down to the water." She turned to Nils. "So this shark's a catch, right? A rarity?"

Nils' face had turned pale. "Like you wouldn't believe. They almost never show their ugly faces. If one's come close to the surface—"

She was first in the jeep, turning over the engine and gesticulating orders for the other team members to hurry.

*

Lea pulled off her headphones and listened for Peter. Still no sound. She scrolled down the filenames on the hard drive. The filesize of the final track was enormous. Whoever had been operating it remotely from the boat must have let the recording run on, afterwards, while she was being hauled out of the sea. Her index finger paused over the mouse button. She turned in her swivel chair and lifted the phone.

The call went to voice mail. She hung up and tried again. This time, after several rings, Nils answered.

"It's Lea. I need to see it."

"Lea? It's— What time is it?"

"I don't know. Late, I guess. Can you send me the footage?"

"Jesus. Are you all right?"

"I'm just not tired, that's all. Got back this afternoon."

"That's not what I meant and you know it. How are you? I thought they were going to keep you in longer."

"It was only concussion, and I couldn't bear it any longer. It was so cold. Hospitals are never cold." Lea shuddered at the thought of her bare feet against the cold, tiled floor of the ward at Queen Ingrid's Hospital.

A pause. "Have you spoken to anyone?"

"I'm not a talker. You?"

"Yeah. I mean, of course. My wife, kids, my two best friends. I spoke to Carl on the phone, too, as soon as I got home. Two days too late to be anywhere near the first to offer commiserations, of course, but—" Abruptly, the phone line hummed with static. It took a few seconds for Lea to realise that Nils was sobbing. "Fuck. Lea. Carl was— I don't know. He refused to blame me. Said I'll be welcome at her funeral. But… Reeta was part of my team. She was my responsibility. If it wasn't my fault, then I don't know who. And then there was almost you, too."

"Almost." Lea tested the word 'blame' in her mind, holding it up against herself and her own actions. "But I'm okay. I am."

"I'm glad," Nils said, sniffing. "I'm so glad. If you ever need anything, Lea…"

"I just need you to send me the footage."

*

The jeep skidded to a halt at the coast. Lea leapt out, jogging to the shore, scanning for corpses. Terence ran at her side, barely able to contain his glee at the prospect of discovering a bear or seal, evidence of one of Eqalussuaq's rare forays above the surface. During the jeep journey, Nils had pulled up Google image results of seals found with rips that corkscrewed around their bodies. As she had glanced at the photos, Lea's only thought had been to wonder what the attack must have sounded like.

They found nothing but the waiting boat. Its three crew members took Nils aside to speak to him, before allowing any of the production team on board. Even then, they remained far quieter than usual.

For three hours, the boat bobbed in the waters at the foot of the Jakobshavn glacier. After the first hour, Lea's eyes grew tired of staring at the roiling waters and her stomach ached from leaning over the rail. She gazed up at the glacier and imagined that she could make out its creep, pushing across the sea towards the boat.

When Reeta volunteered to go below the surface, Lea stood at her side and insisted that she should go too. She held the microphone before her like a staff, as if to demonstrate her strength. Nils protested, of course, but Lea made her case again and again. If Eqalussuaq wasn't down there, then she could simply gather more iceberg and background recordings. And if it was, then wouldn't it be a crime to have video footage but no sound?

*

Lea refreshed her inbox until the email appeared. She followed the link to the fileshare site. While she waited for it to download, she darted upstairs to fetch a blanket, then drank another glass of wine huddled within it. It was getting colder all the time.

She opened the final sound file, *14Sep16_044*, then clicked the pause button before it started.

The video finished downloading. She set it running. The video was far from broadcast quality, as it was the backup from the remote feed the rest of the team had viewed on the boat, rather than the master files. After a dizzying flurry of pixel artefacts and indigo bubbles, the image cleared a little. She saw herself, barely recognisable in her wetsuit, identifiable only by the Tippex marks on her shoulder: DISKO SUCKS.

Onscreen, she held up three fingers. Here, now, Lea copied the pose, then two fingers, then one. Then she clicked the play button on the sound file.

Suddenly, the bubbles produced by her scuba equipment were accompanied by gulping sounds through the headphones. Lea leant close to the screen, trying to judge whether sound and image matched. The underwater Lea tapped on the microphone, twice, producing dull thuds. Perfect sync.

It was as she remembered. Reeta's camera swung smoothly around, performing a three-sixty turn to end up facing Lea again. Lea gesticulated and Reeta spun quicker, losing her balance. Lea shook her head. She hadn't meant to suggest that she had seen anything that should be filmed, she had only meant to tell Reeta to point the camera somewhere other than towards her.

The gurgling sound increased in volume, the only clue that Lea had allowed herself to descend further. Reeta's camera dropped too and the indigo screen darkened. When the bubbles lessened once again, Lea could hear the low grumbles and creaks of the icebergs above.

It was difficult to remember how long they had floated there, searching the darkness for signs of the shark. Even now, watching onscreen, Lea lost track. Her eyelids drooped. If it hadn't been so cold, she might have slept.

A flurry of bubbles alerted her. The video artefacted again as Reeta bounced the camera around. When it stabilised, Lea could see herself once more, in the bottom left-hand corner of the screen, barely visible against the blackness of the lower depths. This tiny Lea was looking up and away from Reeta's camera.

And then there it was.

Eqalussuaq.

Lea felt a swell of disappointment. Even with its entire length visible, the shark seemed squat and small, making a horizontal stripe across the centre-left of the screen. Its tail was only a few pixels in height. She tried to judge the distance between her and it. Ten feet? Five? Both of them seemed to fidget, an effect of the camera shaking.

The shark seemed to hover before Lea, maintaining a consistent distance. The effect was as though it were tethered to her like a balloon. Onscreen, Lea stretched out her arm, pushing the microphone towards the thing. New sounds came from the headphones. Whooshes and hisses. Its fins as it adjusted its position.

Then, both Lea and the shark seemed to grow. Reeta was moving closer. Brave girl. For the first time, Lea felt a stab of guilt about what happened next.

It would be any second now.

The shark edged backwards—she hadn't realised that at the time—before it leapt towards Lea. Her arm lifted to protect her face, producing loud gulps as the weight of the water pushed back against the microphone. Then, onscreen, Lea's head raised to look directly at the shark as it came.

She remembered the sequence of events clearly, up to a point. Her memories filled in what the grainy footage had failed to capture.

She remembered seeing the thin threads that trailed from each of its eyes. Nils had described them during the jeep journey—parasites that itched and blinded the shark.

She remembered the moment in which the shark seemed to travel above her, rather than towards her, before its jaw dropped open.

She remembered the distinct difference between its two sets of teeth: broad and square below, thin and pointed above. An ugly phrase had repeated in her mind: seal ripping.

She remembered opening her mouth just as the shark did, releasing her grip on her scuba mouthpiece, and letting loose a storm of bubbles that almost, but not quite, obscured Eqalussuaq, and she remembered shouting at it. The recording failed to capture the words, but she spoke them aloud, again, now.

"Not me! Take her!"

Abruptly, a squall of sound shrieked through the headphones.

Lea spasmed and one arm knocked the glass from the worktop, spraying red wine onto the screen. She ripped the headphones from her ears.

Onscreen, the open jaws of the shark shuddered, as if the shriek came from within.

What was *that*? Instinctively, she glanced at the waveform. Its shape was smoothly bulbous, without peaks.

She bent the headphone cup to listen with one ear. The shriek began again, even louder than before. Even with the amp dialled down, she could hardly bear to hear it. Now she could make out a guttural growl beneath the shrill static.

She flung the headphones down again.

Onscreen, silent, the shark turned. Now it faced the camera full on.

Perhaps Reeta wasn't so brave, after all. At the moment that it was clear that Eqalussuaq was accelerating towards her, she let go of the camera. The blue light of the screen flashed bright and dark, bright and dark, as the camera spun and dropped down, down, down.

Upstairs, Peter began to howl.

*

She slept badly, imagining herself in the depths along with the abandoned camera. Something was down there with her, sinuous and sleek. It was a bad joke, she thought when she woke. Eqalussuaq, of the family Somniosidae. *Sleeper shark.*

*

The bulky headphones comforted her. As she strode towards the island's coast, she listened to the live recording stream from the binaural microphones fixed to the exterior of the earphone cups. Her footsteps redoubled in her ears, lagging fractionally behind the real world, as if following her.

Lindisfarne could be defined by its sounds. The wind tumbling from the sea and up the rock outcrops. The cries of the gulls and the whip of their wings. The dense, tactile calm within the oasis of the priory ruins. Captured and suitably arranged, it all belonged to Lea.

Her pace quickened as she headed through the sand dunes to the pebble beach, putting distance between herself and home. The Arctic recordings weren't scheduled to be delivered to Nils for another week, after Reeta's funeral, and indexing the sound files would involve only a handful of hours of work. That morning, when she had returned from delivering Peter to school, she had lingered in front of the computer, unable to bring herself to boot it up. Eqalussuaq's shriek had still echoed in her ears.

She had decided to distract herself by concentrating on other projects. Her record label had shown only muted interest in her proposal of manipulated ambient recordings from Lindisfarne, but they hadn't heard even the raw audio yet. Following post-production work in the studio, the tracks could be wonderful.

She was still crouching beside an abandoned boat, leaning in with the binaural mics to capture its dull scrape against the pebbles, when she noted the time. All those weeks away from home had left her insensitive to the timing of the tides. She would have to rush to make it across the causeway and back before the sea made it impassable.

As she turned from the shore a faint sound registered in her headphones. She turned to the boat again. Had its hull made that screech? She turned her head from side to side to locate the direction. It was coming from somewhere out at sea. Shrill. As the high-pitched noise grew in volume, she heard a deep grumble beneath, and she thought of icebergs. She stared out at the water, half-expecting to see a disturbance, something cutting through the waves as it approached.

Nothing. At least, nothing visible.

But the volume increased, all the same. The screech and roar became more insistent. Louder.

Angrier.

After another ten seconds she could no longer bear the shrieking. She pulled off the headphones and sprinted back towards the dunes.

*

Lea sat opposite Peter at the melamine table. He hadn't touched his burger. There were dark shadows beneath his eyes. After the awkwardness of the apology to Daphne and her parents at the school gates, Lea had brought him to a McDonald's in Berwick, but her desperation to maintain the pretence that it was a treat was wearing thin. Peter was a smart six-year-old. He understood that her delay on the island, and the high tide that now covered the Lindisfarne causeway, meant an enforced wait of four hours before they could return home.

"What if you'd got lost when you were away?" Peter said.

Lea flinched. Once again, she imagined herself freezing in Baffin Bay. If she'd found herself trapped down there, would she have prayed for Peter or would her final thoughts have been of her precious recordings?

"I had maps and people to show me around," she said. She noted the petulance in her own voice.

"But you were far, far away."

"Eat your food."

Peter pushed away the greasy container. "Daphne said you weren't coming back."

"And that's why you bit her?"

"I bit her because she's a bitch."

Lea sprung from her seat. "Don't you dare use that kind of language!" She hovered beside him. What was she going to do, hit him?

Peter slumped further into his chair.

Lea sighed. It was fruitless to wonder where he'd learnt the word. She had no idea how he'd been living for the last three months. She would never have thought him capable of running away from home.

"Look," she said, "I was far away, you're right. But I found my way back to you, didn't I?"

Peter's sullen expression changed to one of quiet hope. "Like I've got a homing beacon? So you can always find me?"

"Exactly. I zoomed across the seas, from Greenland all the

49

way back to here. And I won't leave you again." Instantly, she regretted the last part.

That night, after Peter had bathed, he insisted that Lea bring the portable radio into his bedroom. Karen, it transpired, had taken to leaving a radio on low volume, following a phase of interrupted sleep. The mutter of Radio 4 voices was unintelligible but soothing nonetheless, despite the static that wouldn't quite abate, no matter where Lea tuned the dial.

*

Shadows in the depths. Smooth skin and sharp points.

Lea woke in a panic.

That shriek again. It pulsated, echoing around the walls and in her head.

She burst into the corridor and down the stairs. Behind her, Peter's shouts mingled with the scream that seemed to come from everywhere at once.

The shrill sound was even louder as she neared her studio at the back of the house. She staggered with the pressure of it as she entered the room. The huge bookshelf speakers emitted waves of piercing white noise.

Lea lunged up at them. Once they were turned off, her body slumped in delayed shock.

She ignored Peter's wails. In the kitchen she turned on the radio, then flicked it off as the squealing sound began again. The TV in the lounge gave the same result, though the picture was unaffected.

It was everywhere.

With shaking hands, she booted up the computer. She opened one of the iceberg sound recordings at random.

She saw what had happened immediately. Instead of a smooth waveform, the sound editor showed a single block of black, with only occasional slices missing, like shards calved from an iceberg. Tentatively, she lifted the headphones and pressed play. The scream was unbearable, even with the headphones held at arm's length. The plastic buzzed and shook with the force of the sound.

She opened more and more sound files. They all appeared identical—masses of noise, black blots on the screen.

All of the recordings were gone. All of the sounds, eclipsed by a single shout. A shriek. A scream.

"No," she whimpered. "Please. Anything but this."

She staggered backwards. The loss of the recordings felt like grief.

She remembered how the sound had approached as she had stood on the shore of the island. A phrase from the day before echoed in her mind.

…across the seas, from Greenland all the way back to here…

She thought of Sighna, the Inuit guide, his hands clamped over his ears.

She thought of Eqalussuaq, its jaws wide. Its silent scream, back then. Its shriek, on the recordings.

Whatever she had picked up on her microphone, it hadn't been a sound, not in the usual sense. It was something else. Something that she had trapped, or that had— what was the word? Hidden? No… burrowed. Torn and ripped and burrowed, hiding itself within her recordings.

And she had brought it home.

The bookshelf speakers began to rock. Lea shuddered. She could still hear the sound, though only faintly. She pulled the plug from the wall. The sound only grew in intensity.

Anger.

She felt an icy chill all over her body. The sound grew and grew and grew, dizzying, nauseating. It no longer came from the speakers. It seemed to be emitted by the walls, the air, her own skin.

"Stop!" she shouted. "Whatever you are, stop! Leave me alone!" Another phrase, the same one she had used when she had first encountered Eqalussuaq, pressed at her. "Not me!"

The scream stopped.

Lea waited. The calm felt like deafness. Tentatively, she plugged in the speakers and turned them on. Nothing.

Safe and sound.

With shaking hands, she booted the computer, then scrolled

down to the first recordings of that final day in the sea. She selected the first file. A low, warm, creaking sound came from the speakers. The song of the iceberg had returned, pristine and ethereal, its wheezing groan continuing without interruption. No screaming, no anger.

She selected another recording made that same morning, then another. All were unimpaired, the clean, clear sounds matching the smooth waveforms on the screen.

Breathless, she gathered recordings together in the sound editor, overlaying and overlapping them, until the orchestra of soft moaning sounds grew into a single, overwhelming, glorious song. Bubbles rose around her. She felt warmth despite the chill. She danced slowly as if underwater.

Only one unwanted, alien sound penetrated through. Lea finally registered Peter's complaints from upstairs.

As she entered his bedroom, her son reached up blindly with both hands.

"It's okay," Lea said, rocking him against her chest. "It's gone."

Peter said nothing. Tears trickled down his cheeks, making twin spots on her pyjamas. His open mouth worked from side to side. Lea remembered making the same motion herself, as the plane touched down and she tried to restore her hearing.

"Stop shouting," Peter murmured.

Lea frowned. Was he dreaming?

But then he looked directly at her. His voice sounded far away. "It hurts so much, Mum. Make it stop."

She watched him writhe, his hands pressed against his ears and his face pushed into the pillow. She felt a sudden certainty that it wouldn't help.

Peter's body was slack in her arms as she made her way downstairs. She stood holding him, before her computer, watching the undulating shapes of the waveforms on the screen. The iceberg recordings continued playing. Warm and heavenly.

She hesitated for several moments before laying Peter down on the battered studio sofa. Her hands wavered over the computer keyboard.

Peter's mouth contorted with pain, a thin white line pressed tight as if withholding something trying to force its way out.

It felt like a choice. Save the recordings, or Peter. Eqalussuaq was demanding that she choose.

She understood that her hesitation was unforgivable. She understood that she would spend her life attempting to rationalise the fact that she had even considered the alternative.

She looked at her son.

She chose.

14Sep16. Select all.

She wept a little.

Delete.

Peter whimpered as Lea smoothed his hair, then pressed his head further into the sofa cushion. His body shivered and shook. Clearly, he was still in agony.

She yanked out the plug to the computer and clawed at its case.

In the lean-to beyond the kitchen she found a hammer and chisel. As she cracked through the casing of the computer she shouted and wailed, a sound almost as feral as the scream on the recordings. The chisel revealed the internal hard drive, then fractured it. Once it was in pieces Lea turned her attention to the portable drives. In her desperation she shattered them all.

If anything, Peter appeared to be suffering even more now. His knees pulled up to his chin. As he rocked back and forth, his entire body spasmed.

Then his white lips trembled. They parted, showing his teeth.

The scream of whatever had followed Lea from the Arctic burst forth. Peter's head rattled from side to side with the effort of restraining himself against the force of the sound.

Lea gripped his hands. She pleaded.

But she understood. Destroying the recordings wasn't all that Eqalussuaq demanded.

"It's not him you want," she said in a whisper. "It's me."

Peter's eyes opened.

Lea gripped the wooden arm of the sofa.

It hit her. Creaking limbs, something bellowing, screams that knifed through the water.

She clamped her hands over her ears, without any effect. The shriek took swipes at her head and torso, threatening to send her toppling. Her body convulsed with the cold.

*

Peter recovered within hours.

Lea's tinnitus would be permanent, the doctor said, though over time it transitioned from excruciating to deafening to a persistent, wavering drone.

She stood on the rock outcrop at dusk, facing out to sea. She watched a flock of gulls, concentrating on the shifting shapes that they formed, at first a ribbon, then a fat arrow, then a winding river.

She stretched her body upwards, tracking the flock, then winced at a pain in her stomach. She pulled her cardigan and T-shirt up. The thing had left her, but it had also left its mark. If it had ever been a real wound, one might have said it was healing fast. It was clear that the scar would remain, though—a single line of ripped, raw, pink flesh that corkscrewed around her abdomen.

A wave curled into existence and bundled itself towards the shore. Once she might have worn her binaural microphones to capture the sounds of the wind and waves, but the ringing in her ears interfered with the recordings. Now the sounds of the island served only as a temporary mask over the hisses and shrieks.

Above her, for a few seconds, the flock of birds formed a new shape—something sinewy and snub-nosed. It flexed and flicked its tail as it swam across the darkening sky.

Finding Waltzer-Three

A static-filled sigh comes across the comms link. Richard leans close to the speaker housed in the control unit. When his wife speaks, he jolts back in alarm.

"Toss a coin, Rich?" Meryl sounds both fragile and husky at the same time.

Richard thumps the input panel. "You scared me, going quiet like that. What can you see?"

"We were right. I can see her. In fact, I'm standing on her."

"Good grief! You don't mean—"

"I do. Here's the ID plate. *Waltzer-Three.*"

Richard checks and rechecks the array of screens before him. This is the only panel fully operational on the deck of the spaceship, the rest hum in standby. "She's not showing up anywhere."

"Except out here. Toss a coin."

Richard knows better than to ask for clarification. Meryl has a sense of theatre. He pulls a coin from his pocket and flips it with a thumbnail.

"Tails."

"Tails never fails. Right, I'm going in."

Richard leaps to his feet, sending his chair skittering across the floor to thud against another unit. "Are you hell! Gregg stipulated absolutely clearly—"

"So maybe you should wake him up to check."

The captain, along with the bulk of the crew, are scheduled to sleep until May at least. Richard clicks his tongue.

"I'll tell one of the others, then."

"Who, the bursar? As it stands, we're the top dogs, Rich. You and me."

"Then I say no."

"Fine. And I say yes, so the coin gets the deciding vote. The door's open."

Richard pulls at his beard. "Meryl, you've got no right. There's no telling what actually happened to *Waltzer-Three*."

"Smell you later." The tone of the comms transmission has changed, the hush surrounding Meryl's voice replaced with a low hum. Richard hears distant, muted bumps, the sound of his wife clambering into the airlock. In sympathy, he experiences the closure of the outer door as a popping of the ears.

He breathes deep to slow his heart rate. "Check readings." He says this only in order to hear her voice, he realises.

"Centripetal sim-gravity superb. Waltzer by name, waltzer by nature. Toxins normal. Oxygen adequate. Radiation normal-ish."

"Ish?"

"Kidding. Helmet's coming off."

The helmet release sounds like the fizz of an opened lager bottle.

"Keep talking, love," Richard says.

He hears a gentle snort. Meryl is smiling.

"You forget how bare-bones these old ones were," she says. "Bare, moulded plastic, all magnolia. Looks like an intergalactic starter home. It could do with Laura Ashley wallpaper, or something. And the smell of coffee or freshly-baked bread or they'll never sell it. Still, the foyer's pretty big. Room for a pram."

"Meryl."

"Sorry. OK, I'm going all the way in."

He hears another mechanical groan as the interior door opens. Meryl's footsteps punctuate the static.

"Oh." Meryl's voice has become smaller.

"What? What's going on? What do you see?"

"Nothing. Seriously, I mean it. The control room's desolate, not a soul here."

Richard chews his cheek. "What could that mean? All the final transmissions indicated that they were operating normally."

"So I guess the final transmissions weren't the end, then."

"This is no good. Come back, Meryl." Without meaning to,

he ends with a rising inflection, a request rather than a command.

His wife ignores him, or doesn't hear. "It's all pristine, though. No damage, like Ops predicted. There are more blinking lights in here than there are out in the starfield."

The hissy footsteps begin again. Meryl is heading towards the bunkhouses, he supposes. She's a people person.

"Strange," she says.

"Please," Richard says, "Stop saying vague, alarming things. What's strange?"

"It's double-locked from this side."

Richard ponders this. "So nobody could enter the control room?"

"Don't be silly. Of course they could. What earthly good would there be in a door that could be locked tight from only one side? The point is that whoever last came through the door locked it from here."

"So then they left."

"So then they left."

"You should too, Meryl. Don't go in there."

"Too late." The whoosh from the door follows several seconds later, revealing her lie.

"Seriously, love," Richard says. "Talk to me. Where are you now?"

"Just checking the third room, sleeping quarters. Nobody here, but that's not so much what's weird about it. I'm thinking of our room, Rich. It's a pigsty, right?"

"Are you saying it's my turn to tidy it?"

"For the record, yes. But I mean, that's how people live. Clothes draped on chairs, piles of shoes, books on the bed. Not here. Immaculate pile of personal items on each bedside table, everything at right angles. I bet you—yep, I've just opened a drawer. Even the underpants are folded, Rich."

Richard shudders without fully understanding why.

The comms static becomes thick, a grunting squall.

"Door's stuck," Meryl says.

"As in jammed? Locked?"

"Nope. It's a swing-open. At least, it would be if it actually swung." She grunts again. "There. Oh shit."

Richard bends double over the control unit, staring at the speaker as it might give him a view onto *Waltzer-Three*.

"It's a body," Meryl says. "A body blocking the door."

"Get out."

"Hold your horses. What's the big surprise, scaredy cat?"

Richard's mouth twitches into a smile, despite everything. Meryl called him 'scaredy cat' back when they were kids, goading him at kiss-chase in the school playground.

"We expected crew, didn't we?" she continues. "No big deal. The only odd thing is how she's dressed. What year did *Waltzer-Three* go AWOL? Eighty-nine?"

"Eighty-eight."

Meryl humphs. "Well, no disrespect to the dead, but this style of evening gown went out of fashion in the seventies. It's all ruffles, uck."

"Evening gown? The corpse is wearing an evening gown?"

"Rich, that sounds gruesome. She wasn't a corpse when she put it on. And the automated life-support is doing overtime. She hasn't decayed a bit. A redhead, you'd like her."

"Funny."

"Made me laugh. Sorry. You know how I get when I'm anxious."

Richard feels a pang of relief. At least she admits that much.

"So I'm just heading into the canteen. And—"

"And?"

"And there they are."

"Who?" When she doesn't reply, he repeats, "Meryl. Who?"

Her voice sounds strained. "The crew. Twenty, twenty-five of them. Sitting around three big round tables, bigger than in our canteen. Must have been more sociable back then. Hasn't everyone become more cynical nowadays? Nobody likes large groups, people keep themselves to themselves."

"Meryl, please! You're rambling."

He hears her draw three deep, sputtering breaths.

"Rich. I'm terrified, suddenly."

Richard reaches out as if he might grasp her hands. "I'm here.

I'm here."

"They were all eating," she says. "When it happened, whatever it was, they were eating."

"It had to be sometime, Meryl. Does it matter if they were asleep, or in the control room, or here?"

"You don't understand. They knew."

"How can you tell?"

"It's so eerie. Some are face down on the table, but some are still leaning against each other, somehow. And it wasn't just the woman in the doorway. They're all dressed up, Rich. Like it's a prom or something. All the women in gowns, hair done, caked in makeup. Most of the men wearing tuxes, and those that aren't made do with those black engineer jackets. White bowties made from toilet paper. And the food! Roast chicken, potatoes, petits pois. Cut-glass goblets filled with red. Did ships really carry all this stuff, back then?"

Richard's eyes water. "Please, Meryl. Come back. I'll do anything. Don't spend another minute there. If you love me, come back to me now."

To his relief, Meryl's supply of wisecracks has exhausted.

"I'm coming."

*

Meryl pants heavily as Richard helps her out of the bulky suit. Once it has been discarded the two of them topple together, wigwam-like, into an awkward embrace. Richard's hands explore her back, tracing familiar contours.

"I love you so much," he says.

"So you're always telling me." She pulls away, holding him at arm's length. She grins. "Sorry. I love you too, you beautiful oaf."

They walk back to the control room, hand in hand.

"So what happens now?" Richard says.

Meryl pauses. "We should wake the captain."

Richard nods.

"In fact, we should wake them all," she says. "We should all be together."

She turns to look at him. Her eyes are a calm sea. "Rich, I'm hungry."

St Erth

Carmen's forehead bumped the window as the Land Rover Discovery struggled across uneven ground. She scowled and stared at the darkness.

Her younger brother, Asher, continued singing. "Ten man, nine man, eight man, seven man, six man, five man, four man—" He took a deep breath. "—three man, two man, one man and his dog…"

Their mother, Imogen, joined in from the front passenger seat, rising to a falsetto. "Weeeent to mooooow a meadow! How about 'Row Your Boat' next?"

Carmen kicked at the back of the driver's seat. "Stop them, Dad? I've got the mother of all headaches."

The car came to a halt. Michael turned in the driver's seat. "Don't start, you lot. We're here."

Imogen hunched down to peer through the windscreen. "I didn't see the signs."

Asher yanked open the door and leapt out. He made a pantomime retching sound. "It's muddy."

Carmen and her father exchanged looks: a neutral facial expression in place of raised eyebrows or rolled eyes. They'd long since learnt not to signal cynicism. Asher didn't understand it and Imogen wouldn't stand for it.

Imogen had already removed her shoes and pulled on her wellies. "This is going to be such tremendous fun. Getting away from it all for a whole week!"

Michael's fingers still clamped the steering wheel.

As Carmen exited the car, her Cons sunk into soft mud. With difficulty, she followed her brother and mother as they made their way towards a wide wooden hut bearing a faded sign: 'St Erth

Campsite Reception'. No light came from within the building but the car headlights made the windows shine.

Imogen rapped on the door. There was no answer. She tried the handle.

"Hello!" she called.

"Let's go to a hotel," Carmen said. "It's like midnight or something. I just want to sleep."

Asher ran into the reception, opening other doors. "Nobody's here, Mummy." He stood on tiptoes to hit the light switch. No lamps lit.

In the next room, Imogen shone her keyring torch, illuminating a meagre collection of groceries upon a formica counter. "Look. There's an appointment book. No need to wake anyone. It'll tell us which yurt is ours." She rifled through the pages, sucked her teeth, then tucked the book under her arm. "It'll be easier to read in the Discovery."

"That's stealing," Carmen said.

"Nonsense. The campsite owners can come and collect it in the morning."

Back in the car, Imogen announced that their accommodation was yurt number sixteen. The wheels of the Discovery slipped in the muddy furrows that led to the camping field.

Even in the darkness, Carmen saw immediately that yurt number sixteen was in bad repair. Mud streaks rose halfway up its outer wall. A wooden beam had pierced its roof from inside. The canvas door flapped in the wind.

"There must be some mistake," Imogen said. "Michael, dear, make yourself useful and find us another yurt."

Michael slid out of the driver's seat and edged across the field, arms outstretched. He returned, looking forlorn. "They're all empty, oddly enough, but none are in any better state than this one."

Imogen seemed almost triumphant, as if her distress made her stronger. "Then we'll just have to become one with nature, won't we? It's good to leave our creature comforts behind. All we need is ourselves, a canvas roof over our heads, and this wonderfully fresh Cornish air."

An hour later, Carmen curled tighter into her sleeping bag inside the yurt, enjoying the quiet and the chill that stung lightly at her face. Every so often the door of the yurt flapped open wide enough for her to see Asher, her mother and her father, sprawled awkwardly in their car seats, the interior light faintly illuminating their sleeping faces.

*

Carmen woke to the smell of frying bacon.

"Well, they're no use on the kitchen counter, are they?" she heard her mother say.

Michael's reply was an unintelligible mutter.

Carmen ducked further into her sleeping bag as her mother entered the yurt.

"I know you're awake, dear."

Carmen wriggled out. She pushed her hair from her eyes.

"Your father's a fool and forgot the eggs. It'll be no kind of fried breakfast. Be a love and ask the campsite owner for some? Six, and large."

"I don't feel well," Carmen replied. As soon as she said it, she realised it was true. Something in the centre of her stomach felt tight and hard.

"The fresh air will do wonders for you. Breathe deep, Carmen. It's nature's own medicine."

Reluctantly, Carmen pulled on her shoes and left the yurt. In daylight, the churned mud of the camping field looked even less appealing. She ducked into the car to retrieve her parka—Asher moaned at the intrusion and turned away in his seat—and pulled it tight around herself. It lessened her shivering but didn't stop it entirely. The air was colder now than during the night.

Her father had been right: all of the yurts were empty; the few caravans were too, and there were no tents at all. A lone trailer home teetered at an angle, thick mud pushing or pulling at its concrete-slab base.

The reception shack was empty. In the doorway, dark footprints overlapped to make a black ooze, as if the mud outside was gathering itself to mount an attack.

She stepped inside. A layer of grime covered the formica counter and even the stacks of tinned food. There were no eggs.

She returned to her family. A stranger had stopped outside their yurt.

"You big dodo," Imogen said as Carmen approached. "You must have passed Mrs Spargo coming the other way. She says she doesn't have any eggs."

Mrs Spargo's lank grey hair had plastered to one cheek. She didn't meet Carmen's eyes. Her hands clasped tight together as if one was restraining the other.

"I don't have any eggs," Mrs Spargo said slowly.

"What a wonderful campsite you run," Imogen said. "It's... *authentic*."

Mrs Spargo blinked and looked around her at the mud and empty yurts.

"Does your family help you to maintain it?"

Mrs Spargo shook her head. Strands of grey hair whipped across her eyes. "My husband's all dead and gone."

"Oh." Imogen chewed her lip. Then her face brightened again. "Well, I'm sure he's up there looking on."

Mrs Spargo raised her eyes to the sky. Her mouth opened in a kidney-shaped, toothless grimace. She backed away.

"The floods came," she mumbled, "and that was that."

When Mrs Spargo had moved out of earshot, Imogen said, "What an interesting lady. I expect we'll find all sorts of local characters around here and they'll tell us a thing or two about local customs. Superstitions. It's not hard to imagine that a flood might be seen as much a sign of good fortune as bad. You know—the chance to start afresh." Her smile faltered. "Poor Mrs Spargo, though. I hope the grass grows back soon."

"She's stark raving mad, Mum," Carmen said. "Can't you see that?"

"What tosh, darling. We can all learn a lot from Mrs Spargo and her sort. Michael. Are you *close* to having prepared breakfast, my sweet? I'll rouse Asher from his golden slumber."

Carmen gave her father a look. Michael just sighed and began transferring limp rashers of bacon from the camping stove to the plastic plates.

*

Carmen hesitated at the edge of the forest. The bacon sandwich wasn't sitting well in her stomach, even though breakfast had been hours ago and she had only half-eaten hers. She leant against a thick tree trunk. The bark prickled against her palm.

"Come along, sweetness!" her mother called from ahead. "Nature calls!"

Michael sniggered. He gave a pantomime shrug when Imogen turned and glared at him. Asher tramped with his head down. His wellies went up past his knees, knocking with every step.

The yurts were pinpricks in the distance. The camping field had become even boggier as they had approached the forest. Carmen's boots were heavy with filth.

Abruptly, a shiver started at her feet and then travelled upwards along her body.

"I think we should stay out in the open," she said, too quiet for anyone else to hear.

Being left alone was even less appealing than entering the forest. She jogged to catch up.

Imogen held up a hand. "Hush!"

Obediently, they all stopped.

Imogen turned. "I thought I saw something. I hoped it might be a deer." She crouched, scanning the foliage like a big-game hunter.

Carmen listened. The forest was silent.

She flinched at Asher's gasp. "I see a trap," he said, pointing to the right.

It was a spider's web, but like none Carmen had ever seen before. Its threads spanned the space between three trees, making its mass three-dimensional. In its centre the threads intersected in a tangled ball.

Michael and Asher edged closer.

On instinct, Carmen held out a hand as Michael ducked

under the nearest anchoring thread, as if that might stop him. Imogen pulled Carmen against her hip and guided her forwards to the web.

The thick web ball contained a collection of insects. They were mostly flies, but also beetles, daddy-long-legs and even dragonflies. They were bundled into a space the size of a grapefruit, making the dense centre of the web almost uniformly black.

"Mummy, I don't like it," Asher said.

Imogen clutched Carmen's shoulder tighter.

"They're still alive," Michael whispered. He reached out his hand.

Instantly, the insects began to writhe within their prison.

"Don't," Carmen said in a quiet voice.

Michael hesitated, then reached out again. The insects grew feverish in their struggles. The web ball shook, tugging at the threads that anchored it to the surrounding trees.

Imogen leapt forwards, grabbing Michael at the waist and yanking him backwards. He staggered, then blinked rapidly and rubbed his eyes.

Imogen smoothed her hair, then raised both arms to shoo everyone back to the path.

"There's another lesson for us," she said. Her voice trembled slightly. "There's an order to the natural world, gruesome though it may be. We can't intervene, but we can watch and learn. It's wonderful, in a way."

There were tears in Asher's eyes. He gripped Imogen's hand, walking as quickly as his short legs could carry him and dragging his mother along.

Carmen and her father followed behind. Every few steps, Michael shook his head.

"I didn't see the spider," Carmen said.

*

Each new thing that they encountered threatened to erode Imogen's belief in the purity of the natural world. When they stopped to eat cereal bars, Asher sat directly in a wet turd and then shrieked for minutes afterwards. When Imogen insisted that they investigate a potential badger sett, they found it filled with empty bottles and litter. Imogen stared down at a discarded condom, her bottom lip trembling, before announcing that the flood water had certainly done some damage to the area, and didn't that just prove how powerful Mother Nature really was?

Imogen, Michael and Asher all looked terribly tired. Perhaps they would refuse to spend another night in the Discovery. If they wouldn't sleep in the yurt either, perhaps the holiday would be ended abruptly and they could return home to the controlled, safe environment of their Woodstock house.

Then they saw the man. He moved through the trees, further ahead. His back was bent as though he was injured.

"Is that a tramp?" Asher said.

"No, darling," Imogen said. "Homeless people are only in the cities."

"It's a tramp, Mummy. He might kill us."

Following Imogen's lead, they moved slowly towards the man. Carmen kept her eyes fixed on him. Every few steps, he bent down to the ground.

"If it is a homeless person," Imogen said after a pause, "then he probably chose to live here in the forest, that's all. His diet's probably better than ours. We ought to envy him."

Carmen squinted. "There are more of them."

The sunlight penetrating the trees turned the four figures into silhouettes: two larger, two smaller. They bent to the forest floor every few seconds.

"It's a family," Michael said.

Carmen saw them reach down to pick up items from the ground, then stuff them into sacks slung over their shoulders.

"They're clearing up the rubbish!" Imogen said. "See? Community spirit!" She jogged ahead, calling out a greeting.

Carmen winced at a fresh pain in her stomach. With some difficulty, she joined her family. They stood a few feet apart from the family carrying sacks. Mother faced mother, father faced father, boy faced boy. Carmen sidestepped to avoid standing directly before the teen girl.

Their faces were pale and their eyes moist. Their clothes were covered in grime. Loose threads from their jumpers and wayward strands from their unkempt hair, combined with the harsh streaks of sunlight from behind, gave their bodies blurred-edged haloes. They stood upon a blanket of litter that obscured the forest floor.

"Can we help you?" Imogen said, indicating the sack on the mother's back.

The other mother shook her head.

Carmen glanced at Imogen.

"It's wonderful, what you're doing," Imogen said. She stepped forwards.

The new mother and father each took a step, too, narrowing the gap.

Imogen raised her left hand above her head slowly as she bent to the ground. She picked up an empty two-litre milk carton, nipping its handle daintily between her thumb and index finger.

"Get off it!"

The mother of the other family burst forwards, snatching the milk carton from Imogen's hand. She bundled it into her sack and snarled from the back of her throat.

Then, abruptly, her aggression seemed to disappear. When she spoke again, her voice was soft and welcoming.

"Come with us."

Carmen looked at her own family. To her amazement, none of them appeared afraid.

The mother, father and son of the new family paired up with their opposites. Carmen tried to stifle the ache in her stomach as she walked. The teen girl kept pace with her. Her hair was short and frayed. Thin twigs protruded from holes in her thick jumper. She might have been pretty, if her face were scrubbed of filth.

"Stop," the girl said. She reached out her arm, barring Carmen's way.

Carmen shuddered. "What's your name?" she said, just to say something.

"Who cares. Nessa. You?"

"Carmen."

Nessa smirked. "Nice. Carmen, Carmina, Carmine. Meaning

crimson."

She pushed Carmen from the path. Carmen felt weaker than ever. Soon Nessa brought them to a halt.

"There."

Carmen saw only tree trunks and branches. The path was still visible, though her family had disappeared somewhere ahead.

"There," Nessa said again.

She pointed to a trunk that was wider than the others. It was marked by a dark oval the size of a plate, exactly at the height of Carmen's eyes.

"Guess what made that?"

Carmen shook her head.

"My best friend made it. My *old* best friend."

Carmen whimpered as the ache in her stomach grew more fierce. "How?"

"Like this." Nessa placed a hand either side of the dark patch, hugging the tree trunk. She pulled her head back. Then she jerked it forwards.

"Smack," she said. Her forehead stopped millimetres from the bark.

She pulled her head back and performed the action again, twice. "Smack, smack."

"Stop it."

"Smack. Smack. Smack until her head just burst."

Carmen's eyes filled with tears. "Stop it! It's not true. It's not true!"

Nessa stepped back. Carmen almost expected to see blood on her forehead, but there was only the same dried muck.

The girl grinned. "Yeah. It's not true."

*

They caught up with the others at the far side of the forest. Carmen squinted into the sunlight.

A wide river wound from left to right, curling around the forest. It shone like a mirror. Water sat in stagnant pools at its edges, barely troubled by the current. The flood water must still be seeping back from the land, dragging the soil along with it, turning the river black.

Structures had been erected on the strip of land between the forest and the river. Carmen saw a few tents, but most of the buildings appeared more solid. Planks, branches and sheets of plastic formed huts, wigwams and yurts, caricatures of the ones in the campsite.

Figures tramped around the shanty buildings, slopping wet muck. Some weaved from building to building and others moved to and from the forest. The latter carried bulging sacks.

The pain in Carmen's stomach become unbearable.

She bent double and puked on the ground.

*

Something leant over her. She covered her eyes until it retreated.

"Carmen?"

"Mummy?"

"My sweet. Hush. All's well."

Carmen sat up, grimacing at the sensation of something heavy sloshing inside her belly. She pointed at the single lamp on the ground. "Is it nighttime?"

"I suppose it's morning, but only just. The wee hours."

"Tomorrow morning? I mean, how long have I been asleep?"

"A night and a day and then another night. You were worn out. All this fresh air."

Carmen noticed that there were walls around them: pale canvas. "We're not in the yurt?"

"It was awfully draughty. And the Discovery's a little cramped. Your father's been awfully proactive, darling. He just appeared with the tent under his arm."

"He went out and bought a tent?"

"Well, I shouldn't have thought he'd have stolen it!" Imogen's voice faltered a little. "He bought it from one of our neighbours, I believe."

Gradually, Carmen became aware of murmuring sounds: running water and voices.

She struggled to get out of her sleeping bag and to stand. The tent was taller than head height. It must have cost a lot of money. Her father was normally agitated by unnecessary spending.

She pulled the canvas door.

The shanty buildings were lit by torches, some battery-operated, some flaming. Any walls made of plastic sheeting sparkled with reflected light. Low drumbeats underpinned a hubbub of chattering voices. Dark figures came and went from hut to hut. To the left of this strange village the river was a black streak, a blind spot.

"Where's Asher?" Carmen whispered.

"He's playing with the other children."

"But it's black dark out there. You never let him play outside after dusk."

"There are no dangers here. This is the natural world."

"And Dad?"

Before Imogen could reply, Carmen saw him. He emerged from one of the shanty huts. The mud sucked at his bare feet. He wiped his mouth with the back of his hand, took a lungful of air, then entered another building.

*

"It's simple," Michael said, when the sun had risen and turned the black river golden. "We'll gather wood—or whatever we come across—and add it around the tent. There's no hurry. But soon enough we'll have made a hut, more or less like the others, and we can just pull down the tent."

"I think I'm rather attached to it," Imogen said in a quiet voice.

Michael stretched out, not appearing to mind the mud oozing around the edges of the camping mat he had dragged outside.

Just before dawn, when Imogen had finally fallen asleep, Carmen had crept out of the tent for the first time. Even without entering the shanty village, she had identified the chattering voices as the sounds of people having sex. Through the doors she had seen bare limbs, shining with sweat. She hadn't seen her father. A couple of hours later, Michael had woken her with a cheerful "Rise and shine!" as he flung open the door of the tent.

"Why are we even here?" Carmen said.

"For our holiday," Michael replied. "Though we could always push it longer than a week if we're still having fun."

Carmen glared at him. "I don't mean St Erth. I mean here here. Why are we camping out with a load of hippie freaks in a bloody fucking bog?"

Imogen gasped. "Young lady!"

Michael put one hand on the back of Imogen's neck and the other on Carmen's. He drew them both closer. "Your mother was right all along. You have to respect nature. And all those people out there know it, too. The flood was a warning. There's stuff out there that came up from the ground when the waters rose, stuff we can barely glimpse."

"But shagging random strangers helps you glimpse it?" Carmen said.

Imogen spluttered but didn't scold her. She watched Michael with a terrified expression.

The fingers around Carmen's neck gripped tighter.

Abruptly, the canvas door flapped open. The fingers released. Carmen toppled backwards, rubbing at her neck.

All three of them turned.

Asher stood there. His eyes were wild and his hair stuck up in clumps. Dried mud coated his face, hands, arms and bare feet.

Michael grinned. "I bought something for you, boy." He reached into his sleeping bag and pulled out a leather pouch. "Your own hunting knife."

Imogen began to weep softly.

Asher leapt forwards, pulling out the knife and discarding the leather pouch. He brandished the blade for a moment, then turned and scampered away, whooping.

Carmen stared at Michael in disbelief, then followed Asher.

"Carmen!" her mother cried.

"Leave him, girl!" her father bellowed.

Asher had already joined a group of youngsters racing towards the forest. Carmen lowered her head and charged after them. Her boots slipped in the mud. She half-turned to see that Michael had set off in pursuit, followed by Imogen.

The forest seemed darker, despite the fact that the sun was high in the sky. The tree trunks had become more densely packed.

Carmen hurtled through the forest, listening for sounds of the children. Branches scraped at her arms and roots threatened to trip her. She held her hands out as protection. She thought of the dark oval that Nessa had shown her.

She found the six children crouching around the hole that Carmen's family had investigated two days earlier. Litter made a wall behind the youngsters, where they had dragged it from the hole. Five children made a semicircle around the sixth.

Asher.

He bent to root around inside the hole. The other children shouted encouragement.

"Stop this!" Carmen shouted.

Asher emerged from the hole. He was dragging something after him.

It hadn't been a badger's sett, then, but a foxhole. The fox's head hung limp from Asher's shoulder. He flung it onto the ground, bringing up a shower of bark chips. Then he drew his knife and fell upon the fox. He ripped with the knife and, when the animal had been torn into shreds, he ripped with his teeth.

Carmen realised that her mother and father were standing at her side.

On a sign from Asher, the five children descended on the fox. It disappeared beneath the mass of their bodies.

Carmen realised that the pain in her stomach had lessened, as if putting distance between herself and the black river had restored her health.

"We have to go home," she said. "This isn't natural."

Imogen stared down at Asher. Both of her hands were clamped over her mouth. Michael blinked rapidly.

"I—" her father spluttered.

Imogen sucked in gulps of air.

"Mum? Dad?"

Michael turned. "What do you think, Immy? You always know best."

Weakly, Imogen nodded.

Working together, they were able to pull Asher from the writhing group of children. The knife had been lost somewhere in the pile of bodies. Asher struggled as they dragged him away. His clothes had been torn and the fox's blood made a thick film on his chest.

To Carmen's surprise, they were only a minute's walk from the edge of the forest.

"Look, there's the Discovery," she said.

They didn't stop to collect their belongings from the yurt. Asher writhed as they bundled him into the car, but then became more docile once he was strapped in tight.

They travelled along the narrow lanes to the M5 in silence. After that, the calm was punctuated only by Asher's occasional growls.

Tunnel Vision

It's not dark but the school is so empty it feels like night.

Miss Henson must still be in the staffroom. In there, the teachers sit on saggy red sofas instead of classroom chairs too small for their big behinds. It smells a bit like cigarettes and a bit like the seaside.

The classroom feels massive with nobody but me in it. When I was little I thought teachers lived at school, but now I'm ten and old enough to know better. But I'm standing in the middle of the room and it feels empty at the edges.

I swing from side to side in Miss Henson's padded chair. Seeing the classroom from this angle gives me a queasy feeling, like looking down at your own street from above. I look over at my seat. I'd be facing Miss Henson, if she was sitting where I'm sitting and I was over there. There's another wave of sickly surprise as I imagine my own face looking up at me.

I shake my head to clear it, like in a cartoon. I came in early for a reason. For a moment I think I've lost the envelope but there it is on the desk, mixed in with the exercise books and worksheets as if it needs opening and marking.

I hear a thump to my right. A dark shape appears against the glass panel of the door to the playground, wobbling as whoever it is shakes rain from their coat. I jump out of the teacher's chair, whip the envelope from the desk, run to the side counter and slip it into the tray marked Anita S.

*

Anita hasn't sent me a card. I almost wish I could take mine back, but it's propped up in front of her and she's been talking to Debbie about it, all excited. My cheeks glow as she reads the poem aloud again, even though it's nothing soppy: *Roses are red, violets are blue, Some poems rhyme, But this one doesn't.* Pretty funny. She doesn't read out the bit underneath where I'd written something about love. I wish I hadn't written that, but it's just what you do.

After break-time a card has appeared in my own tray. Anita must have had it all along but just didn't think to come in early like I did.

She sits directly behind me with her back to mine. I'd have to turn to speak to her, but since break-time I hadn't turned around once. What happens next? Two people sending Valentine's cards to each other, that means something, right?

My face aches from the glowing and the keeping still. I thumb the edge of Anita's card where it sticks out from my maths workbook.

I have to speak to her. We're boyfriend and girlfriend now, or something.

I only manage to half-turn. "Hey Anita? Thanks for the card. But you know that honey is spelt H-O-N-E-Y, not H-U-N-N-Y?" I'm speaking much louder than I'd meant to. "'Hunny bunny', that's what you wrote."

Anita doesn't say anything. I turn fully but all I can see is red hair.

"Who says I sent it?" she says quietly.

I turn back to look at my workbook.

*

Anita doesn't speak to me for the rest of the morning. At lunchtime, even though it's not raining any more, the school fields are muddy and out of bounds. The playground seems tiny and there's nowhere to stand that's out of sight of Anita and Debbie and their friends. They keep glancing over to where I'm standing with Mousey.

"Cylinders: eight," Mousey says.

Anita doesn't look nearly so pleased about the Valentine's card now. I'm sure her friends are laughing at me.

"Cylinders: eight," Mousey says again.

I glance at my own Top Trumps card and back at Anita.

"Come on then. Hand it over. There aren't any others with eight cylinders."

I hand over the card without even checking to see which it is. "I'm sick of Top Trumps. It's stupid."

Mousey shrugs. "I don't even like cars. What *is* a cylinder in a car, anyway? Johnny's got Top Trumps with Marvel superheroes on."

I can't stand the looks I'm getting from Anita's friends. I push Mousey in the shoulder with the palm of my hand. "Tig! And no tigging the butcher."

"There's no one else playing," Mousey says, rubbing his shoulder. "So who can I tig?" But I'm already halfway down the playground.

The game draws in other boys until there are twelve of us hurtling around the playground and paved area beside the school doors. Anita's eyes follow me, making my cheeks sting with heat.

Today I'm all limbs and speed. Soon I'm the only one left untigged. The other eleven shout and groan as I slip away again and again. They close in but I duck and weave. My winding, zooming route takes me towards Anita's group but I turn away even as I run toward them. Casual and cool.

When my head thwacks against the wooden post of the doorway awning, like a ball against a rounders bat, it's the surprise that takes me down, not the pain. I lurch backwards and hit the ground. Eleven boys tig me all at once with shouts of 'Pile on!' and Anita's face disappears in the gaps between the bodies.

*

After lunchtime we're marched to the tiny music room. It's too hot with twenty of us in there and our glockenspiel-and-maracas version of 'Yellow Submarine' makes my ears ring. I stay at the back, shaking my maraca only when Mrs Pearson looks my way. I'm sleepy. I raise my hand, waiting for the teacher to notice me.

"Mum, I need the loo."

Anita and Debbie turn, but it's not just them laughing, it's almost everyone. What's so funny? Has Anita shown my Valentine's card to them all?

The tiled bathroom feels small but it's not the room that's narrow, it's my view of it. I lean on the sink. The cold ceramic is shocking against my palms. The edges around my reflection in the mirror are hazy. I can't see anything outside the shaking image of myself looking back. It's not blackness exactly—there's just nothing there. I look left and right. The rest of the bathroom appears, bit by bit, as the circle of vision follows the movement of my head.

I leave the bathroom on shaky legs and take my place at the back of the music room.

I should say something to someone.

I can still hear quiet sniggers. Mrs Pearson shoots me a look which is partly annoyed, partly worried.

I'm telling nobody.

*

I leave as soon as the bell rings, stumbling through the gate and ignoring a hello from Mousey's mum, who comes to meet him every day because she thinks he's still a baby. I keep looking straight ahead, partly to stop the sickly feeling from spreading, and partly because everything at the edges is getting more invisible all the time.

Aldenham Road seems too long to bear. I take the cut along Roxby Avenue, past the place where an older boy once stopped me on my bike, said he had a secret to tell me, then leaned in close and spat in my ear. I cross to Lealholm Way and the embankment that I once worried was haunted, where me and Mousey sheltered from a lightning storm, certain we'd be struck and not minding.

Mrs Lilley from next door doesn't notice anything wrong when I ring the bell to collect the house key. And then I'm home, alone, heavy and dim.

The house is all corridor, just tiny circles of clear vision surrounded by mist. My head is like an enormous iron wrecking ball balanced on my body. I stagger up to my parents' bedroom, feeling the way. I look into the full-length mirror on the wardrobe door and something ghostly looks back.

I don't believe in God. It's all just stories. At the mirror, I pray to God, or something. Then I sit on the edge of the bed to rest.

I've always liked the wallpaper in here. The brown is broken up with curled vines, a pattern that repeats every five leaves upwards and three side-to-side. If you know where to look, there are faces in the spaces between the vines. Berries for eyes, wisps of stalks for mouths. One is laughing, one is worried, one is jealous of the others, I don't know why.

"You know what this is?" the worried one says.

I stare.

"It's bad," he says, without moving his stalk mouth.

The jealous face nods without nodding. "It's bad, really bad." I don't know why he seems so jealous about that.

I look for the happy face. I can only see vines and leaves.

I'm dying. This is what it feels like. Soon I'll only see a pinprick of light ahead of me and then even that will close in and everything will be black, or just nothing, and then that'll be that.

I'm only ten. People don't die aged ten. But I'm dying all the same.

Why aren't mum and dad home from work yet? Where's Michaela, my sister? Even she would do.

Mousey once said that if he knew he was dying, he'd kill as many people as possible before he snuffed it. If he was going to die then they could too. He'd read about making a bomb from washing powder and it couldn't be all that hard.

Mousey's a nutcase.

But I'm dying and I'm on my own and nobody's home and I'm hungry too.

I'm back downstairs without knowing quite how I got there. I'm not all that hungry after all, just sleepy.

But I'm ten years old. I don't want to go to sleep.

The sunlight through the kitchen window makes me wince but wakes me up a bit. I fumble with the handle to the back door. The air is cold in a good way, because my face has got all fiery again. I stumble on one of the broken slabs that dad laid out ready to crazy-pave the path. Out in the garden the hazy nothing around my circle of vision seems even stranger. The bright greens and oranges bleed into blindness.

I try not to think about mum and dad and Michaela. They'll cry for ages, but what do I care? I won't be there to see it.

A scuffling sound comes from the shed. I'm not on my own after all. I open the door to see Michaela's rabbit, Roderick, looking up at me. He's as white and ghostly as I was in the mirror. Rabbits don't live long and he's already six. But I'm dying today and Roderick might live for years yet. Is that fair?

Dad promised I could write my name in the wet cement. Tomorrow.

My eyes sting. I heave one of the loose paving slabs into the air. It's thick and heavy and digs into my fingers at the jagged edge.

I lurch into the shed and raise the slab over Roderick's head. Then I drop it on him and there's no going back from that.

Back inside, I crawl up the stairs and into bed. The thought crosses my mind to leave a goodbye note but I'm very sleepy now and I don't have a pencil.

*

The glow of light through the curtains and the noise from the street tell me that it's still afternoon, not morning. I hear the front door close and then mum and Michaela talking.

My bedroom's big again. It's as though I can see everything all at once—not just what I'm looking at but things around the edges. Things and things and things instead of hazy nothing.

I'm not dead, or dying. I'm ten years old and I'm going to get older every day.

I hear the back door *thunk* open, then the door to the shed.

Seconds pass.

Michaela screams.

The Eyes Have It

Flashes from the giant neon spectacles in the window shone through the shutters and into the opticians clinic. The light made a pattern of oblong shapes on the tiled floor.

Glenn helped himself to coffee from the pot. This would be his only cup, with green tea to follow. Two months ago an anonymous suggestion slip had warned him about his coffee breath. Now he always swilled mouthwash before the first customers arrived.

"Hey-ho. Who's first?" he said.

Adele stood before the data entry computer at the rear of the clinic. "Caroline Klein, Mrs Solomon, Peter and Sheila Dawson and the twins, then lunch, then—"

He held up a hand. "OK. That's enough to be getting on with, thanks."

Adele turned back to the screen. Her hands lay motionless on the keyboard.

Glenn retreated into his office. He pulled handfuls of paper towels from the dispenser, pressing them into one armpit and then the other. He switched to his newer pair of glasses. They made him less authoritative and more approachable.

Caffeine and anticipation made his heart race. He could hear voices—Adele and another, softer, female voice. He wiped his damp palms against the rough fabric of his chair.

Normally he liked to make patients wait, to reinforce an impression of behind-the-scenes work. He glanced at the clock. Thirty seconds. Good enough.

The door rattled as he yanked it open. "Miss Klein!" Too eager. "Do come in."

Caroline Klein settled herself into the faux-leather chair. Glenn kept his gaze fixed at face level, determined not to stray to her stockinged thighs. She had changed her hairstyle to Mia Farrow short. It suited her, making her features even more elfin.

"Hi, Mr Withers."

"Glenn, please, Miss Klein. Caroline."

A flicker of a smile, a leap of the heart.

"How are you? Well? Your hair is very— How are the new glasses working out?"

Caroline took them off and turned them in her hands. "Oh, you know. They're good. Everything is awfully clear."

"But you're back very soon after your last appointment. It's been only two weeks—or so—hasn't it?"

"Mm-hmm. Yes, it's all just a bit..." She passed a hand over her face.

"Okay, well, let's go over it again."

He flicked off the light. His hands trembled a little as he fitted the thick test glasses. A friend had once confided in him that, when an optometrist leaned in close, the dim lighting and the proximity of his looming face made her instinctively want to kiss him.

Caroline gazed directly ahead. Sometimes, when her image appeared to him in daydreams, she would be wearing these glasses with their interchangeable lenses. Her hair smelled of citrus.

"Right. These lenses are the same as your current prescription." He indicated the Snellen chart opposite. "From the top?"

Caroline recited the letters on the test chart confidently and accurately.

"Okay. Let's move on. Which is clearer, the circle on the red or the green?"

After a long pause Caroline said, "They're both fine."

He pulled out one lens and inserted another. "And now?"

"I don't know. The red? No, the green. I don't know."

"Not to worry. Mind if I take a closer look?"

Deep furrows crossed Caroline's forehead.

Glenn put away the test glasses and leaned in with his retinoscope. Such large pupils. He could lose himself in there.

"All seems well!" He steepled his fingers in an authority-figure pose. "But you obviously feel that something's amiss. Could you explain the problem?"

Caroline's face clouded. "Everything looks all right. It's just all a bit—" She made a raspberry noise.

"I'm sorry, a bit what?"

"It's all just *stuff*. You know? No, perhaps not. Listen. In this morning's post I received a picture my nephew had painted. It was of the two of us travelling on a train, waving. And it barely meant a thing to me! I mean, I could see it all right. But there was something blocking me from really *seeing*-seeing it, you know?"

She slumped back, exasperated. "Mr Withers, you know me pretty well, don't you?"

Glenn nodded stiffly.

"So you know that I'm normally excitable. I'm interested in what goes on around me. Well, I just can't see those things any more, Mr Withers. It all just looks like *stuff*."

Glenn's stomach did something complicated. "Miss, I mean, Caroline. I'm an optometrist and I know about eyes and I like to think I know you well, as you say. But I think that maybe what you're experiencing is not so much a vision problem as a, well, another problem. The eyes and the brain work in tandem. What the eyes see is only half of the story. It's what the brain does with the information that matters."

He had slid onto his knees on the floor, somehow, in a parody of a proposal. "Caroline, I think this may be about happiness."

She gazed down at him with wide eyes. A pained expression flickered across her face.

"I need to go," she said. She teetered towards the door, using the counter for balance. A rack of lenses wobbled and nearly clattered to the floor as she left.

Glenn followed, but Caroline had already left the clinic. Adele stood in the waiting area. Her head was tilted up to the television on its bracket in the corner and her face was set in deep concentration. He glanced at the screen. A weatherman stood before a row of smiling sun-faces.

*

After work Glenn collected his car from the multi-storey. He reread emails on his phone whenever the clogged traffic stopped dead. It took him forty minutes to make the fifteen-minute journey to The Meadows.

Usually, as he parked up, he would see the silhouettes of residents or nursing staff, but today all the windows were empty. He rang the bell and waited more than a minute before he heard the buzz of the remote door lock.

"Afternoon, Maureen!"

The reception desk was unmanned but through a door marked *Staff Only* he could see the back of Maureen's head. She didn't answer. She leant forwards towards the ancient computer that the staff of The Meadows shared. A clutter of advertising pop-up windows filled the screen, the type offering telesales work and porn websites. Maybe next time he visited he would help clean up the computer and install a virus program, but not today.

"I'll just pop through, then," he called. There was no response.

He knocked softly on the door to Room 6, then turned the handle when no answer came. There was nobody in the small apartment. Glenn straightened the sheets rumpled at the foot of the bed.

A heavy photo album fell open to the floor. A single print showed a young couple on the steps of a chapel. The woman, his mother, beamed as she ducked a whirl of confetti. His father wore a tight grimace that could have been good-natured or testy.

Glenn turned the pages. He recognised his childhood home. His parents held their first child, Glenn himself, plump and grinning.

He wiped his eyes and placed the photo album carefully on the bedside table.

He found his mother in the common room. The room had a musty fragrance, a smell he associated with claustrophobia. Unusually, all of the seats were taken. None of the fifteen or so residents acknowledged his arrival. They were fixated on the small TV set in the corner.

His mother sat at one end of the horseshoe arrangement of chairs facing the TV. From the look of it, nobody had dealt with her hair today. Her dressing gown was lopsided and her ankles were bare above her slippers.

Glenn knelt on the floor beside her chair. Behind him a man with tortoise-like features craned his neck to continue watching the TV.

"Mum?" Glenn placed one hand on her arm.

His mother didn't turn away from the screen. The TV seemed far too loud. David Attenborough's voice was a foghorn boom.

"I saw that you were looking at the old photo album," Glenn said.

"—known more commonly as caterpillar fungus—" David Attenborough said.

"Some memories, huh, Mum?"

"—the vegetative part of the fungus invades the tissue—"

"Have you been thinking about Dad?"

"—eventually replacing the tissue, affecting the behaviour of the host—"

Glenn squeezed her thin arm. It felt like there was only bone underneath the padding of the dressing gown.

"—the ant climbs the plant, attaching itself before it dies—"

"Looks like you're all really enjoying this show, Mum. I've never seen the room so full."

"—so maintaining an optimal temperature for the spores to sprout—"

"So I'll come and see you again in a couple of days. Maybe I'll bring more photos too."

Once Glenn moved out of the way, the tortoise-man settled back into his chair without taking his eyes from the screen.

*

"Morning, Adele. Who's up today?"

It seemed to take Adele several seconds before she noticed him. Her head tilted oddly. She said nothing.

"Who's first?" he said. "Not Garry Robinson, I hope?"

She seemed reluctant to meet his gaze. Her eyes kept travelling to somewhere behind him. To the TV. "No. Not Garry Robinson.

Hilary Brough Paul Repper Dulcie and Mina Capp and Larry Hart."

A smear of foundation marked Adele's collar. Normally she took great care over her appearance.

He reached up to turn off the TV. Adele blinked rapidly.

"Are you okay?" he said. "You seem out of sorts."

After a pause she said, "I'm fine, just a bit... you know." Her pupils appeared dilated.

"Do you think you might step into my office for a moment?" Glenn said. "It's been a while since you had a checkup. And if we can't look after staff then what's it all coming to?"

Adele sat stiffly in the chair as he went about his work. The tests indicated near-perfect vision. Glenn leant in with the retinoscope. Her eyes showed no damage but the pupils seemed larger than they ought to be, even in the dim light of his office. He shined the light directly into each eye. Her pupils barely contracted.

"Is this light bothering you?"

She shook her head.

"How peculiar. I've never seen pupils react so sluggishly to changes in light intensity. You haven't been— I mean—"

She stared at him.

"Well, I do have a right to ask, I suppose. You haven't taken drugs, have you?"

"No. Would that help my eyes?"

"That's not what I meant. I'm just baffled." He pulled a reference manual from a shelf. "I'm not even certain what I'm looking—"

He glanced up.

Adele's neck contorted to allow her to stare at the pages of the textbook. Her pupils were even larger than before. She had stopped blinking.

*

The next few hours passed in a blur. Several times, Glenn found himself scrolling through unimportant emails, just for something to read. The morning's patients had few complaints but they seemed nervous. Paul Repper, in particular, was terribly clumsy. He tripped over a chair in the waiting area and then banged his head on the lightbox.

Glenn took an early lunch. After collecting a sandwich from the nearby deli he headed back to the clinic. Halfway over the pelican crossing an instinct made him leap backwards again. The bumper of a car grazed his right leg.

The middle-aged driver of the car wore a creased suit and crooked tie. He gripped the steering wheel tightly as he peered upwards through the windscreen. He was looking beyond Glenn and hadn't even appeared to notice him.

Glenn turned. Behind him, *25% OFF* stickers were plastered over the window of a sports shop. In the centre of the window hung a huge video screen displaying a looped animation, a cross-section of a sports shoe. The car swept past him but the driver's eyes remained fixed on the video screen. His neck twisted awkwardly.

When Glenn reentered the mall he barged into Caroline Klein. Her skin looked deathly pale.

"Caroline? Are you all right?"

She stood at a kiosk in the centre of the mall, opposite the entrance to the clinic. Behind the counter a teenager chewed gum slowly. The hoarding announced that paintball lessons were at an *ALL-NEW LOW PRICE* and offered *A DAY YOU WILL NEVER FORGET*. A Perspex stand on the counter held pamphlets. Caroline bent forwards to study the terms and conditions in tiny print.

"Excuse me? Caroline. Can you hear me?"

She made no sign of recognition. He took a pamphlet from the counter and Caroline's head twisted to follow it. His hands had begun to shake; Caroline's head oscillated slightly with the corresponding movement of the pamphlet. Her pupils were so large that he could barely make out the colour of her irises.

"Please, won't you come with me?"

He took her arm. She remained expressionless as he led her toward the clinic.

Despite Glenn's assurances, a cup of tea did nothing to revive Caroline. She sat in the waiting area with the polystyrene cup clasped in both hands. Now that he looked closely, she seemed a little shabbier than the day before. Her short hair stuck up at one side. The toes of her boots were badly scuffed.

Glenn knelt before her. As gently as possible, he lifted her chin. Her blue-grey irises were all but eclipsed by the pupils. The circumference of each pupil was an undulating curve that rippled like the crest of a wave. These dark peaks licked like a tide encroaching upon the iris.

"My God, Caroline! What's happening to you?"

She stared at him blankly. After a while she said, "I'm fine, I'm fine." Her gaze shifted to the name badge fixed to his breast pocket.

He glanced down.

Information. Data. That was all she wanted to see.

But no, that wasn't it, quite. Caroline herself didn't seem interested. It wasn't her who latched onto the text on his badge.

It was only her eyes. Only the unsettled darkness within her pupils.

A voice nagged at the back of his mind, a half-memory of soft tones spoken as loud as a foghorn.

—*eventually replacing the tissue, affecting the behaviour of the host*—

He leapt to his feet and half-pulled, half-dragged Caroline from the clinic.

*

The journey to the hospital took only ten minutes, but Glenn was sweating profusely by the time they arrived. Other cars on the road had seemed too close, as if they were veering towards him.

Cars jammed the hospital car park solid. Until Glenn honked his horn and forced her to move, its entrance was blocked by a woman crouching to read a newspaper discarded in the gutter. A group gathered around the ticket machine, examining the information about parking charges.

Somebody stood on the roof of the hospital—a workman, Glenn supposed—with one arm raised to the sky and the other clinging to a TV aerial. Glenn shivered.

—*the ant climbs the plant, attaching itself before it dies*—

He parked in the ambulance bay and, when she didn't move from her seat, he bundled Caroline out of the car and into the building.

He paced the corridors. He reread emails on his phone. He browsed the advice leaflets in the waiting rooms and he snuck glances at the charts of patient statistics behind the reception desk.

Caroline reappeared at intervals. The nurses and doctors seemed as calm about her condition as she was herself. Grudgingly, they agreed to take her in for tests. She would be kept in overnight, they said, and the best thing Glenn could do would be to go home and get some rest himself. He only relented when a voice over the tannoy demanded that the car blocking the ambulance bay be moved.

There were three workmen on the roof, now. One of them had shimmied up the TV aerial.

*

As he drove he turned to catch glimpses into the houses lining the streets. In living room after living room he saw flickering screens. He saw people watching, unmoving, with their mouths slackly open and their eyes glazed.

All he wanted was to curl up on his sofa and watch rubbish on TV.

The Forge

Richard paused on the threshold of the lobby. His mouth was dry, in contrast with the clamminess of his palms. His fingers had become smeared with ink transferred from the document folder.

He turned. The darkened glass made it difficult to see the street outside. He could only just make out Lola's silhouette at the far side of the road, facing the doorway. She raised both hands. Two thumbs up.

"I'm just not the kind of person who does things like this," he had said to Lola that morning.

She had laughed at that. "Isn't that the point?"

Richard took a breath, then stepped fully inside. He walked towards the desk that swept a curve around two walls of the wide lobby. A young woman dressed in a dark suit sat behind the desk, her fingertips brushing over a touchscreen. She looked up as Richard approached. He flinched when their eyes met. Her green irises shone, despite the dim light. Her red hair was pulled back tight. For just a moment, she had looked like Zoe. A cruel trick of the mind.

He cleared his throat. "My name is Richard Handler. I've brought all the documentation." He placed the folder flat on the desk.

As the woman leafed through the paperwork, he said, "I hope it won't hurt? I don't know what to expect. Has it been fully tested?"

The woman arched an eyebrow.

"Of course, you're right," Richard said. "Sorry. I'm not casting aspersions, really I'm not. It's only that—"

I'm just not the kind of person who does things like this.

"—I'm scared, I suppose. A bit."

The woman watched him for a few seconds before she spoke. "I'm sorry, Mr—" She glanced down at the folder, "—Handler."

Richard exhaled, as if her sympathy gave him permission to breathe once again.

"I'm sorry," the woman said again, "Which company are you looking for?"

Richard glanced around the lobby. For the first time he noticed a large black letterboard fixed to the wall behind the desk. It contained more than a dozen company names printed in a neat typeface.

"They're called the Forge," he said in a quiet voice. "But I don't see that name on the list."

As the woman handed him back the folder, Richard tried to interpret her expression. Empathy? Disgust? How much had she understood of what she had seen?

"Third floor," she said in a neutral tone. "Last door on the left."

*

The third floor was gloomy and claustrophobic. Richard had met nobody in the lift or in the corridors. The silence suggested abandonment rather than the sterile calm of the lobby.

The last door on the left was unmarked and windowless. He listened but heard no sounds from within. He stood for nearly a minute before knocking and then another minute before accepting that there would be no response. He pushed open the door.

Two tall floor lamps cast overlapping pools of yellow onto wood-effect linoleum. The only other items of furniture were a pine desk with a computer terminal on top, and a circular stool.

"Hello?" Richard edged forwards into the room.

On the left wall another door broke up the plain expanse of woodchip wallpaper. Its brushed steel surface glistened and turned the reflected light grey.

This must be a waiting room. He sat on the stool.

After a couple of minutes he stood up, knocked on the steel

door, then retook his seat.

Silence.

He studied the computer terminal. Perhaps he was expected to input his registration details? Maybe nobody knew yet that he had arrived.

He could see no keyboard or mouse but, at a single touch, the computer screen turned from black to green. In its centre were two words in a tiny font.

INSERT DOCUMENTATION

Richard looked down at the cardboard folder clutched in his lap. Built into the pine desk was a chute with a narrow slot, around half the depth of a letterbox. Hesitantly, he removed from the folder the uppermost form, which contained his registration details. He slid it face upwards into the slot. His fingertips remained in contact with the paper until it disappeared fully into the chute.

Nothing happened. He pulled out another sheet which included his bank details. He had been amazed at the low price, but Lola had been adamant that it was correct. He slid the sheet into the slot.

Nothing.

What about the rest of the paperwork? None of that had specifically been requested. These printouts were just hard copies of the dataset, along with his notes made in preparation for the session. He had felt terribly anxious carrying them here and didn't relish the idea of doing so again on the way home. Slowly at first, then in a thoughtless hurry, he stuffed the sheets into the chute slot.

The text on the screen remained unchanged. Richard rubbed at his forehead, where sweat had broken out. He dropped to his hands and knees to look under the desk. Its underside contained a bulky rectangular box directly beneath the chute slot. His paperwork must be in there, still, just out of reach.

What now?

Then he noticed another feature in the raised surface of the chute. Beside the letterbox was another opening, less than an inch in width. The wood at the edges of this slot appeared slightly ragged, as though the hole had been inexpertly sawn.

He patted the breast pocket of his shirt, pulled out the USB stick, and inserted it.

A humming sound came from somewhere beneath the computer screen.

CONFIRMATION OF NAME, the readout said.

Was that a statement or a question? After a fruitless search for any kind of input device, Richard said his own name out loud.

CONFIRMATION OF TERMS AND CONDITIONS

"Yes," Richard said quickly. He mustn't allow himself to dwell on the small print. Lola had had to prise the printouts from his hand to force him to leave his house.

TARGET DATA PUBLIC DOMAIN

"Yes," Richard said, but a gulping cough made the word unrecognisable. He wished that he could still see Lola and her two thumbs up. "Yes."

CONFIRMATION OF TARGET

"Simon Macmillan," Richard said. Was that specific enough? "Simon Francis Macmillan, of one hundred and twenty-four—"

The text had already changed.

CONFIRMATION > ENTER BOOTH

Richard tapped his fingers on the work surface, rose, wavered, and opened the steel door.

*

"Tell me everything. How do you feel? What was it like in there?"

Lola leant forwards over the table, reaching for his hands. Her blonde hair made a wild halo, backlit by the sunlight that streamed through the café window.

Richard pulled his hands away and pressed them onto his knees, ignoring Lola's hurt expression. It seemed as though his hands—in fact, his whole body—were still vibrating.

"It was very small," he said.

"What was the sensation? Did it feel you were being prodded at, anything like that?" She tapped at her forehead.

Richard shook his head. It hadn't been as literal as that. He had only experienced a hum that seemed to come from within his own body rather than from any external stimulus. The booth beyond the steel door had been little bigger than a store cupboard and had been almost empty, with only a wooden rail for him to sit on and barely room to turn around. The sense of being trapped had been overwhelming at first, as if he was a household pet trapped in a microwave oven. But the whole process had taken so long that eventually boredom became his overriding response and the vibration became less and less upsetting. It was just as well that a green light had appeared to signal that he ought to leave. If not for that, he might still be in there, uncertain whether the procedure was still going.

"There's nothing much to report," he said.

Lola snorted. "Oh, sure! Nothing much to report, my arse. Come on, Rich, spill the beans."

"I don't feel like talking."

"You never do. So that's not changed, then."

"I should get to work."

"Can I meet you afterwards?"

"I feel like being alone."

"Tomorrow, then? Same time, same coffee mug?"

Richard paused, then shook his head.

Lola pulled at an earlobe. This was her customary sign of having taken offence. "Right. Sure. You've got what you wanted, is that it? So you don't need to hang out with me? For fuck's sake, Richard. We've spent at least three hours a day in each other's company for the last fortnight. I've passed up dozens of work offers to help you. Broken the law several times too. And now that we've actually pulled it off, you're just going to blank me?"

She reached into the satchel that leant against a chair leg and pulled out her laptop.

"I guess I was naïve to believe that we're close. But no. It was just a freelance gig, right? Mates' rates, meaning free, but other than that a professional relationship, albeit profoundly bloody illegal." She clicked on the trackpad of the computer, then swung the screen to face Richard. It displayed a spreadsheet crammed with figures. "So should I just delete all this?"

She was right, of course. He'd exploited her. Lola had always boasted of her technical skills, but once Richard had actually asked for her help, he'd been staggered at her proficiency. The browser histories and keyboard characteristics—in fact, all the data harvested by Lola—had formed the fundamental core of the dataset. He'd been the one to insist they also include his own scrappy video footage, though Lola had made clear that the extent of her research made his redundant. And she ought to know. She was the one who had found out about the Forge in the first place.

Lola's dedication to the task had humbled him, then embarrassed him.

He shrugged. "I have a copy."

Lola's face crumpled. Her eyes darted around as she examined his face. "Yes. You have a copy."

He laughed, even though he wasn't sure that she was making a joke. Backups were irrelevant now. He had the data safe and sound, thanks to the Forge. He had it inside his head.

He found himself fascinated watching a single line that appeared and reappeared at one corner of Lola's mouth. If one could parse this code, one might know her absolutely. Normally he'd have missed a little detail like that. He frowned as she lifted her coffee cup, hiding the line.

"All right. I'll let you go, then." Lola jammed the computer back into her bag and stood up. "But tell me. Do you feel different?"

Richard realised that his hands no longer shook. His palms were dry. Before he answered Lola's question he took a sip of coffee, enjoying its bitterness.

"I feel absolutely fine," he said. "I feel good."

"You're avoiding the question. Do you feel like *him*?"

Richard thought of the video footage and spreadsheets contained on the USB stick and the printouts that he'd fed into the slot in the wooden desk. Hours and hours, reams and reams, of evidence and data about Simon Macmillan.

"I've no idea," he said, truthfully. "I really don't know what he's like."

He turned to look out of the window. From this slightly

raised angle, the commuters hurrying outside made a stream of movement that might have been choreographed in its weaving fluidity. Though he and Lola had often met here for coffee, around this time of day, he had never noticed that before.

*

As soon as Richard arrived at the insurance office, time began to drag terribly. He stood unmoving before the wall shelves packed with policy folders, unable to select one in order to begin work. Even though he had stood like this many times before, dwelling on his inertia, something now seemed different. He felt none of the usual sense of hopelessness. Processing and updating each policy and assessing the condition of the pieces were achievable tasks. More than achievable. Trivial.

This slight change in his attitude wasn't enough. What had gone wrong? He had hoped for a flood of new sensations. Purpose and ambition. Perhaps he had picked the wrong target after all. Perhaps Simon Macmillan had no more motivation than himself—or rather, than the old Richard Handler. If the differences were only superficial then the entire procedure had been for nothing. The Forge had done nothing more than compound his character flaws with somebody else's.

Lola had been right. He ought to have picked a target that represented a known quantity. A proven talent or a much-loved philanthropist. She could have harvested data from anybody famous via broadcasts and published writing. Ignoring her protests, Richard had insisted that if he were to adopt somebody's characteristics and behaviour—that is, if he were to become more like any one person—it must be Simon Macmillan.

He sighed and turned away from the shelves, then tapped a code into the keypad beside the secure rear door. The air inside tasted fresh and still. As he leant towards the first rack of paintings he noticed a richer smell. Carefully, he slid out one painting after another, holding each at arm's length. Most were already familiar to him from the catalogues. Nobody could ever have accused him of being a philistine. Understanding technique, composition, historical context and—yes—beauty were all aspects of his profession.

But now he realised there was more to see. The cracking and discolouration of the paint, rather than simply demonstrating fragility or provenance, were themselves beautiful. He revelled in the heft of each heavy frame, the crenellated surfaces that nipped his fingertips.

He wept.

Theodore McCullough, the head of the insurance company, protested when Richard handed in his notice. Richard only smiled and nodded as Theodore finally relented and began to speak about notice periods. He left the office an hour early, certain that he would never return.

At home, he paced the length of his dining room. The vibration he had felt in the steel booth echoed through his body, jittering his fingers. Several times, he picked up the phone and replaced it. Who could he call? Lola might have been the one who had introduced him to the Forge, but she could hardly appreciate his situation now that he had gone through with the procedure. And as for Zoe... no. He couldn't trust himself, yet. He had no proof that he had become a better man.

Only one person might truly understand him. But, of course, Simon Macmillan was strictly out of bounds.

He found himself browsing files on his computer. He selected a video that he had recorded several days ago. Though high-resolution, the footage was shaky. It had been captured by a tiny, discreet lens built into a head-mounted band. The video lasted for only fifteen seconds, ending as Simon Macmillan reached a corner of the gallery building and disappeared out of shot.

He played it again. Simon's long strides demonstrated his confidence. At one point in the video his head turned slightly. His face wore an expression of confident disinterest. The kind of attitude that gets people to do whatever you say. Simon had turned to watch a girl pass, but she had been cropped out of the frame along with any other humans who appeared in any of the videos, discounting Simon himself.

Richard looped the clip and, still watching the screen, resumed his pacing around the dining room. Had his manner of walking altered? It was impossible to be dispassionate and compare two people when one of them was yourself.

He closed the folder labelled *Simon_M* and opened another that contained a few dozen photos. They had been taken the previous year, when he had first bought the head-mounted unit. After that point, the camera had lain unused until he had started to follow Simon.

Almost all of the photos featured his ex-girlfriend, Zoe. Badly composed and oddly angled though they were, the images represented an almost comprehensive documentation of their final few days together. In many ways, the photos were better than memories. Judging only from these images, last summer had been a golden lens-flared sequence of delightful moments. Zoe's features shone in the sunlight, fascinating and overwhelming despite her wistfulness.

Richard pulled in a deep breath to head off a sob.

He flicked the scroll wheel of the mouse. Another image appeared, still sunlit, though it had been taken inside the house. Zoe's face filled the frame, angled at ninety degrees, her cheek creased into the pillow. He had never slept wearing the camera but he remembered pulling it on first thing that morning, then lying down beside Zoe to capture her expression of contentment, her total abandonment to sleep.

He stared at the photo. It was a perfect replica of what he had seen with his own eyes that morning. He leant closer so that the image filled his field of vision.

No. Not perfect.

He placed his head sideways on the desk, as if he still laid beside her. He allowed his eyes to lose their focus. Zoe's features duplicated and overlapped.

*

Zoe frowned. "Why now?"

"We haven't seen one another for more than a year," Richard replied.

"You said that's how you wanted it to be. You said that you couldn't bear the thought of me being with someone else."

"I was wrong. I've changed my mind. I've changed."

Zoe turned forward to face the path that wound through the centre of the park. "I can see that. You're different."

They walked in silence for a minute before Richard said, "In what way?"

"You seem calmer."

"I was calm before. You said that that was what was so infuriating about me."

"True. But back then it was like your body had stiffened while you were sinking into quicksand. You know? Like you'd just given up. Now it comes across differently. Acceptance, but without the defeat."

Richard smiled. Other people had told him similar things during the weeks following his procedure at the Forge. It was a shame that nobody knew both Simon and himself, in order to compare and contrast. Only Zoe could do that, but he couldn't allow himself to make the suggestion.

Zoe slowed her pace as they reached a bench. They sat side by side.

"You understand that I'm not saying anything's going to change between us," she said.

Richard nodded. "Like you said. Acceptance without the defeat."

"It never was like that. You never were defeated. I didn't leave you for Simon. There were two whole months in between."

"I know," Richard said. "Simon didn't win you. I lost you. Or maybe even that's wrong. We just weren't meant to be together. It's not enough for only one of us to think that we were right for each other."

Zoe turned. One eyebrow raised. "I'm impressed, Rich. Really."

Richard pulled a folded piece of paper from his pocket and held it out.

"What's this?"

"Something to impress you even more. I'd love for you to be

there, if you're free."

He waited as Zoe scanned the flyer. Other than the heading—*Introducing Richard Handler*, then in only slightly smaller font, *A Tremendous New Talent*—it contained little information. Only the name of the gallery really mattered.

"Good God," Zoe said. "How did you manage this?"

Richard grimaced. It didn't pay to blow one's own horn. Simon wouldn't. "The curators at Folly have been very kind. They were the ones who approached me about the show, in fact. I'm lucky, that's all."

"Hidden depths, huh?" Her expression clouded. "Isn't Folly one of Simon's galleries?"

"It is. I hope that's not awkward for you."

She watched him carefully before speaking again. "Was Simon involved in signing you up for an exhibition?"

Richard shook his head. "I don't suppose he knows a thing about it. Folly's booking operations are pretty autonomous, I gather. There's no reason that the founder, or any of the other board members, would be involved in a show as small as mine. My work will only fill one corner."

Zoe grinned, a mixture of relief and something else. "Okay. Sure. Yes, I mean. I'll be there."

Richard could tell that she was struggling to hide her admiration, but he knew better than to milk it. Simon would simply gloss over the praise and move on. Though people often spoke of Simon's artistic abilities, Richard knew nobody who had seen any evidence of it.

"Anyway," he said, waving a hand, "I'm pleased that we can talk like this without arguing, finally. I'd like to keep you as a friend, if that's possible."

Zoe played with the tassels at the end of her scarf. "We'll see."

He judged the tone of his next words carefully before speaking. "How's it all going with Simon, anyway?"

Zoe flinched. This was probably what she'd been preparing for, since he'd asked to meet. She was more than likely steeled to scold him for failing to move on.

Instead of the expected defensive statement, she said, "We

broke up."

Abruptly, Richard registered the bite of the cold November air on his cheeks and lips.

Shit.

"You broke up," he said, without inflection.

Zoe nodded, chewing her lip. "Look. If you're being straight with me about acceptance, then I can talk to you about this, okay? Consider it a test, to prove that you understand that you and I are through. So. We broke up. You were wrong about most things, but you were right about Simon."

"In what way was I right?" Richard's voice had become little more than a whisper.

"He was bad. Bad for me and... just bad. I fell for the façade, but behind it he was rotten."

Shit.

Richard sensed individual electrical impulses triggering within his brain. Two distinct groups of them, identifiable as members of one set or the other. His own impulses, smooth and slow, and then the ones alien to him, the ones that the procedure at the Forge had introduced. Impulses that rightly belonged to Simon. Fast and jagged. Rotten and bad.

*

Faces filled the gallery. Richard moved amongst them. He had half-expected Simon to make an appearance and was grateful that he hadn't. He kept a façade of humility, absorbing visitors' praise and reflecting it back towards them. The room echoed with laughter and the chink of glasses.

Zoe arrived more than two hours after the official opening, as the party was beginning to quieten. Richard knew her well enough to see that her casual outfit was a signal. It showed her resolution to not get fully involved in the event. She couldn't have foreseen that Richard would be the only other person in the room not wearing formal attire.

She waited patiently as he extricated himself from a trio of well-wishers.

"So. Are you going to give me the tour?" she said.

Richard took her arm. "Sure. It'll take all of two minutes."

He sensed her displeasure as they approached the first collection. Each canvas contained a photo of his left hand. Single words or phrases had been written there in black felt-tipped pen, as though noted as a memory aide. *Sleep. Forget. Deliver diatribe. Speculate. Desist.* Though the placement of these photo prints in the corridor correctly identified them as worthless, several had been stickered as sold already.

Zoe nodded and smiled. Her tension had dissolved to become undisguised relief. She understood that Richard had played the game, that was all. There was nothing to see here.

"What are those people listening to?" she said, pointing beyond the photo prints and into a room where visitors bent to listen to earphones wired into a central console.

"It was just a daft idea of mine. I'd been listening to some music at home. Trojan dub. When I went to the kitchen, the music merged with the washing machine. The rumbling made a sort of additional melody, in a funny way. Those people over there are sticking different earphones into each ear, trying out combinations to see what comes out. Engine noises and birdsong. Laughing and footsteps and sermons and merry-go-rounds."

Zoe mustered a supportive smile. "It's a sort of comment about the mush of different sounds that always surround us, I suppose."

"Sort of. Sure." Richard squeezed her arm to show that, like her, he recognised it as a sham. Surely even Folly's curators couldn't have been taken in by his concept. But the audio project bolstered the collection and pushed the necessary buttons for the Arts Council. If there was one thing Richard understood since the procedure at the Forge, it was how to play the system.

"Come on," he said. "The stuff I wanted to show you is back here."

He held back to allow Zoe to enter the third and final room alone. Her shoulders stiffened and then grew slack as she turned to look at each of the three walls on which his paintings hung.

The eight paintings had been arranged in strict sequence. Each showed Zoe's face, turned at ninety degrees. In the leftmost image, faint, feathery lines represented her closed eyes and the creases on her cheek and on the linen of the pillow. In the next canvas her eyes were still closed, but a furrow on her forehead suggested consciousness. As the sequence progressed, her eyes opened and her lips parted. Then, in the eighth and final image, she smiled.

None of this would have given any more insight into Zoe's character than the original photos, if not for the additional effect that Richard had introduced. Each painting in the sequence was more abstracted than the previous one. In the leftmost canvas, the representation of Zoe appeared more or less realistic. By the third, the duplication of her features became evident. In the fifth and sixth, her two wide eyes had become four, with the faintest pair slipping off the side of her face entirely. By the eighth canvas, two of the eyes overlapped to become one, darker and doubled, at the bridge of her nose. Only the central strip of her face was flesh-coloured. Her cheeks were near-translucent and merged with her red hair. Her lips contained two cupid's bows, side by side.

Zoe kept quiet, hugging herself.

"It was infuriating, you see," Richard said, "Those photos were so close to how you'd appeared to me at that moment, but somehow they were still utterly false. The problem was that I could never have seen you with that kind of objective clarity. In bed, with you right there, only inches from me like that, the moments I felt closest to you would have been the moments when my vision relaxed. When I lost focus. Clarity isn't everything. That's the theory, anyway."

She turned. Like the Zoe in the paintings, her features blurred.

"I understand," she said.

She rubbed at one eye with a thumb, covering her face in the process.

I'm so close, Richard thought. She's so close. I can take Simon's place, the place I lost.

It had been an elegant plan, using his rival's own mind in order to defeat him. And in the process, giving Richard the inspiration— or whatever electrical impulses encouraged inspiration—to create these artworks, of which he felt very proud. He couldn't—or wouldn't—have created them before the procedure.

They stood facing each other in silence as the exhibition visitors trickled around them. Then Zoe stepped backwards to stand in the centre of the room. She rotated slowly on the balls of her feet, gazing at each painting in turn. Richard watched her with satisfaction, as if this were a dance for his benefit.

It didn't matter that Simon and Zoe had already split up. Zoe had loved some parts of Simon, after all. All he had to was identify which of Simon's characteristics were required and which must be discarded. From the best parts of two men he could become somebody entirely new. Somebody perfect for Zoe.

He felt a tug at his left elbow. He pulled away. "I'll be with you in a moment," he said.

"No. Now," a familiar voice said. "I need to speak to you."

He turned to see Lola. Her waterproof coat and her cheeks glistened with rain.

"I'm sorry I haven't called you," Richard said. Did the disdain in his voice come from Simon or from himself? "I've been busy with the exhibition."

Lola shook her head. That wasn't why she was here. "Is there somewhere private?"

Richard smiled. He kept one eye on Zoe, who hadn't seen Lola enter. Other visitors floated around the gallery, barely glancing at the paintings. "These people are nobody. They're wrapped up in their socialite pantomime. We can speak right here."

Nevertheless, Lola leant forwards before speaking, so that her chin grazed his shoulder. He sensed the tremor in her voice even before she spoke.

"Simon's dead."

*

Detective Inspector Cave retrieved a notebook from his breast pocket.

"Right then. Tell me again when you last saw Simon Macmillan."

Richard stretched his legs beneath the metal desk. He stifled a yawn, despite his feeling quite alert. Perhaps it was some kind of fear response. Or perhaps it was a response inherited from Simon.

"I've never met him," he said.

"And Zoe Forbes?"

"Yes. I've certainly met her." Ordinarily this might have sounded self-effacing. Now Richard knew that it came across as cynical and that his smile appeared more of a leer.

"Are you making a joke, Mr Handler?"

Richard shrugged. This was serious, he knew. But something in him refused to cooperate, despite his instincts to do so.

Cave's smile suggested that all of this was in good fun. "Ms Forbes has stated that, when you last met, she informed you that she and Mr Macmillan were no longer a couple. Could you confirm that this meeting was the first that you knew of the fact?"

"I can confirm that. Yes."

"And what was your reaction to this news?"

Richard tried to arrange his features appropriately. What had his reaction been? Mostly fear. Fear that he had introduced Simon's rotten personality traits into his own head. And fear that doing so had been for nothing, if it made him no more appealing to Zoe.

"Surprise," he said.

"Surprise," Cave repeated. "Well. Let me try and surprise you still further. Although Simon Macmillan's body was discovered yesterday morning, various factors indicate that he'd already been dead for some four days. When was it that you met with Zoe Forbes?"

"Thursday," Richard said. "Three days ago."

Cave nodded. "So Ms Forbes' news was unexpected, you say. Good. Here's a hypothetical. Might this surprise have felt more profound if you had visited Mr Macmillan at his apartment only the day before? And if he hadn't revealed to you this detail about their separation?"

"I can see why you might think that," Richard said. Inwardly, he cursed himself. He must try to be more direct, more straightforward. He wasn't coming across as an honest man.

Now it was Cave who leant backwards in his chair. His catlike stretch was an echo of Richard's own posture. "An interesting fellow, this Simon Macmillan. And an interesting case all round. Of course, I'm biased. I wouldn't be in this job if I didn't find the criminal mind fascinating."

Richard scowled. "I'm not a criminal. I'm innocent."

"Quite. And, as yet, you've not been accused of anything. But you misunderstand me. I'm talking about Mr Macmillan himself. Generally speaking, the wealthy elite are a dull bunch, wouldn't you agree? But this chap... Well." Cave leafed through his notepad. "Non-existent galleries used for laundering of cash, smuggling of priceless artworks, sale of forged artworks to private collectors... It's the stuff of espionage thrillers."

Richard clamped a hand onto his right knee. Its fidgeting had begun to shake the metal table. "I don't know about any of that."

"Indeed. Although, coincidentally, it was Folly—one of Mr Macmillan's own galleries—that was kind enough to display your recent artworks."

"I didn't know Simon Macmillan."

"But perhaps you might have understood how his mind worked?"

Richard's eyes widened. He felt the corner of one eye twitch. What did Cave know?

But the Detective Inspector only sighed. "Okay. That'll do for now. Please inform us if you'll not be at home."

*

The phone rang for more than thirty seconds before Zoe answered.

"I don't think I should talk to you," she said.

"You told the police that I murdered Simon."

The poor phone reception made her gasp a stutter. "No! All I told them is what we talked about."

It certainly sounded like genuine shock, but Richard ploughed on. "Then you have to tell them that I'm innocent."

"I need to go, Richard. I have a meeting."

He channelled Simon's mannerisms and assertion. Nobody

could say no to him. "Go to the police this afternoon. They'll believe you. You must do this for me, Zoe."

A pause. "I don't know you, Richard. I haven't known you for a year."

Richard felt his control over his impulses slacken. "And you think I could have killed Simon? To stand a chance of getting back together with you? Do you realise how fucking stupid that sounds, you deluded... you self-absorbed harpy?" Richard took a breath and struggled to locate his own thoughts amongst the mess of Simon's. "You do know me. You do. I'm not the kind of person who could do a thing like that."

Maybe not. But what about Simon Macmillan? Could he have done it, if the roles were reversed? Could he have made himself commit murder, along with his other crimes?

Increasingly, Richard's sympathies lay with the police. Nobody could blame them for suspecting him as the kind of person who *could* do a thing like that. And maybe they'd be right. Sure, he was innocent of the murder. But if he had actually found himself in a position to kill Simon...

The line became so silent that he was convinced that Zoe had hung up.

"I have to go."

And then she did.

*

Richard's lawyer raised a hand, then turned to face him. "You don't have to answer any more of these questions."

"I'll answer them," Richard said, glaring at the CCTV camera in the corner of the bare room. "I'll answer any fucking question they like, because I'm innocent and I'm telling the truth and the truth can't implicate me. Okay?"

But Richard could see clearly that this was no longer the case. His responses to Detective Inspector Cave's questions were reasonable enough, in theory. But he understood it was his mannerisms that had secured him in Cave's mind as a suspect. Before the procedure, he would have cooperated fully and would now be a free man, despite the wealth of circumstantial evidence against him. But Simon's jagged electrical impulses were stronger and more insistent than his own. They controlled the articulation of his words. They controlled the muscles of his face.

"Thank you. I appreciate that," Cave said. "So please, go ahead and enlighten me. Why does the hard drive of your computer contain more than ten hours of video footage, all exclusively of Simon Macmillan, all filmed illegally using your own recording device?"

At least the police mustn't have discovered Lola's spreadsheets, which would only have made matters worse. Or perhaps they just hadn't recognised what the dataset represented. The near-complete map of a human mind, gathered from external evidence. More insight than anybody should reasonably expect to have about anybody. A comprehensive template to forge a copy, or to overlay those characteristics onto one's own.

There was only one way out of this mess.

"I've never seen that footage before," Richard said. "But perhaps I can help, after all. The computer and camera have only just been returned to me. Over the last month, I'd lent it to a friend of mine. I'm afraid to say that she has a history of rather illicit activities online. Maybe you have a file on her already. She's called Kent. Lola Kent."

*

Two days later, Lola approached him in the street outside his house.

"Don't come any closer," Richard said.

She kept walking towards him. He held up a hand. It shook uncontrollably.

"Good God," Lola said, "You look dreadful."

He tried to fend her off with flailing arms. "Why are you here? Did the police let you go? I didn't say anything to them. It wasn't me."

When Lola reached him, she put her arms around his waist and pressed her face into his shirt. The rhythm of her steady breathing contrasted with his shivers and fidgets.

"It's over, Richard." It seemed as though her words came from inside his chest.

He held her at arm's length, long enough to examine her face. This wasn't a rejection. She was referring to the murder inquiry.

"For you, maybe," he said.

"For both of us. For all of us."

"I don't understand. What about the dataset?"

"I explained everything to them."

"About the Forge? The procedure?"

Lola began to speak, halted, then said, "The police weren't concerned about that. They were sceptical about whether it was even possible."

Richard shivered. He wished that it hadn't been possible. He wished that Lola had never told him about the Forge. She had been wrong to hope that it might help him recover at a point when his self-confidence had been at its lowest ebb.

Lola spoke quickly, perhaps to distract him from these thoughts. "Anyway, they accept that you're innocent. I'm not sure you ever were a suspect, really. The case is closed."

Richard just stared over Lola's shoulder, focusing on nothing.

Lola continued. "Simon was murdered by one of his European contacts. Some Belgian guy, I don't remember the details. Considering the number of rackets he was mixed up in, he was due some comeback. Turns out he wasn't just prone to cheating art collectors out of money. He was cheating the cheats, too."

Richard found that he still couldn't speak. So he was innocent in the eyes of the law. So what? The more he learnt about Simon Macmillan, the more he understood that he, Richard, was no longer himself. His mind held the personality of that crooked, unloved bastard, overlaid upon and overwhelming his own.

"Zoe's refusing to speak to me," he said. "I'll never see her again. It doesn't matter that I'm innocent. It doesn't matter that Simon's gone. I see that now."

Lola nodded. "I'm sorry. And I'm so, so sorry about the Forge. But it's like I always said. You've got to move on."

Richard rubbed hot tears from his eyes. "I can't do that. And

I don't mean because of Zoe, not really. I can't move on because I let Simon Macmillan into my head and I can't get him out again. I went back to the Forge, Lola, the day after I met Zoe the first time. The whole thing's gone. Disappeared. Not a trace. The office managers denied that any such company was ever there. And now Simon's dead but he's still hanging around inside my head and he always will and—"

Lola embraced him again. "Hush. Let's try one more time. I'll come with you."

*

Richard paused on the threshold of the lobby. He turned to see Lola standing on the other side of the road. Two thumbs up.

Rather than speak to the receptionist, he walked straight to the lift at the rear of the lobby. His leg movements felt stiff and unfamiliar. Sweat made his underarms and the area between his shoulder blades slick.

The third floor was dark and silent. His pace slowed as he reached the last door on the left.

He paused. He wiped his damp palms on his trousers.

He knocked.

"Come in," said a muffled voice from within.

A young man wearing a smart white shirt and pink tie sat behind the wooden desk. Despite the outfit, Richard recognised him immediately. He had seen him only once before, in some nightclub in the city, dancing madly amongst a group of coders celebrating Lola's thirtieth birthday.

What did this mean? Had Lola's friends been operating the Forge all along? Or Lola herself?

He bit his cheek. He had to believe that there was still hope.

"I had a procedure here," he said. He nodded to indicate the brushed-steel door at the side of the room. "And it didn't work out."

The man behind the desk nodded. Gordon, was that his name? Graeme? "And you'd like the procedure to be reversed?"

"It's possible?"

"It's not trivial. But yes, it's possible. To be frank, we're winding things up here."

Richard gave an appropriately grateful smile. "I didn't know if I needed a particular form," he said, passing a sheet of paper over the desk, "So I just noted all the details I could think of."

The young man nodded and glanced at the printout. He tilted his screen display so that it was angled away from Richard's line of sight. As he tapped on the screen with one finger, his tongue protruded from one side of his mouth in a parody of concentration.

Richard concentrated, trying to remember details of Lola's birthday party. After they had left the nightclub, most of the group had ended up at the house that Lola had, at the time, shared with a few other people. He had drunk tequila shots, slamming each glass down onto the pine table in the kitchen. That table was very much like the one he now faced, except that that one hadn't had a letterbox chute dug into it.

One of the faces around the table that night had been this young man. Gordon, Graeme, or maybe Gywn. They had talked for a while. This man had told Richard that he felt out of his depth here, because he wasn't a techie like the others. He worked as a barman by night. By day he auditioned for and failed to secure acting roles.

Electrical impulses fired in Richard's mind. Not jagged, not rotten.

"Why is the Forge closing down?" he said.

The young man took a deep breath. When he spoke, his tone sounded rehearsed. "We've had several customers return. In some cases the effects of the procedure have been more pronounced than anticipated. It's certainly no fault of the user. Our technicians are concerned that video footage may sometimes overwhelm an otherwise robust dataset."

The part about the video footage was a neat detail. In Lola's original conception of the plan, all that would have been required would have been a spreadsheet filled with meaningless numbers. No stalking, no surveillance. That had been Richard's idea alone.

He understood now. The whole thing had been a sham,

from start to finish. Lola had invented the Forge in an attempt to pull him from the depths of depression. And he had ruined everything, first by selecting Simon Macmillan as a target and then by making the lie even more destructive than his self-pity.

He forced his expression to remain impassive, for this young man's sake, and for Lola's.

"Okay. This all checks out," the man said finally. "The booth is prepped and ready."

Richard wished that he could still see Lola and her two thumbs up.

He tapped his fingers on the work surface, rose, wavered, and opened the steel door.

All I Can See Are Sad Eyes

Exactly one year ago, I turned and saw her waiting in the queue. I smiled, despite the coffee spilling from one cup and scalding my fingers. Didn't I know her? From my office, or Miriam's?

Miriam had bagged a corner table and was already absorbed in a magazine.

"Is that a friend of yours?" I said, gesturing as I deposited our drinks.

Miriam scanned the queue, then shrugged.

I shrugged too. "One of those faces. I must have just seen her about."

As the woman took her seat I stole another glance. Not unattractive, with her dark hair and sad eyes, but that wasn't it. I felt sure I'd seen her in some other context. University, perhaps, or even school.

Miriam turned her magazine to show me photos of a wedding. Shabby chic, cotton bunting, toddlers in waistcoats. Low in expense but rich with perfect moments. When I looked up, the woman had finished and left.

I saw her again, only hours later. She stood at the opposite side of Iffley Road, cheering on the half-marathon runners. My friends in the race hooted and jeered as they passed. I blinked myself awake and called out, too late.

*

When I noticed her at the winter market, I raised my hand in an instinctive wave. How many times do you have to see a stranger for them to be no longer a stranger? There's nothing wrong with acknowledging a familiar face.

The woman only frowned, her features made strange by the glow of fairy lights.

*

"You're going to think this is weird," I said to her, a couple of weeks later. I kept one arm around Miriam's waist to demonstrate that I was no threat. "But I'm certain I know you."

The sad-eyed woman flinched. "Really? From where?" More guarded than interested.

Miriam pressed into my side, tipsy and scanning the crowd for anyone yet to see the ring.

I waved a vol-au-vent. "I thought maybe you'd know. Have you ever done any freelance work for Hargreaves?"

The woman shook her head. She raised herself on tiptoes to look around. "Sorry," she said.

"OK. But how do you know Lil and Gary?"

"Friends of friends. I don't mean to be rude, but I think someone's calling me."

When the woman left, Miriam spun to face me. "We've only six months to practise, otherwise we'll embarrass ourselves in front of everyone," she said. "So ask me to dance."

*

The next time was a month later, in a London pub, sixty miles from home. Drinks with Ryan, mock-pleading for him to go easy on arrangements for the stag.

"What's she doing here? It's as if she's following me," I said.

Ryan looked over, sizing her up. "Not bad. Sure it's not the other way around?"

The woman glanced up from her phone, then hurriedly down again.

*

"We can't," Miriam said. "It's insane."

"But in the best possible way," I said. I framed the Holywell building with my joined thumbs and forefingers, making a photographer's viewfinder. "And we knew a cancellation was the only way the place would become available."

"But this weekend? What about all our—"

"They'll make it, I'm certain. And you've already sorted the important things, the dress, the…" My joints cracked as I slid down to kneel on the pavement. "You're perfect, Miriam. We are. And I want it to be as soon as it can be."

*

She was everywhere.

*

"Look, I'm sick of it," Miriam said. "What are you trying to tell me here?"

I held up both hands. "No subtext. Promise. I'm genuinely weirded out, that's all, and I wanted to tell you. Isn't that what marriage is about?"

Miriam squinted against the afternoon light to where the sad-eyed woman sat alone on a park bench. "She's not your usual type."

"That's not it at all. You're my type."

Miriam puffed her cheeks. "It's not normal, noticing other women all the time, when you're committed. It shows me that something's wrong."

"But it's not other women. Just that one." I paused, recognising the danger too late.

"You're saying you're obsessed with her."

"I'm not. Anyone would be."

Miriam pushed me away. "Just go and talk to her, for God's sake."

"What are you saying?"

"You know what I'm saying."

*

She was everywhere, though, abruptly, Miriam was not.

*

Hi. Is this the number for Citizen's Advice? I don't know if you can help. I have a few questions about my rights. I'm being followed, I think.

A woman.

I don't know.

No.

I don't think so. She seemed familiar at first, but—

No violence, no.

No, no threats.

Yes, briefly, at a party. I did.

I understand. But, you see, I can't continue like this. Everywhere I turn, she's—

I see. I'm sorry. Thank you.

*

She started to back away as I approached. I placed myself between her and the bus laden with colleagues waiting to be delivered to the office party.

"You have to stop this," I said.

"Leave me alone," she said, trying not to meet my eye.

"I broke up with my partner of four years," I said, "Because of you."

"I'm sorry. But I don't see how it—"

I thrust out an arm to prevent her from boarding the bus. "Why did you take a job here? Wasn't it enough for you, following me around the streets?"

Finally, she looked at me. I felt painfully aware of my stubbly beard and the clothes I had been wearing for the last three days.

We both spoke as one.

"You have to stop this."

*

A lot can change in a year.

I tend not to go out a whole lot. Better to stay in the house. I'm not as bored as you'd think, even after cancelling the broadband. My Facebook feed had become filled with her face.

Even though it's a quiet enough street, people pass by more than I'd like. Sometimes they ignore the notices on my door. Their silhouettes shrink as they bend down. I shrink too, in the hallway, keeping out of sight.

The letterbox opens and all I can see are sad eyes.

Winter in the Vivarium

The angle of refraction through the thick, curved glass made it difficult to see into the bedroom. Byron Bright rechecked the motion sensor strapped to his right arm. A single green dot appeared, faint and unmoving, every couple of seconds. If there was anybody in there, they must be asleep. He pulled himself onto the gantry for a better view.

The single occupant of the room, a middle-aged man, lay on a wide bed with his arms and legs outstretched. The covers had been thrown off and were bundled in a heap on the floor. Behind the headboard, a fan blew green-leafed plants gently from side to side. The sleeping man yawned, turned, and settled again. His flesh looked pink and warm.

Byron sighed.

Snow whipped at his parka. Ice-cold air stung the exposed parts of his face. He ought to be wearing his goggles, but they became so easily fogged. At least the thick fur trim of his hood protected him from the worst of the wind. Its narrow opening gave him tunnel vision.

He pulled a flat-edged scraper from his pack and began clearing snow from the curved window. When the sleeping man woke, he would have an unobstructed view of the mountains for the first time in several days.

Sidestepping right along the gantry, Byron crossed the boundary between this apartment and the next. With one bulky gloved finger he made a circle in the snow that covered the glass. The darkness—both inside and outside the Vivarium—made the reflection of his own face eerie, illuminated from below by the light from his motion sensor.

He noticed the appearance of the green dot a second too late.

A figure appeared, framed in the doorway to the bedroom. A woman. She stared up at the window. She saw Byron.

He expected her to scream, but instead she reached for the bedside phone.

Byron dropped down from gantry. The fabric of his trouser leg caught on an exposed bolt and tore. With shaking hands, he bound the tear with gaffer tape from his pack. Even though his long-johns hadn't been ripped, the cold wind that whistled around his thigh made him wince.

His earpiece communicator bleeped.

His first thought was: *How did she get my number?* He almost laughed at that. He had no number. The woman had no way of reaching him, even if she had wanted to.

He jabbed at his neck, pushing the Receive button through his hood.

"Bright?"

Mr Collins sounded angry. That woman, whoever she was, had worked fast. She must be in some position of authority to have contacted the management directly.

"Sir. Before you say anything, I can explain," Byron said. "My motion sensor's on the blink, I think. I didn't know—"

"Are you saying you claim responsibility?" The tinny voice stuttered with each new blast of icy wind.

"Well, I can't blame anyone else, sir. But she only saw me for a second. I've been careful, I always am. All the others were asleep or away from their apartments."

Mr Collins didn't respond. Byron tapped at his hood to check that the earpiece was still attached.

"Sir?"

"Destroy them, Bright."

Byron hesitated. Was this some kind of test of his loyalty?

"Do you hear me?" The shrill voice made his ear buzz. "They've already upset several residents. Get over to the lagoon this instant, and destroy them, you hear?"

"Sir, I think we may have got our wires crossed—"

Mr Collins's voice hardened. "There are a dozen Outfielders who would welcome the chance to do your job. Do not push your luck. Do you understand me?"

"Not fully, sir."

"Go!"

The comms line cut out.

"Yes, sir," Byron said.

The leisure quadrant was diametrically opposite the apartments, more than sixteen miles away. Byron steered his snow-scooter far wider than the perimeter of the circular city, keeping below the level of the ha-ha that obstructed views of the town from the Vivarium. It was imperative that he stayed out of sight. Even if that woman's complaint hadn't yet reached Mr Collins, he would hear of it soon enough. Byron couldn't afford to make another mistake.

Once he was certain that he mustn't be visible from any of the apartments, he killed the engine and climbed the ha-ha on foot.

The grandest feature of the leisure quadrant was the tropical lagoon. Many of the residents spent whole weekend days lounging in the reclining chairs or splashing in the shallows of the huge, kidney-shaped swimming pool. Creepers climbed the inner surface of the enormous domed window. The leaves of giant taro and palm trees sweated with condensation.

The entire leisure quadrant closed at five each morning, only to reopen an hour later to provide breakfasts and massages to the residents. It was now five-fifteen. Most of the lights of the tropical lagoon had been dimmed. Reflections from the pool refracted through the curved glass and made a shifting, shimmering pattern on the snow outside.

Byron stopped dead.

Three people stood facing the enormous curved window of the lagoon. Outside.

"Hey!" he called. "You can't be here. You're miles within the exclusion zone!"

None of them turned around. Only their shadows moved with the ripples of the reflected light.

"I know you're not residents. Mr Collins is already furious. You'd better head back to town, right away."

His boots sunk into the snow as he stepped onto the flat

snow bank. None of the people acknowledged him. As he moved around to one side, he saw that the blue light reflected from their faces, their torsos, their limbs. They shone like diamonds.

These weren't Outfielders, or residents. They weren't even people.

They were statues.

He reached out to touch the closest one. His gloved fingers skidded on the icy surface of its chest.

They had been sculpted from packed snow. Rather than crude snowmen, they were ice sculptures. At their thinnest parts— the arms, legs and necks—the snow had hardened and become translucent. They had no features except for two hollows to represent eyes.

It was no wonder that they had unnerved the residents. They appeared to be watching the Vivarium.

Byron remembered Mr Collins's words. He returned to the scooter to collect a spade.

Each of the statues shattered in a thousand sparks of ice.

*

"Spill the beans, By," Garry said as he handed over a pint of hot beer. "Was it really you?"

Byron glanced at Jess, who had already taken a stool. She leant forwards over the bartop.

"I don't know what you're talking about," he said, taking a sip of his drink. He wiped at the hot foam caught in his moustache.

Jess rolled her eyes. "The statues, Michelangelo."

"How did you hear about them?"

She smiled. "We might not be able to get close to the dome, but we still hear what's going on over the comms. They're talking of nothing but the statues."

"And the same goes for Outfielders, now," Garry added.

Byron's eyes widened. "You've been listening to the Vivarium's internal comms? That's impossible."

"It would be," Garry said, "If not for the two-way in your room. Doesn't take much tinkering to tune out old Collins and tune in the Domers' headsets, if you know what you're doing."

Byron thumped the table, spilling beer on its already sticky surface. "That communicator was given to me to allow me to fulfil my duties. I don't know what to say. My own brother! It's a terrible crime to listen in—"

Garry held up a hand to stop him. "Sure. Yeah. You swore a solemn oath. And so on and so on."

"But don't you see that I'll lose my job?"

"You'll lose it anyway, the way you're carrying on. And you can do better than scurrying around outside the dome. You could help the people that really matter. Your family, your—" He paused. Perhaps he couldn't bring himself to say 'friends'. "You don't have to be a hunter. We need technicians too, to convert more cars to snow-runners."

Byron gripped the edge of the table. His hands were shaking.

Jess prodded Garry with an elbow. "Leave him be, lover. Give him time. You've already accepted that you were wrong about Byron. He's not a dome-dreamer after all."

Byron just stared at her. "Is that what you all call me?"

It was his brother who replied. "What do you expect? You spend all your time staring into that bloody Vivarium, and then you come back and tell us all about what you've seen, every sodding day. Oh! The restaurants, the bowling alleys, the lights and lights and lights. People wandering around in the heat, wearing only their undercrackers. We figured either you're obsessed, or you're just trying to rub our noses in the fact that we couldn't get within pissing distance of the exclusion zone, even if we wanted to."

"That's not fair. I—"

"But you're not listening," Jess said. "We don't think that any more. We think you're sort of a hero."

Byron frowned. He looked at one smiling face, then the other.

"You've upset the Domers, big time," Garry said. "Those statues? Elegant, that's what they are. A beautiful idea."

"But I had nothing to do with them," Byron said.

Garry waved a hand. His voice sounded as though it was coming from far away. "So us Outfielders can't get close to the domes? So the Domers don't want to be reminded of the rest of us, shivering our nuts off in the snow?" He grinned. "Those statues will remind them. A peaceful fucking protest. I could almost kiss you, brother Byron."

*

Each night, Byron skirted the perimeter of the Vivarium on his scooter. Each night, he discovered more of the ice statues. They stood watching the lagoon, the hair salons, the children's crèche, the bedrooms.

"It's not me who's building them, sir," Byron insisted.

He destroyed each of them with a single blow of his spade. Their bright shards disappeared into the snow drift.

"I'll prove that it is," Mr Collins hissed. "And then I'll have you hung in the piazza."

"You'll bring me inside?"

"Of course not. Out there in the wilderness, then. You'll be swinging from a tree. And then I'll get some other fool to clear the windows and maintain the vents. Anyone could do it."

Byron smashed the statues, then returned to his usual duties. When he had finished clearing snow, he pressed himself up against the glass of the Vivarium and imagined that he was warm.

It was almost dawn. The snow had stopped falling and the rising sun tinged the white ground with red.

He turned.

A statue stood watching him.

*

"I heard some Domer woman describe them in detail, on the phone to a friend," Jess said. "I couldn't get the phrase out of my mind. 'Like they had risen out of the ground,' that's what she said."

Byron thought of the statue that had appeared, the night before. He shuddered.

"They're more than just a reminder of us Outfielders, aren't they?" Jess said.

The people at the neighbouring table had stopped talking to listen. Byron sipped his drink. Nobody in the inn had believed him when he had tried to deny involvement. They all knew of Mr Collins's certainty about his guilt, heard over the hacked internal comms. The trouble was, keeping quiet wasn't an option, either. The less he said the more Jess and Garry and the others celebrated him.

Everyone was waiting for him to speak.

"They're just ice, like everything out here," he said. Surely that couldn't be a contentious comment?

Garry clapped his hands in delight. "See, Jess? I told you!"

Jess grinned. "So you're making a link between the Outfielders and the natural world itself, is that it?"

Byron shrugged.

She tapped her chin. "No, that's not it, quite. It's a bigger statement. About nature itself, about the ice age, the changes. The world is watching the Vivarium. All of the other domes, too. No matter how much Domers would like to deny it, there's still a world outside. Continuing, thriving."

*

"I think you're wrong, sir. I don't think you'll find anyone else to do my work. Everyone I've spoken to, they hate the Vivarium. And most of them hate me, too, because I work for you."

His earpiece only crackled in response.

"And there's another thing you don't understand," Byron continued. "It's no wilderness out here. It's cold, but we're all doing okay. I live in the same house I did when I was a boy."

When he had finished destroying the statues that had appeared overnight, he cleared the windows as quickly as he could, then checked that the air intake vents were in good condition, then he retreated. The artificial light from inside the Vivarium hurt his eyes.

He shouldered his pack and returned to his scooter. Three more ice statues had appeared on the flat bank, watching the lagoon.

What did they find so interesting in there?

He stood back to back with one of the statues. If only they faced in this direction instead, they might see something far grander than the avenues and leisure facilities inside the Vivarium. Through the squalls of falling snow he could make out the white foothills and the mountains that made a horseshoe around his home town.

He revved the scooter and headed to the hills.

When he had been young, before the ice age began, he and his friends would camp out here. They slung hammocks between the trees or slept under bivouac shelters. They sang invented songs to welcome the dawn of the solstice.

The trees were still here, somewhere, beneath the blanket of snow. But only the tips of the tallest protruded now, like tiny shrubs.

The runners of the scooter hummed as he navigated across the undisturbed snow. Why was it that he never travelled out in this direction, these days? Without the foreground distraction of the Vivarium, the hills were more beautiful than he remembered. The hillocks and valleys weren't uniformly white. The sunlight filtered through the falling snow turned the ground blue, grey and gold. The hillside appeared like the flank of a great, bruised beast.

He stopped at the top of the foothill. It must have been somewhere near here—beneath where he now stood—that he and his first girlfriend had shared their first kiss. He had been terrified and her lips had tasted of liquorice.

The snow had buried all landmarks. When it had begun, those fifteen years ago, it had seemed to Byron that his past was being erased. Other townspeople, Garry and Jess included, had welcomed the change, once they had accepted that they couldn't afford to enter one of the Vivaria. They revelled in the challenge. They altered their ambitions to fit the new world. Instead of worrying about climbing corporate and housing ladders, they concerned themselves with hunting, fishing, sharing time with the people they loved. They began to feel sorry for the Vivarium residents, who had recreated a caricature of the old world in their bubbles. And they felt sorrier still for Byron, who longed to be in there with them.

In the distance, the sheer face of the mountain glittered, like constellations changing every second. It had never seemed so glorious when it was just rock.

The falling snow thinned a little. Byron's breath caught as a rainbow appeared, making a shimmering bridge across the valley.

It was beautiful. Utterly, overwhelmingly beautiful.

A nagging thought hardened into certainty.

Those statues back there, they weren't watching the Vivarium, at least not in the way that he did. They didn't want to get inside.

Could it be that they wanted the Domers to come outside, for their own good?

*

By the time he reached the ha-ha, there were two dozen ice statues at the lagoon window. Byron stood before them. He made a show of laying his spade on the ground.

"I'm sorry that I hit you," he said. "I shouldn't have done that."

The statues watched as he made his way to the air intake unit at one side of the enormous window. This unit, and the others like it, dragged in freezing air from outside, then super-heated it before pumping it directly into the Vivarium. Without this new intake, the air conditioning systems would recycle the same air indefinitely, degrading it with each circulation and allowing viruses to thrive.

He trod carefully to avoid slipping on the ice patches, where the suck of the fans had smoothed the top layer of the snow. He removed the cover and set to work with his screwdriver and wrench. He felt the warmth of the heating appliance through the thick fingers of his gloves. Nobody understood the workings of these air intakes better than he did. It took only twenty minutes for him to jerry-rig the unit so that the fans remained operational, but the air bypassed the heating appliance.

He replaced the cover and climbed back onto the flat snow bank, where ten more ice statues had appeared. The curve of the window obscured any view of the vent inside the Vivarium, but he could see immediately the effects of his work. The air that whistled into the lagoon was a white streak. The leaves of the plants nearest the vent glistened with ice veins.

Byron's earpiece bleeped. Instinctively, he tapped at his neck to receive the call.

"Bright! My dashboard panel's lit up like a Christmas tree. Air intake warnings at the south-west radial. Get over there right—"

Byron wiggled his hand into his hood and plucked out the earpiece. The buzz of Mr Collins's voice reduced in volume and was overwhelmed by the sound of the wind.

There were eleven other vents. He worked steadily, making his way around the circumference of the Vivarium. By the time he reached the fifth vent the sun had risen fully. Residents rose from their beds and stared in horror at Byron in his thick, fur-hooded coat, wielding his wrench. He waved back at them.

By the time he had returned to the lagoon window, the snow bank was packed full of statues. He threaded his way carefully through the crowd to reach the curved window.

A crowd of Domers faced him. They stood in the shallows of the swimming pool in their bathing costumes.

No. They weren't facing him. They hadn't even noticed him.

The foliage closest to the window had become encrusted with snow and ice. Byron followed the trail of white that spread on the ground, making a chevron away from the air intake unit. It cut through the green grasses and creepers of the tropical jungle.

A single ice statue stood at the tip of this arrow of snow. Its limbs were thinner than the statues outside. It wobbled a little in the gust produced by the fans.

As Byron watched through the window, and as the Domers watched from inside, the statue seemed to become more substantial. White powder collected upon its spindly frame, accumulating on its arms, body and head.

High above, where three lamps made an artificial sun, it began to snow.

Lines of Fire

When he saw the look on Patrick's face as he opened the door, Matt wished he'd stayed at home. What was the word? Triumphant— that was it.

"Didn't think you'd actually show up," Patrick said with a smirk.

"I told you I would."

Patrick snorted. "Scout's honour, right? Dib-dib-dib, dob-dob-dob."

Matt felt his cheeks redden. He was a head taller than Patrick, following a growth spurt that his mother put down to a bumper spinach crop from their garden allotment, but somehow it seemed that it was Patrick who towered over him, not the other way around. The fact that Matt was wearing shorts—it was July, and hot, wasn't it?—and Patrick was dressed all in black made him feel much younger than his twelve years.

"Leave it out," he said. "If you don't want to invite me in, then don't. I've got plenty of things I could be doing instead."

"I bet. Pressing wild flowers. Combing your doll's hair."

Matt turned. His mum's car was only just pulling out of the long gravel driveway. If he was quick, he might catch her.

But Patrick held his arm. "I'm just yanking your chain. Which is what I was doing to myself, before you showed up. Get it?"

"Yeah. Funny."

Other boys at school talked about that sort of thing, too, but Matt avoided those conversations. A couple of months ago he'd tried to join in with the jokes. His friend Davey had said something about Hugo hiding under the table, wanking. Matt had said, 'Sure, but who with?', and then his four mates were just staring at him like he'd told them he was an alien or a trannie or something. They laughed, but not in a good way.

"Come on in, then."

Reluctantly, Matt followed Patrick into the hallway. The farmhouse had looked huge from outside, with its long driveway winding through fields, but in here it was dingy and small. He tripped on a pair of boots hidden behind the door.

Patrick had already disappeared into the house. His voice echoed. "You want a cheese sandwich?"

"It's nine o'clock in the morning." Matt stumbled through a dark dining room to find Patrick in the kitchen. A cat with matted fur prowled along one of the work surfaces.

"Figured you must love cheese sandwiches," Patrick said. "It's all I've ever seen you eat."

"You've only known me for three days."

"Yeah, but you should see the look on your face when you open your lunch box and see that little cheese sandwich sitting there, all lovingly made by your mum or whatever." Patrick pulled a block of cheese from a plain white packet and held it up. It was covered in crumbs and little hairs. Matt glanced at the cat. He shook his head.

"It is your mum, isn't it?" Patrick said.

"What is?"

"Who makes your sandwiches."

"Yes, but that doesn't make me—"

To his surprise, Patrick didn't seem interested in making a joke about being a mummy's boy. He bit off a chunk off the cheese and munched it in silence.

"So are we going to play videogames?" Matt said.

"It's a summer's day. It's burning hot outside."

"Yeah. But—"

"We could play skittles. Some kids left a set behind. Or we could collect ladybirds."

"But that's why I came here. You said we could play videogames." In fact, that topic was all they'd ever really talked about. Miss Moran had asked Matt to help Patrick find his way around the school when he first showed up on Monday, three days before the end of term. Patrick had barely spoken unless it was to insult Matt or the town or the school, until Matt had mentioned videogames. Then Patrick started boasting about his skills and his massive collection of games.

"God! You're so easy to kid around," Patrick said. "You seriously think I want to play outside? Course we'll play games, you big girl."

Matt sighed with relief. Hopefully, playing videogames would mean speaking less to Patrick. Even so, it would have to be an amazing collection to make his visit worthwhile.

Patrick pulled a keyring from a wall hook. Beside it was a framed family photo that must have been taken several years earlier. The older kid had to be Patrick; he had the same narrowed eyes. His parents were looking down at him but Patrick was scowling straight at the camera. He had an arm around a younger boy, who looked pretty uncomfortable.

Patrick pushed open a glass-panelled door. Matt saw rows of cottages outside. They must have been hidden behind the farmhouse.

"Where are we going now?"

Patrick had already left. Matt hurried to catch up with him as he strode along a path running between the buildings.

"Is this all part of your house?" he said.

"Houses."

"Why do you need more than one?"

"Because there are like thirty people in my family."

"I thought you only had one brother. I saw a photo in the kitchen."

Patrick stopped. "Jesus. It's like you've got a blind spot for lies. These are holiday cottages, obviously."

Matt's face flushed. He shielded his eyes to peer into the dark windows. "But it's the middle of summer. Why aren't there any people? Holidaymakers, I mean."

"Because I live here now. And I don't want any little brats running around or fat bastards sunbathing in my garden."

Before Matt could ask any more questions, Patrick set off at a run. Concrete paths criss-crossed each other at right angles, separating each cottage from its neighbours. Empty crates and metal cylinders were stacked against the walls of the buildings in untidy piles. Soon Patrick had disappeared in amongst the cottages.

Matt followed at a walking pace. He wished he could just cut back through the farmhouse and leave, but it was miles back to his place. He was trapped until four o'clock, when his mum would show up with the car.

He found Patrick standing before a tall man who bent down to speak to him.

"You haven't been leaving the lights on in the house, have you?" the man said.

Patrick didn't answer. He tried to move past without stepping off the concrete path.

"Because every penny counts," the man said. "You know we can't afford—"

Patrick noticed Matt. "*Shut up,*" he hissed.

The man looked up. "Who's this?"

When Patrick didn't introduce him, Matt said, "I'm in Patrick's tutor group. Miss Moran made us sort of team up. She said we should be 'buddies'."

The man reached out a hand to shake Matt's, but Patrick batted it away.

"You're friends?" the man said. He had deep creases around each eye that looked rough and itchy.

"Well—" Out of the corner of his eye, he saw Patrick glaring at him.

"We're going to play videogames," Patrick said.

"I don't think you should," the man said.

"Then you can go to hell, can't you?"

The man looked as though he'd been punched in the stomach. He took a step backwards, off the path. Patrick pushed past and Matt followed.

"Ignore him," Patrick said, "He's just the caretaker."

Matt frowned. "But I saw him in the photo in the kitchen. Isn't that your dad?"

"Bloody busybody," Patrick said, but Matt couldn't tell if he meant him or the man.

He heard a scuffling sound to his right. Turning sharply, he saw a thin, speckled dog—a greyhound, perhaps—scrabbling on the bare ground in the shade of a cottage.

Patrick noticed his panic and laughed. "He's just hungry."

He jogged over to the dog. A rope held it to a metal ring fixed into the bricks. He kicked at the animal's side. Before the dog could lunge at him, he darted back to a safe distance. He knelt down beside the porch and returned with a bowl of dog food, which he placed on the ground. The dog pulled at the rope. Its mouth stopped short, a few inches from the bowl.

Patrick snickered and kept walking. He turned left at the next junction of the concrete path. After checking that Patrick wasn't looking, Matt nudged the bowl towards the dog with his foot. The dog slurped at the food gratefully.

He found Patrick standing in an archway. It connected the cottage area to an open space where low, white-walled buildings surrounded a swimming pool with a tall diving board. The pool was thick with leaves and green slime that shifted slowly on the surface of the water.

"Do you ever swim out here?" Matt said. He walked around the pool.

Patrick shook his head. "Does it look like it? The heater's conked out." He pointed to a door behind Matt, which was hanging off its hinges.

Matt pulled the door open. Inside, wood had been piled from floor to ceiling. Other than splinters and dirt, the only other item in the room was a large iron furnace with a thick door grille. It rattled violently.

"Want to take a dip?" Patrick said.

Surprised, Matt spun around. He hadn't heard Patrick sneak up behind him. He shook his head.

"Then let's play games."

Patrick unlocked the door of another of the white-walled buildings and went inside. Matt glanced into the pool as he passed. There were dark shapes in there. Perhaps animals had fallen in, along with the leaves.

"Welcome to the games room!" Patrick's voice called.

As Matt entered, the fluorescent ceiling lights flickered twice, then blinked off entirely. It was far darker than seemed possible, given the bright sunshine outside. The only source of light came from a square of blurry static at the far side of the room.

He walked past a ping pong table and a yellow fibreglass train, some kind of children's sit-on ride. Patrick stood with one hand resting on the panel of an arcade cabinet. He looked proud, like an adult showing off a fancy car.

"So, here it is."

Matt chewed his cheek. "Here what is?"

"I promised you videogames, didn't I?"

The screen flickered as the machine booted up. A logo appeared but Matt could barely make it out. The screen was filthy and the curve of the old-fashioned monitor made all the straight lines bent. He looked from the arcade cabinet to Patrick and back again.

"Patrick."

"Shut up."

"Why did you lie to me?"

"I'm not a liar."

Matt thought of the 'caretaker' at the cottages. Patrick had begun to fidget. He looked like he might cry.

"It's okay," Matt said. "My dad won't let me get a console either. Not until sixth form. He says, by then I'll be chasing girls, anyway."

He waited. To his surprise, Patrick didn't make a crack about him being gay.

"It's not that he won't buy me one," Patrick said. "It's that he can't. We don't have any money."

Maybe it wasn't Patrick's choice to wear those plain black clothes. "I'm sorry. I didn't realise. But doesn't the holiday park bring in money?"

"Nobody stayed here last summer. The year before, there was only one family, and they left early."

"Then why don't your parents sell it?"

"No chance. The park has a bad reputation." Before Matt could speak, he said, "And it's *parent*, not *parents*. My mum left years ago. It's just me and dad now."

Matt felt utterly out of his depth. He thought of his own parents and house. Even if they were boring, at least that made them safe. He remembered the photo in the kitchen. "And did you mum take your brother with her when she left?"

Patrick scowled. "Are we going to play videogames, or what?"

Matt was glad of the distraction. The screen had now turned the same bright blue as the sky outside. "Dyna Blaster? I've never heard of it."

"Bomberman. Same thing."

Matt shrugged. "This machine must be like, what, fifty years old?"

"Who cares? It's a classic."

Patrick ducked down and fumbled with the coin slot. He prised its front away with a tent peg. When he stood up he was holding two old-fashioned ten pence pieces. His face had the same triumphant expression that Matt had seen earlier. This time it seemed fair enough. He jammed the coins back into the slot again.

The screen filled with a grid of grey squares, with brown blocks at irregular intervals. A character stood in each corner, one white, one black. Blobby alien figures, which must be non-player enemies, patrolled areas separated from the characters by the brown walls.

Patrick grabbed one joystick and moved aside to let Matt take the other. Matt moved the joystick experimentally, guiding the white character around the maze. He pressed the single button. A bomb appeared on the same square as his character. It exploded. His character reappeared in the corner. The same thing happened again. The third time, he dropped the bomb at a junction in the grid and moved his character away. When the bomb exploded, lines of fire shot out along the grid in four directions. A moment later, Matt moved his character into the path of the firestorm a moment too soon. The words 'GAME OVER' appeared on the screen in warped, curved text.

Without saying a word, Patrick bent down to the coin slot. He fumbled with the tent peg and pulled out the two coins, then inserted them again.

"I think I get how it works now," Matt said. "But what's the aim of the game?"

Patrick didn't turn from the screen.

"I'm going to kill you," he said.

Matt glanced at Patrick. The boy's face was lit blue by the screen. His teeth clenched tight in concentration as soon as the title screen disappeared. The grid reflected in his eyes.

So it was going to be like that. He should have guessed that Patrick would be ultra-competitive.

Matt frowned at the screen, trying to see patterns in the grid and the layout of the destructible blocks. It seemed best to ignore the blobby enemies, for now. If he was careful, he ought to be able to avoid freeing them from their areas, at least for a while.

He was aware of the black character darting around at the bottom-left corner, and of Patrick's hands tapping at the joystick in careful, precise movements. Matt's own character, the white one, dithered in the top-left corner. Patrick's firestorms began to eat away at the brown blocks that separated them.

Matt placed a bomb in a junction of the grid and sped away. It was a wasted effort—the fire-lines didn't quite reach to the brown blocks.

"Is that a power-up?" he said, pointing to a boxed, cartoon picture of a flame at Patrick's side of the screen.

Patrick didn't answer, but directed his character over to collect the token. His next bomb produced fire-lines that stretched further in each direction.

Matt worked carefully. He dropped his next bomb directly beside a destructible block, alongside one of the grid squares rather than at a junction. He nodded in satisfaction. It was possible to be methodical and precise, without needing to send fire in every direction and risking death. A flame power-up appeared but he continued to play safe, destroying blocks one by one rather than trying to achieve too much with each bomb.

The next block produced a different power-up. Instinctively, Matt directed his character away from it.

Patrick snorted. "That's not a bomb, dickwad."

"It looks like one."

"Collect it."

Matt directed his character to the power-up, which blinked away as he passed over it. He dropped a bomb and moved away. "Nothing's happened."

Patrick didn't look away from the screen as he leant over. His index finger jabbed at the button on Matt's side.

A second bomb appeared. Panicked, Matt tried to move his character away, but became trapped between the two bombs. A couple of seconds later, he was dead.

"That's not fair," he said.

"Are you going to cry about it, little girl?"

Rattled, Matt found his concentration broken. Within thirty seconds he made a needless error and trapped his character between a bomb and a dead end. The white figure blinked away, then reappeared in the top-left hand corner. Matt punched the button with his fist and dropped another bomb at the character's feet. It exploded and the 'GAME OVER' message appeared.

"You did that on purpose," Patrick said.

"I'm sick of it. Does this thing have any other games?"

Patrick had already knelt to retrieve the coins from the slot. "No. Try harder this time. You didn't even give me time to break through the blocks to get to you. I didn't get a chance to kill you."

Matt moved away from the arcade cabinet. He looked around the games room. Perhaps he could convince Patrick to play ping pong instead? But there were no bats or balls on the table and no obvious place where they might be kept. Other than a few discoloured chairs, the only other items were the child's train ride and a freestanding bookcase.

He pulled out a book at random. It looked like the kind of thing his Auntie Diane would read. Its pink cover had cartoony pictures of high-heeled shoes and handbags. He bent to a lower shelf, where he glimpsed corners of dog-eared comics. They were ancient issues of *Bunty*.

"Who reads this stuff?" he said.

"Why do you think they were all dumped out here in the games room?" Patrick said. He pulled out a large, hardback book.

"This is the only one worth reading. It's just as well nobody else would bother with it, though."

Matt frowned at the cover. "'I Can Make You Thin', by Paul McKenna. Are you serious?"

Patrick leafed through the pages, tilting the book so that it was lit by the blue of the screen. Loose pieces of paper had been inserted into the back of the book. They must have been ripped out of some magazine. Matt saw pictures of flesh and lips and hair. He saw women with their legs held wide open.

He sensed that Patrick was watching him. His cheeks felt oddly cold. He had no idea how to react to the pictures.

"Look," Patrick said, turning to another page. "Erect nipples!"

Matt blinked rapidly. He glanced down at the picture, but only for a second. The blue light from the screen made the woman's skin look like weathered stone.

Patrick looked as though he was waiting for him to speak. Matt thought he should probably make some kind of noise to show how exciting he thought the pictures were.

He said the first thing that came into his head. "Nipples don't get erect, only willies."

Instantly, his eyes became hot and itchy. He knew he had said something wrong.

Patrick sniggered. "Willies?"

"Cocks. Dicks. Penises."

"*Willies*? How old are you, five?"

"Shut up."

Patrick placed both his hands on his own chest to hold imaginary breasts. "How does this make you feel? Is your little willy erect? Or maybe you'd say 'standy-uppy', or something like that?"

"You shouldn't have those pictures," Matt said. His voice trembled.

Patrick mimed lifting his invisible breasts and licking them with the tip of his tongue. "Oh, Matty. Show me your little willy."

"Stop it."

"I'm erect and wet and all those other things that you don't understand."

Matt shuddered. He didn't want to hear any of those words applied to girls. It was all terribly wrong. When he daydreamed about that sort of thing, he thought about kissing and maybe touching boobs. Not this.

"I'm going home," he said.

"Your mummy's gone away. You can't go. I don't want you to go." Patrick reached out an arm. His fingers wiggled slowly. Matt had no idea any more if he was still pretending to be a lady. He turned away. He rubbed at his eyes.

"Are you… Are you *crying?*" Patrick's voice had become high-pitched, but now he wasn't doing an impression. He was just delighted.

Matt ran to the door. He pulled the handle but it wouldn't open. The lock must have clicked when it closed.

"Give me the key," he said.

"Turn around."

Matt pulled at the shoulder of his T-shirt to wipe his eyes. Reluctantly, he turned around. He held out his hand.

Patrick took the key from his pocket. Before Matt could reach out, he snatched it away again.

"I'll play you for it." He pointed to the arcade cabinet.

"That's stupid. You've played the game loads of times, and I've only had one go."

"Then you'll have to try really hard."

"I won't win."

"Then you won't get the key, will you?"

"You'll have to leave, too, sooner or later."

"True. But that doesn't mean that you will."

Matt watched Patrick carefully. If he was bluffing, it was pretty convincing. There was no way Matt was going to be able to argue with him. With a sigh, he returned to the arcade cabinet. Patrick placed the keyring onto the control panel of the machine. He fed the coins into the slot and the game began.

Matt's hands shook and his palms felt clammy. Within moments he made a silly mistake and lost a life. Then he did exactly the same thing again, trapping the white character between a bomb and a wall.

"You'd better try harder," Patrick whispered. It sounded more like a threat than advice.

Matt did try harder. This time, he slowed his pace. He dropped bombs only when he was certain that he could escape to safety. The brown blocks became fewer and fewer, although it was Patrick who destroyed far more of them than he did. Even so, it was Matt who was the first to release one of the blobby enemies from its area. The alien chased him around the grid. He didn't even get to drop another bomb before it cornered him in a dead end. GAME OVER.

"Don't cry, little Michael," Patrick said.

"My name's Matt."

"Okay, Michael."

"You're being really weird."

Matt tried to snatch the keyring. Patrick yanked it away and dropped it closer to his joystick.

"But I won the game," Patrick said. "Fair and square."

"Give me the key."

"I told you, I like winning. Let's play again."

Not knowing what else to do, Matt nodded.

They both turned at a sharp sound from behind. A ping-pong ball had fallen from the table and bounced across the floor. Hadn't the table been empty, before? Matt shook his head, trying to clear his thoughts. Even though it was unlikely, winning the game would be the simplest way to get out of this awful situation.

The grid appeared again. Matt dropped only enough bombs to collect a few power-ups. Minutes passed in silence. Patrick snarled as his character died in a crossfire of his own making.

When the black character reappeared, Matt waited and watched as he worked away in the opposite corner of the screen. Patrick obviously enjoyed making the fire-lines as long as possible, destroying several blocks at a time. It was a risky way to play.

Now Matt moved his character only a little, without dropping any bombs. Each of the times he had died, it had been his own fault. It was time to let Patrick make some mistakes of his own.

The black character cleared block after block. He bombed one of the enemies. Patrick grinned gleefully as he edged his character towards the top-left of the screen. His finger jabbed at the single button on the control panel. He dropped more and more bombs, making his character dance away from the chain reaction of fire-lines. The first two times he managed it, but not the third. The character blinked away and reappeared in the bottom corner.

"You're not trying, Michael," Patrick hissed. "Play the best you can, so I can win properly."

Matt frowned. There was something very, very wrong here.

He let the black character come towards him again. His fingers tensed on the joystick. He waited.

The moment that Patrick's character came within range, he moved. He dropped one bomb directly in front of him, then skirted away along the only free route. He placed another bomb at the junction, then darted to the space just behind the character before Patrick could react. One more bomb and then the black character was trapped.

Patrick turned. His eyes were wide with anger.

GAME OVER.

"I won," Matt said, trying to stop his voice from trembling. "So give me the key."

Patrick shook his head. He cupped one hand over the keyring and peered at the screen. Instead of the title of the game, it showed a scoreboard. Patrick must have racked up a decent score, even though he had lost. Three letters beside the number ten blinked. Patrick flicked the joystick to enter the letters P A T.

All of the other positions were filled with the same three letters. M I C. The difference between Patrick's high score and the next one up was huge.

M I C. Michael.

"So who's Michael, then?" Matt said.

"Nobody."

"Is he your brother? From the photo?"

"I don't know anyone called Michael."

"You called me Michael."

Patrick spun around. In the same movement he reached into his back pocket and pulled out something that glinted red. It was a penknife. Matt saw the Swiss Army cross on its side.

He jolted backwards, banging into the bookcase.

Patrick gripped his arm. He was stronger than Matt would have expected. "Do you *want* to be Michael?" he said, spitting the words.

Matt just shook his head.

Suddenly, Patrick smiled. It was no less terrifying. "We'll make it best of three matches. If you win, you can leave."

"And what if I lose?"

Patrick pushed the blade open with his thumb.

"If you lose, then you lose," he said.

Matt shuddered. "What do you mean? That doesn't even make—"

Patrick pointed the knife downwards. "Let's see. You could lose a toe… Or a finger… Or a little willy."

"Get off, you nutter!" Matt wrenched himself free.

There was a noise from behind him. Orange lights blinked on and off, reflecting on the beige walls and in Patrick's shining, wide eyes. Matt turned to see that the child's train toy had lurched into motion. It began rocking back and forth, matching the rhythm of its blinking lights. Chugging noises came from some hidden speaker.

"Stop it!" Patrick shouted. He was speaking to the ride, not Matt. He pushed his way behind it but emerged again before Matt could grab the keyring. In his right hand Patrick still held the knife. In his left he held a flex of cable with a plug dangling from it. He looked utterly confused. He kicked at the ride. It stopped rocking but the lights still flicked on and off.

In a much quieter voice, but still looking at the train, Patrick said, "I'll do it all over again, you hear me?"

Matt glanced at the door. The glass panel looked thick. He doubted he'd be able to smash it, let alone get through before Patrick caught him. He glanced at the keyring, judging the distance. If he played along, perhaps Patrick would become absorbed by the game. Then he could grab the key and get out. It might be his only chance.

"Patrick."

Patrick seemed not to hear him. His whole body shook.

"Patrick. Let's play another game. I want to."

Silently, Patrick took his place at the arcade cabinet again. He inserted the coins. The two of them stood side by side. The only sound was from the creak of the joysticks.

This time, Matt paid less attention to tactics. He turned just enough to be able to watch Patrick, only checking the screen every so often to make sure that the white character was safe. He stretched his right hand as far as he dared from the joystick, towards the keyring and the Swiss Army knife.

He flinched as Patrick thumped the panel, making the keyring rattle.

"Fucker!" Patrick shouted. The black character blinked away and reappeared in the corner.

Within seconds, Patrick had directed his character straight into a waiting enemy.

He picked up the knife and held it in his fist. Then he jabbed it down so that it dug into the painted wooden panel, in the centre of the metal ring attached to the key.

Matt slipped his hand away and watched the screen. Perhaps Plan A would work after all. Patrick was playing so badly that Matt might actually win.

Except Patrick seemed to be concentrating much harder now. Matt watched as he destroyed block after block and wiped out the enemies that stood between their two characters. Matt hadn't even collected any power-ups. His hands shook. He kept glancing at the knife.

He seemed not to be able to move—either his own body or the white character onscreen—as Patrick closed in. Patrick gave a high-pitched giggle.

Matt watched the screen, wincing. There was nothing he could do.

A bomb appeared in front of the black character. The white character was still far away. Matt hadn't dropped the bomb.

Patrick gasped. He smacked at the joystick, turning his character away just as the firestorm appeared.

A second bomb appeared. Patrick pushed upwards, only to be stopped by another one.

"No!" he shouted.

Now there were four bombs trapping the black character in their centre. Where had they come from?

"Cheat!" Patrick shouted.

Matt lunged for the keyring, but Patrick smacked his hand so that it scraped along the knife blade instead. Matt pulled his hand back. His palm was bleeding.

He heard a fluttering sound. Comics wafted from the bookcase as if blown from behind. They were followed by hardback books that thumped onto the floor.

Patrick's eyes widened.

The train began to rock again, faster than before.

A white ball rolled past Matt's feet, then bounced upwards and onto the ping-pong table.

Out of the corner of his eye, Matt saw movement on the arcade cabinet screen. It showed the leaderboard again. The letters at the tenth position blinked and then changed, even though neither boy was touching either of the joysticks. It spelt out the letters M I C.

Taking advantage of Patrick's distraction, Matt knocked the knife onto the ground and kicked it under the cabinet. He grabbed the keyring. Patrick bellowed.

Matt fumbled with the key in the lock. He heard Patrick scrambling behind him.

The key turned. Matt burst out of the games room. He blinked in the dazzling daylight.

A rattling, rumbling sound echoed around the buildings that surrounded the swimming pool.

He spun on the spot, disoriented. He was now facing the door that hung off its hinges. The door shook with each of the thudding sounds that seemed to come from everywhere at once.

The only way out must be through the metal gates, past the cottages and through the farmhouse.

Before he could turn, something smacked into his lower back. His arms windmilled as he fell forwards. All of the breath left his body. His face smashed into a wall.

But if it was a wall, why was he still falling? Why did he feel icy cold, suddenly? And why couldn't he get his breath back?

His arms swung in slow motion. It was several seconds before he realised that he was underwater. His lungs ached as he righted himself and pushed upwards to the surface.

Through the carpet of leaves on the surface of the swimming pool he saw Patrick's face leering down at him. Matt had only just emerged when the boy's hands pressed down on the top of his head, pushing him under again. He struggled desperately. He felt the warmth from the sun on his hands as they clawed upwards and out of the pool. He took a mouthful of water and found that he couldn't even splutter to push it out again.

And all the time the thudding, rattling sound continued. It merged with the pounding of his heart and the bubbles produced by the spasming of his arms and legs.

From somewhere above he heard Patrick's voice, muffled by the water.

"I hate you, Michael! I told you I'd do it again!"

Matt felt his body weaken. Even keeping his eyes shut against the pressure of the water seemed like too much effort.

He saw a shape.

A body. A boy, younger than Matt.

He was face down and white, almost transparent. The body twisted in the water, like cream in a cup of coffee.

Matt tried to call out but could barely hear his own voice over the thudding sound.

The boy was more like a white shadow than a real body. The more Matt looked, the less certain he felt that there was really anything there at all.

It was Michael, Patrick's brother, no older now than he had been in the photo.

The hands pressed down harder on Matt's head. His body twitched and so did Michael's white shadow.

Above him, the leaves glowed orange. He felt Patrick's hands release their pressure slightly.

He kicked off the wall of the swimming pool, pushing himself upwards and to one side. The leaves glowed again. He burst through them and pulled air into his lungs. Each breath felt like a knife in his chest. The air was hot.

Patrick was standing at the side of the pool, staring over Matt's head.

Matt's arms felt ridiculously weak as he clambered out of the pool. He grabbed at the metal support of the diving board steps. His fingers skittered on its cold surface.

Dimly, he realised that Patrick was coming around the pool, moving towards him.

"Stop!" he gasped. "Patrick, please stop. You don't have to do this. I know what you did to Michael."

But Patrick didn't seem to hear him. The rattling, thudding noise was louder than ever.

Matt reached up with shaking arms to fend off Patrick. But instead of attacking him, Patrick ran straight past. He raced through the metal gate and between the rows of holiday cottages.

Matt turned. The door to the white building had now fallen away entirely and lay on the ground. The walls of the building shook with each of the thudding sounds. Through the doorway Matt saw the huge iron furnace. It glowed bright orange and spat sparks.

Something burst up through the leaves on the surface of the pool. It was Michael's white shadow. It hovered above the water for a moment, then whipped away, rushing towards the furnace. It left a streak in the air like a contrail.

He realised he was still gripping the metal struts of the diving board. He clambered up the steps.

The white shadow shot through the grille of the furnace. The furnace rocked on its iron feet. The thudding grew even louder.

From the top of the diving board steps, Matt could see over the wall and towards the holiday cottages. He saw Patrick running along the straight concrete path from the gates, heading directly towards the farmhouse.

The greyhound lunged from its shelter, snapping and barking. Patrick stumbled backwards. Without slowing down, he took a left turn and kept running with his head down.

The furnace rattled and stamped and howled.

Matt climbed up onto the diving board and hunkered down

to keep his balance. The board shook with each of the thuds. Below him, the swimming pool had become a roiling mass of waves and leaves.

Orange flamed licked out from the furnace and through the door of the building. Matt gripped the sides of the diving board to stop himself from being flung off.

More flames emerged, funnelled into a line by the narrow doorway. They shot out over the pool. The fire reached as far as the metal gateway on the opposite side of the water.

Matt could see Patrick still running along the paths between the cottages. He kept changing direction. His eyes were wide and wild. He stared in horror into the windows of the cottages as if he had seen a ghost. Matt thought he saw something in some of the windows, too; reflections of big, black, spherical objects.

Inadvertently, Patrick had turned four corners to double back on himself. He was running back towards the gateway and the swimming pool.

The flames burst through the gates again. They snicked at the edges of the metal canisters that leant against the wall of a cottage.

In an instant, the canisters caught light. The chain reaction made a fire-line that sped along the pathway.

The fire hit Patrick head on. His strangled shout lasted only for a second or two. His blackened body dropped forwards onto the concrete.

Abruptly, the firestorm abated. The thudding sound stopped, too. Now Matt could only hear a faint rattle that came from the white building.

With shaking limbs, he climbed down from the diving board. He edged towards the white building, stepping carefully over the door that lay on the ground.

He peered through the doorway. The iron furnace had blown itself open.

A shimmer of heat-haze obscured the front of the furnace, but he could see something through it, inside the blackened oven, something left there.

Matt peered closer.

It was a pile of thin bones.

'Honey spurge': Confidental report into dispersal, growth and catastrophe

[for Secretary of State's eyes only]

Executive summary

This confidential report documents causes and consequences of so-called 'Honey spurge', first manifestation Dec 2019.

Instigating factors
- *Q4 2019* – Outbreak of root-knot nematodes (plant-parasitic nematodes; genus *Meloidogyne*) affecting *Euphorbia pulcherrima*, commonly known as 'poinsettia'.
- *Nov 2019* – Failure of UK crops and shipping delays (esp. routes from Australia and Egypt) result in lack of availability of poinsettia, popularly used in Christmas floral displays.

Development of 'Honey spurge'
- Evidence of genetic modification of poinsettia with existing shrub in 'spurge' family: *Euphorbia x pasteurii* (NB itself a cross of *E. mellifera x E. stygiana*).
- Timescale of development unknown.
- Contradicting sources re: centre of operations. Possibilities inc. commercial laboratory; garden centre; amateur enthusiast.
- Location: Westmorland and Lonsdale, Cumbria.
- 'Honey spurge' crossbreed characteristics (likely intended):
  o Resists root-knot nematode;
  o Hardy;

o   Honey scent;

o   Retains distinctive poinsettia features inc. vivid red leaves.

- 'Honey spurge' crossbreed characteristics (likely unintended):

o   Increased regularity of seed production;

o   Retention of *Euphorbia x pasteurii* explosive seed pods;

o   'Hybrid vigour'.

Events of Dec 2019

- Crossbreed 'Honey spurge' evidently popular with Christmas consumers. Widespread uptake in Westmorland and Lonsdale region.
- Multiple theories relating to causes of spontaneous dispersal of 'Honey spurge' seeds:

o   Over-watering;

o   Effects of central heating / likely increase of body heat from large family groups;

o   Proximity to other heat sources e.g. Christmas tree lights.

- First accounts of seed dispersal: 25th Dec 2019.
- Furness General Hospital A&E notes minor injuries from explosive seeds.

Subsequent events

- *Mid Jan 2020* – Appearance of additional 'Honey spurge' plants. Locations inc. gardens; public land; refuse sites.
- *Late Jan 2020* – 2nd phase seed dispersal quickly results in additional 'wave' of plants. Some accounts of parkland entirely given over to 'Honey spurge'.
- *Feb 2020* – 3rd phase new plants; rapid seed dispersal of existing and new plants. Anecdotal accounts of extreme accelerated growth in 2nd/3rd phase plants.
- *Early Mar 2020* – Formal identification of exponential nature of plant population increase.
- *Mid Mar 2020* – Honey scent overwhelming in Westmorland and Lonsdale region. Some accounts of suffocation.
- *Late Mar 2020* – Armed Forces fail to repel 'Honey spurge' / limit propagation via burning/bombing.
- *Apr 2020* – Westmorland and Lonsdale evacuation proposal

rejected in Commons. South Lakeland District abandoned.

Status May 2020
- No signs of limitation of dispersal/growth.
- Quarantine initially extended to Pendle Forest; area enlarged to include south extremity of Forest of Bowland. Drone footage of 'Honey spurge' on northernmost parts of Bowland Fell.
- Commons proposal to evacuate Blackburn at earliest convenience. Ongoing discussions with Mayor of Greater Manchester.
- Time estimate for spread to entirety of UK: Dec 2020

Next steps
[to be confirmed]

By the Numbers

Three hours to wait and no free seats.

Henry Polter shifted his laptop bag onto a less aching part of his shoulder. The bodies of sleeping backpackers littered the floor of the waiting lounge. Only the occasional wail of a child rose louder than the unhappy murmur.

A winding metal staircase led to a dining area suspended above the waiting lounge. Here, the only restaurant not packed with diners offered 'a taste of the Savannah'. Henry wasn't hungry but took a seat at a two-seater table in the corner, facing away from the rows of corpse-like backpackers laid beneath the mezzanine. He ordered the smallest possible dish, bread and smoked snoek pâté, and coffee. As the surrounding tables began to fill up, Henry placed his laptop bag on the unoccupied seat and unfolded his copy of *Private Eye*.

"'Scuse me—is this seat taken?"

Henry's brow wrinkled in apology. He didn't look up. "Sorry. My friend's just ordering."

He took tiny bites of bread and pretended to be engrossed in the magazine, aware of the stranger's hovering shadow. The man pulled the laptop from the chair and sat down.

"You haven't got a friend."

The man looked in his early thirties and wore round, John Lennon glasses. One of those guys who'd once been skinny and it still showed, a narrow head above a body full of bulges. Henry bristled but returned to his feigned reading. He sensed that the man was watching him.

"So what's new, Henry?"

Henry stiffened. "What?"

"It's been a while."

The man wore a checked shirt over a Sonic Youth tee. His blonde hair parted in the centre, slicked to his forehead on either side, a style that hadn't been fashionable since—

"Shit—Giles? It's you, isn't it?"

Henry held out his hand. Giles Freeman glanced down at it, snorted, and ignored it. That attitude hadn't changed, then.

"What are you doing here? I mean, where are you going?"

"Edinburgh. You?"

"Philadelphia, for work," Henry said. "Wow. It's been, what, fifteen, sixteen years? It's good to see you, man. Do you live nearby?"

"Mainly Edinburgh. Rhodes in the summer." Another grin.

"Doing pretty well for yourself, then? What do you do?"

"I own a recruitment company. Pharmaceuticals. *Vezeera.*"

Henry reddened. "I've heard of you. I'm in pharmaceuticals myself. Editorial, terms and conditions, that sort of thing."

When Giles didn't respond, Henry continued, "I don't mean to sound—you know—but you never seemed the type back at school. 'The boy most likely to...' You were sort of withdrawn."

Giles laughed. "Withdrawn? That's a fucking understatement."

"Yeah. But we were friends, right? On and off. Swapping comics." Even as he said it, his certainty evaporated. "But—wow, I haven't thought about this for years—I've got this mental image of you, from way back. At the copse beside the playing fields, you with a huge tree branch, chasing me down." He felt his cheeks blanche. "A look on your face like a demon. God, what were you even upset about?"

An expression difficult to pinpoint flickered across Giles's face.

"I've thought about that day, over the years," he said. "I wondered about it too. What you'd done to make me so angry. And I did work it out, eventually."

"Oh? What, then?"

"Don't look so terrified, Polter. It wasn't anything you did. Blood sugar issues. Nothing serious, but enough to affect me if I fuck up my diet. On that day, do you know how many times the normal sugar amounts I'd had? Four times, Polter! Blood sugar problems plus adolescence equals one massive hissy fit."

Henry relaxed a little, his shoulders unknotting. "I'm glad to hear it wasn't me. Shame, because I don't think we really hung out after that. I remember thinking you were a psycho. Hold on though—how do you know what you ate that day? Who remembers stuff like that?"

Giles smiled. "Hold on a sec. Just off to the pisser."

Henry stared at the rolled up magazine, thumbing the pages. From the waiting lounge, announcements of gate changes punctuated the rising hum as backpackers roused themselves from sleep. His flight wouldn't be called for another half hour or more, but he felt a sudden compulsion to be alone, away from this unwelcome echo from the past. Might he be able to lose him downstairs in that crowd?

When Giles returned and took his seat, he leaned across the table with both elbows on the plastic surface.

"You know how you said we used to swap comics? Do you remember how many you lent me? Eleven. And how many of mine do you think I gave you? Forty-four, Polter. And seven of those you never gave back."

His voice had attained a harsh edge. Henry put his magazine down.

"Next question," Giles continued, "If we were such good friends, how often do you reckon you sat with me at lunchtime rather than sit with your mates? No idea? Four. Thought it was more, did you?"

"Giles, what's this all about?"

"Hold on, one more. You knew how fucking hard life was at home, didn't you? Course you did." A bead of sweat trickled from beneath Giles's slick hair. "So how much time did you spend in my house or on the phone with me or hanging out with me outside of school?"

"I don't—"

"Of course you don't. But I do. It's less than you'd think, Polter. Fifteen hours, that's all. And that's rounded up. Fourteen hours, fifty-two minutes. Can't remember the seconds."

"For Christ's sake, Giles, what is all this?" Henry eyed the exit.

Giles beamed, all trace of animosity gone.

He rubbed his face. "It's all right. I'm just yanking your chain. Like I said, it was ages ago. Impressive, though, right?"

Henry weighed up the benefits of playing along. But why should he humour this trumped-up little shit who belonged in the past?

"Impressive? All those numbers? Not really. No one remembers that kind of detail." He shot Giles a look. "You don't, do you?"

"Nah. No one does, you're right. But those numbers, they're one hundred per cent accurate, promise."

Henry didn't answer, but his expression must have said it all.

"Fuck it, I'm bored of teasing you, you stuffy old prick," Giles said. "Are you sitting comfortably? So. School was shit and college wasn't any better. Took me until uni before I worked out that not only was I a pussy, I was wasting time. The comics, internet, wanking, you name it. So I pulled myself together, figured I'd do something about it."

"What'd you do? Stop masturbating?"

"That's not it. It's about knowing yourself, knowing your weaknesses, seeing the patterns. Ever heard of 'the quantified self'?"

Henry shook his head.

"It's on the web. It boils down to a bunch of people all figuring out exactly what makes them tick, just keeping tabs on everyday details."

"Like how often you masturbate?"

"Shit, give it a rest. But yes, that, or how much TV you watch, or how many calories you eat. Collecting all the raw data. Every day."

Henry glanced at the exit again. Five strides and he could be away. But to where?

Giles drummed his fingers on the table. Enthusiasm, not impatience. "It's the bit afterwards that matters. Once you've got the data you can start extrapolating, start seeing patterns. For instance, whenever I had breakfast more than half an hour after I woke up, my mood stayed foul for the whole day."

"OK, I'll concede the point," Henry said. The moulded plastic seat seemed suddenly uncomfortable. "That actually does seem useful."

"I learned a shitload about myself. Hold on." Giles pulled the phone from his pocket, prodded at it for a few seconds, put it back.

"I'm still not seeing the link to your memory trick," Henry said.

Giles glanced around before continuing. "Here's the thing. I get this email one day. Looks like the usual spam, except without spelling mistakes. It mentions 'quantified self' in the subject line, so I open it." He leaned further forward. "Here's a tough question. How much would you pay for all the data—everything numerical—about your life?"

"Like tax returns?"

"Don't be a dick. This is what the email was offering. *All* the raw numerical data about *me*."

"The number of hours you watch TV each day?"

"Going all the way back to the first time I ever saw a TV."

"And how many times you've wanked?"

Giles nodded.

"Everything?"

"Everything."

"But nobody could have that information."

"Forget logic for a second. What I asked—what the email asked—was how much would you pay for it?"

Henry watched Giles's twitching face. An accumulated shuffling sound from the waiting lounge below signalled another departing flight. He checked his watch. Still twenty minutes to go.

"Interesting. I guess it could be useful. You could learn a lot about yourself."

"No shit."

"How much?" This could be okay. Just play for time. "I guess... five hundred?"

"Five hundred?" Giles sneered. "We're talking every bit of data from a whole human life, Polter."

"All right, a grand then. No, two."

"That's more like it. So the email just had the blurb and then asked that question, 'How much would you pay?', and then a box to type into."

Another droplet of sweat emerged from Giles's hairline.

Just how much of nutcase was he? "You can't type into an email someone sent you," Henry said. "How would that even work?"

"I wasn't taking it seriously either."

"So you typed in a number?"

"Yup."

"How much?"

Giles paused, drumming both thumbs on the table. "Bear in mind that I was already really into this shit. I was spending an hour each day just logging what I was doing in the other twenty-three."

"How much?"

"I took the question in the spirit it was asked. How much did I think it was worth, hypothetically? A lot, that's how much."

"Oh, for God's sake, come on."

"Ten. Ten grand. That's what I thought it was worth."

Henry snorted. "Bloody hell. Well, whatever. So what's the point of this Aesop's fable?"

Giles stretched backwards in his seat with a mock yawn. "An email came back straight away," he said. "Not much in it, just the words 'payment accepted'. That made me laugh. Ten grand's a fair whack."

"It is. But what does it matter? It was only hypothetical."

"Hypothetical, yeah. It was, until I checked my savings." He picked up Henry's cup and slurped cold coffee. "Gone."

"Fuck!" Henry was sitting up straight now. "But how? You didn't give them your bank details, did you?"

Giles shook his head.

"What'd you do then? Call the police?"

Another shake. "A third email came through. And there, in all its glory, it was."

Henry found that he was gripping the melamine edge of the table.

"The data, Polter. My data. All of it."

Henry forced his fingers to release. "So you're saying that the same person who magically stole ten grand from you then sent you a magical spreadsheet? With lists of figures about every aspect of your life, from birth onwards?"

"Yup."

"Jesus, Giles. You were kind of nuts at school, but compared to this... Are you on something? Medication?"

"No. Hold my seat would you? Need the loo."

As he waited, Henry spun the coffee cup in its saucer with one finger. He glanced around the restaurant. Now, all the nearby tables were occupied. He picked up *Private Eye*, then put it down again. He beckoned a waitress wearing a leopard-print apron and ordered two fresh cups of coffee and, in response to the glaring waitress, two slices of milk tart.

Giles returned. "So?"

Henry reached back, scratched his neck, winced. "I've still got a while to wait for my flight. There are no other free seats in the whole terminal. And I'm kind of into your story, despite myself. So go on."

With a look of satisfaction, Giles put his phone in his pocket and settled himself back into the moulded seat.

"Where was I?"

"The email, the data. What did it look like?"

"You know you get tabs at the bottom of spreadsheets, linking to different pages? There were tons of the fuckers, hundreds. But all locked, couldn't see any of them except the first sheet. And all that contained was an empty text box with a flashing cursor."

"That doesn't sound worth ten grand."

"Right. So I'm kind of in shock about the money, but still in that hypothetical frame of mind too. What do I do? I type in a question."

"What question?"

Giles laughed. "You'd think it'd be something rigorous. Something revealing my inner nature. Nah. 'How many fingers do I have?'"

"Fair enough. A question that could fool any crappy AI, I suppose. And did it answer?"

"It did. Ten. Written in big red digits underneath the text box."

"Now we're starting to see where the money went!" Henry grinned. "What did you ask next?"

"Well, I'd been logging data for the day anyway. So I tried asking about something I'd just put on my own chart. 'How many hours of sleep did I get last night?' Just wrote out the question like that. And there it was, seven-point-three-two hours, or whatever the fuck it was, in big red digits."

"And you're saying it was right?"

"It wasn't what I'd recorded it the table. But then how do you know exactly when you fall asleep anyway? What's the exact dividing line between sleep and awake? But it was pretty close to my own number. Then I try a bigger question. I ask it how many times in my life I've said the word 'kettle'. Only just over two thousand, quite a surprise."

Slow down. Maybe humouring him might do more harm than good. Maybe he was an escapee from some asylum or other.

"Giles, anyone could have made up a number in answer to that question. It doesn't mean anything."

"True enough. But it sounded halfway plausible. If it had told me I'd said 'kettle' six times, that would have blown it. So I asked a question that I knew the answer to. 'How many different women have I ever made love to?'"

"Nice. How many?"

"Doesn't matter. But it was right. At first I thought it was one out, then I realised that I'd counted one that didn't really qualify as sex."

Henry widened his eyes in mock surprise. "Still. Wow, that's pretty great."

"Yeah, so I'm getting really excited now. I try a different kind of question, something like, 'What was the first word I spoke as a child?'"

"What was it?"

"'Rabbit'. At least, so my mum tells me. But the dataset doesn't give any answer at all. Cursor just keeps flashing. I reread the email and sure enough, it's only numerical data that it can give, nothing else. I ask how far the Sun is from the Earth. Nothing. Fair play again—it can only give me answers about me, my own life, not general knowledge."

"No good for pub quizzes then."

Giles shrugged off the comment. "But then I input a load of questions about me, all with numerical answers. And it's all coming out right, or at least right enough to sound real. The number of miles I walked that day, that week, year, ever. The volume of shit I'd produced in whatever time period. The whole thing was fucking true, Polter!"

Henry slumped down again into his seat. "You know what? For a minute I was getting carried away with you, can you believe that? But this is mental, Giles. You didn't really believe all this?"

"It wasn't a matter of believing. It was just happening. Now, think about it for a second. I could ask it anything and use the answer to sort myself out for the better. It wasn't just a novelty. I had a job interview coming up a few days later. I got down to business using the dataset, analysing all the other interviews I'd ever done. Which things helped me get the job and which didn't, even down to the number of times I said the interviewer's name. All gold. Cruised through the interview with total confidence."

"Nothing like being prepared is there?" Henry said. "All right, I can buy that. Ever heard of the placebo effect?"

"Fuck off. Anyway, so I started the new job. Call centre manager, nothing swish. But the dataset helped me work out how to deal with people. Went down a storm. Course, I still wasn't prepared for what I discovered next. I was still logging all my normal data in the old-fashioned way at that point, Microsoft Excel sessions every night after work. Saw it as keeping the dataset up to date. And what do you know? They matched. The dataset had already updated."

"You mean they sent you another one?"

"Nope. The same spreadsheet I'd saved to my PC, up to date with information about stuff that had happened that day, even."

"That's ridiculous." Henry struggled to think straight. It was ridiculous, wasn't it?

"I guess. But there you go."

Henry spoke slowly, spelling it out. "Okay, so the magical spreadsheet is magically updating all the statistics of your life, every second. There must have been a fairy following you around with a clipboard, right?"

Giles shrugged. "Haven't really thought about it."

"Oh come on. Listen to yourself! This is the biggest imaginable pile of bollocks."

"All right, I'll be off then, if it's going to be like that." Giles stood up.

"Whoa, okay, okay. Sorry, all right? Sit down." Henry felt oddly uncertain which of them was wasting the other's time.

The moulded seat squeaked as Giles settled down again.

"So, you realised you had all the information about yourself, updating instantly forever more…"

"Pretty much," Giles said. "But it was hard. Knowing so much about yourself, I mean. Kind of like looking into a mirror all day long. So I tried to turn it to my advantage again. Maybe it could help me get women."

"Your plan was to get a girlfriend using the power of statistical data?"

Giles affected a wounded look. "It's not so crazy. Anyway, I was just interested in knowing my own mind, remember? Stands to reason the dataset could help me order my thoughts."

Henry stared blank-faced.

"Use your imagination, Polter. There were a truckload of girls in that call centre. Some I got on with, some that wouldn't give me the time of day. And in all the other departments of the company too, hundreds of them. I was in and out of meetings the whole time. Maybe I was losing my nerve, not trusting my own mind. Seemed easier to consult the oracle, as it were. How many glances a day did I give to each of the girls on my team? How many minutes of conversation had I had with each? How many times had I come while thinking about them?"

"Good grief. I hope you mean when you were safely back home."

"Very funny. But the point was that the dataset knew about my innermost thoughts. Unbelievable, right? And all the data seemed to point to one particular girl. Marianne, in HR. Pretty and all, but not outstanding, at least so I thought at first. But once the oracle had spoken, I was all eyes for her. Turns out that she was a real sweetheart. We just fucking clicked."

"You started coming on to a girl because a spreadsheet told you to? That's messed up."

"Don't be fucking facetious. It wasn't a spreadsheet. It was my own mind I was looking into, I just hadn't picked up on the signs. Every night, I analysed the day's data about her, about our conversations and whatnot. The next day, I was even better at sweet-talking her. I was looking out for the little things. Number of laughs. Number of pauses longer than two seconds in conversation, showing one of us had lost interest. Number of times she touched her face when we were talking. If I phrased the question right, I could even work out how many times she'd glanced at me across the office, as long as I'd actually seen it with my own eyes."

This was getting worse by the minute. "And you didn't think this was a little, just a little, like stalking her?"

"Everyone does it. Only most people don't know the answers for sure."

Henry thought of his own attitude towards women, back in the day. It was a tricky point to argue. "Whatever. Presumably there's a happy ending to all this? You and Marianne are married? Does she know about your little helper?"

"Never told her. And no. I don't know where she is now. Still at her desk at the call centre, for all I care."

"The girl of your dreams?"

"This is just an example, Polter. She wasn't for me. Turned out that the more I talked to her, the less interested I was."

"But all that data showed that she was your perfect match. What about the glances, the laughs?"

"That's how it was at first, anyway. Time moved on and I was thinking about her less and less. Other girls' faces, you know."

"So the dataset told you that that you didn't fancy her? How about the pauses in conversation and all that?"

"Long pauses, Polter. Long fucking pauses."

Henry snorted. "And you don't see what happened here? Was there any conceivable chance that the very fact that you had all this information might have changed the way you acted towards her? You don't think that she might have weirded out a little when you kept acting like a stalker?"

One of Giles's eyebrows twitched. "Sounds like you believe me now, at least."

Henry struggled to keep his voice level. "I don't know what to believe. But I do know that this story of yours is deeply, *deeply* sickening. I'm guessing you've still got your dataset? Do you use it every time you fancy someone?"

Giles shrugged yes.

"So here's a question with a numerical answer. Since you got your spreadsheet, what's the longest time you've spent in a relationship?"

"You've got to understand that with this data I can get pretty much whoever the fuck I want, Polter. It made me who I am today, made me rich."

"How long?"

"Three, four months. Three."

Henry shook his head and took a sip of coffee. "Three months. Quite a success story, Giles."

Abruptly, Giles grabbed Henry's hand across the table. "Listen to me. *Listen* to me. I thought you'd get it. They're everywhere, and all you have to know is what to look for. Even here. Do you know how many women I've seen in the airport this morning? Three hundred and thirteen. How many I glanced at more than once? One hundred and thirty-five. How many looked back at me, meeting my eyes? Forty-eight, Polter." He pulled his phone out from his pocket, brandishing it.

"Get off me." Henry whipped his hand away. "So you've got the dataset on your phone, then? That's what you were doing when you said you needed a piss, wasn't it, checking data? About me as well as all those unsuspecting women?"

Giles grinned.

"And what are you going to do with all that information, you nutcase? Look around you," Henry swept his hand as if to indicate every woman in the terminal. "These women don't care about you, Giles. And if they did, your data isn't going to make any difference. They're human beings! Prick."

Giles's eyes darkened. He leant back, head upturned to the strip lights, then stood up. He slipped the phone into his pocket, took a couple of steps away, then turned.

"Whatever. So long."

Henry remained alone at the table, both palms flat on the surface to stop them shaking.

It couldn't be true.

Giles was just obsessed enough about analysing himself, so focussed on his own navel that he'd invented a story to rationalise his actions. Right? All this about 'quantified self'. He'd become nothing but his own collection of stats, corrupted like cheap software.

A week or so ago, someone in the pub had told Henry about a self-experimenting scientist. Some ridiculous name. *Sanctorius Sanctorius*, Jesus. He'd lived in Italy in the sixteen hundreds, studying human metabolism. After deciding to quantify how his body processed food and turned it into waste, he'd spent thirty years sitting in giant weighing scales, measuring his own excrements.

Henry fished under the table for his laptop bag and turned to look at the departures board. The waitress with the leopard-print apron collected his payment. As he stood to leave, their eyes met.

He counted the seconds.

The House Lights Dim

On the morning of the white light I was working in my study, the room that Catherine would have designated the nursery, if she'd had her way. I worked as a theatre script editor, but cancelled the day's read-through meetings to remain at home. I'd given the excuse that my wife had fallen ill and needed regular attention, but in Catherine's absence the real reason was the attention I gave to my wine cellar.

When it happened, I wasn't even looking at my manuscript, but gazing out of the window behind my desk. The cul-de-sac was calm, as usual. Peter, an elderly neighbour, struggled to restore his wheelie bin to its correct position. I didn't consider the possibility of helping him.

Abruptly, a burst of light fell upon me like a crashing wave. The thought flashed through my mind that this must be a precursor to a blackout. I'd drunk myself into a stupor several times in the preceding weeks, but it was mid-morning and I was sober. The piercing brightness washed over me. My eyes flickered shut but the light shone through. I held up a hand to shield myself. My fingers appeared as thin grey silhouettes, haloed with absolute whiteness.

*

I don't know how long I lay unconscious on the floor of the study. It couldn't have been more than a day as I had no sense of hunger when I woke. Even through my closed eyelids it was clear that the intensely bright light continued to stream in at the window. A pain in my forehead throbbed in regular pulses, seconds apart.

Tentatively, I opened one eye a fraction. The pain doubled

and my hand raised instinctively to cup my eyes. Under my palm I felt the dampness of my swollen cheeks. Tears ran in rivulets through my fingers.

In fact, the curtains were tightly closed. When Catherine and I had prepared for our final holiday as a couple, I'd feared for the security of our house. After installing a cheap (and, as it turns out, faulty) alarm system and timed, automated curtain closers at the two front-facing windows, I had lost interest. The curtains were heavy and thick but the light penetrated them as if they were tissue paper. Still, without them I'm not certain I'd have regained consciousness at all.

I kept one hand clamped over my face as I groped around the small sofa beside my desk. That morning I'd returned from a short walk (excruciating, due to my hangover), coming directly to my study. I felt beneath the coat that hung limply from the back of the seat to find my woollen scarf. Fighting another spell of faintness, I wrapped the scarf four or five times around my head.

My eyes ached from the tension of the scarf, but it relieved the pain from the white light. Blindly, I swept my arm to clear the desk. I ripped the manuscripts and papers from a low bookcase and hefted it onto the desk. Once I had fitted the bookcase into the window frame I loosened my mask. An eerie grey light bathed the room. It had none of the warmth of normal sunlight. A knife-edge of searing light framed the bookcase. I pulled the scarf back into position, curled up on the sofa with the coat over my head, and slept.

*

When I woke the light hadn't dimmed. I turned on the radio to hear only jeering static. I moved around the house cautiously, blind due to the scarf still covering my eyes, barricading each room against the seeping light using wardrobes and upturned tables.

At the glass-panelled front door I paused before applying the thick layers of cardboard I'd discovered in the garage. I opened the door a crack with my eyes averted. The cul-de-sac was always quiet, but the silence had now become somehow more complete. In ordinary circumstances I would have heard the hum of the road that passed through the residential estate, and the sound of birds in the trees.

I called out into the void. The only response was a strangely tinny echo of my own voice.

The house now as secure as I could manage, I felt my way to the kitchen. I switched on the small television set on the counter. The box hummed into life for only a moment, then sputtered to silence. The electric oven didn't power up at all. I found a tin of peaches and ate greedily. I sat at the kitchen table with my head resting on the crook of my arm.

*

I'm sitting in the same room now. It's changed beyond all recognition. Wooden planks nailed to the far wall totally obscure the small window. I'm resting in a wing-back armchair taken from the lounge. The lounge is the largest room in the house, but is uninhabitable. Not only does it have a large window at the north end, at the south is a patio door leading to a conservatory. The white light carries no heat but the conservatory magnifies its intensity to a degree that no amount of barricades can block totally.

If I keep to the other rooms I can use my eyes, more or less. Rather than the woollen scarf, I now wear a gauze bandage which reduces the intensity of the light but allows me to make out objects. I've become used to seeing in monochrome.

The kitchen is the room best insulated against the light, so that's where I rest when my chores are complete. I listen to my parents' records on a wind-up gramophone. Keeping daily routines is my way of marking the passing of time in the absence of night's darkness.

My meals are eaten raw. Right away, when it was clear that the light wouldn't abate, I realised that my food stores wouldn't last long. I transplanted crops from my garden allotment to a row of pots just outside the back door. It was a struggle. Even with my face protected with thick blankets I barely made it back to the house after each short trip.

At first the plants grew at extraordinary speeds, but yielded less each week due to my reluctance to spare water for them. It never rains any more. Incredibly, the taps in the kitchen still operate, but the water is looking more and more suspect. I use an arrangement of filters made from old sheets to purify the water as much as possible. I eat less and less, and when I look in the mirror my silhouette looks hopelessly gaunt.

I've no idea how widespread the light may be. Does the power and communication outage mean that the whole world is affected, or just Britain? If the Sun has become more powerful, a supernova, shouldn't it have enveloped the Earth totally?

Sometimes I imagine that I, along with everyone and everything else, really did die in a sunburst, and that I am only a ghostly echo. Sometimes I spend days convinced that the light is a trick of the mind and that I've inflicted madness upon myself.

When I get to thinking like that, I venture outside. The light burns the mind as well as the eyes.

How many other people survive? It's been four months now. Many who fed themselves at first must have died by now. Might Catherine still be alive, down south, with her new husband? I often lie awake in bed looking up at the streaks of escaped light upon my ceiling and imagine that she is pressing against my side, fidgeting in her sleep.

My supplies won't last indefinitely. I have only a couple of tins of food and I've stopped watering the plants to save the water for myself. I have no choice but to leave the house. If I wait much longer, my strength will be diminished and my chances of finding food far lower.

I've spent the last few days poring over maps of the neighbourhood at the kitchen table, examining them as closely as I'm able through my gauze mask. There's a corner shop a few streets away from my house. I barely used it in the past as its supplies of fresh fruit and vegetables were terribly limited, but beyond its newspaper racks I remember shelves of tinned food.

Catherine used to joke that some of them looked old enough to have been rations from the war. Now the thought of those dusty tins of carrots and pineapple make my stomach leap in anticipation.

Back then, my route to the shop would have been along the cul-de-sac, then right and right again onto the main road, tracing three sides of a square. I've tested how long I can be outside. I wouldn't be able to make it before succumbing to the awful pressure of the piercing light.

The maps show that there's a more direct route. Only one house would stand in my way if I were to walk to the end of the cul-de-sac and navigate through that property and out the other side. It's still a great risk, but the house itself may be a source of food or, at least, temporary shelter.

I gather together another roll of gauze, blankets, a winter coat and a large hiking rucksack filled with tools. If I fail my chances of returning to the house will be low, so I eat the remaining vegetables, a cherished tin of baked beans, and a pint of filtered water. I wrap gauze around and around my head, then a scarf twisted thickly, then a woollen hat to hold it all in place. I wear the coat backwards so that the hood covers my face, and the blanket on my shoulders, ready to hoist it over my head.

Even prepared like this, I gasp as I remove the cardboard from the front door and wrench it open. Immediately, the light seeps through my eyelids. The ringing in my ears that has been a dull constant now amplifies, disorienting me even more. I shake my head and plod carefully down the driveway and along the street. The air inside my hood is stale and the silence unnerving. The only noises are my footsteps and ragged breathing. I clear my throat. The sound echoes, reverberating with a strange metallic tone. I use the echo to estimate my distance from the buildings on either side of the street.

I stumble. I reach down and touch something cold, yielding and rotten. I'm strict with myself and don't allow myself to imagine what it may be.

After a dozen more steps I detect grass beneath my feet. The pain in my head is almost unbearable. Even with my eyes squeezed tight shut it's as though I'm staring directly into the bulb of a powerful lamp. But I'm nearly at the fence and so halfway to my neighbour's house.

The fence isn't high but I struggle to climb it due to dizziness and exertion. My trouser leg snags on the rough wood. For a moment I feel like resting there, uncomfortably straddling the fence. I throw the blanket over the fence to free both hands, but this allows more light to assault me. With a great effort I hoist myself over, ripping my trouser leg. I scrabble around for the blanket and huddle for a few moments in a shivering igloo of fabric.

More from weakness than caution, I cross the length of the garden on my hands and knees. I pause every few paces to rest and clear my thoughts, fighting an overwhelming desire to lie down and sleep.

I reach a concrete patio and drag myself forward, suddenly terrified of encountering a locked door, or, worse still, one reinforced like the doors of my own house. My fingers claw weakly at a plastic ledge. The door is wide open. I haul myself into the house and kick the door closed behind me. The light isn't much diminished—there are no planks or barriers to block the light seeping in at the edges of the doorframe—but it's enough to restore my energy.

I doze fitfully for a while in a wash of whiteness. I pull myself upright and move cautiously along the corridor. The house is built to the same specifications as the others in the estate. By stepping one pace into each room at the end of corridor I find that the linoleum floor, and therefore the kitchen, is on the opposite side to the one in my own house. The curtains must be drawn, as the intensity of the light is bearable, but I leave my scarves and coat in place as I grope around.

The first two cupboards contain only crockery, but in the third I grasp at cold tins and heavy cardboard containers. I place a couple onto the kitchen table and then fish around in my rucksack for a can opener and spoon. As I open the first tin I whisper brief thanks to my absent neighbour.

The spoon hasn't even reached my lips when I hear a noise. I freeze. The sound came from within the building. I imagine that it's my neighbour, but then I remember the full cupboards and my breathing becomes shallow and fast.

Then—again—there! It comes from within the main part of the house, a sound like air escaping from something under pressure. I steady my breathing. Perhaps some long-abandoned gadget is still working, somewhere within the house? But still I don't begin eating.

The third time, the noise is closer to hand. The low hissing sound ends with a languorous rattle. My skin prickles. I turn my head from side to side, listening, trying to locate the source of the sound. It rings out twice more.

Even before I hear the rattle again, I sense that the source of the noise is now in the kitchen. I fight the urge to pull the scarves from my face to try to catch a glimpse of whatever it is. Now the only sound is a gentle tapping of something settling on the linoleum. Then, the hiss and rattle, more malevolent than before.

Should I strike out? I'm conscious that I'm trapped in a seated position behind the large table and am brandishing only a spoon.

The movement is a swift flurry. After a frenzy of tapping on the linoleum the creature strikes. I bolt from my chair, tipping over the table and then swinging the blanket from my head. I feel the heavy fabric swat at something hard before it gets tangled, or snatched, and I dodge around the perimeter of the room, aiming for the doorway. My left foot is pulled backwards sharply. My head strikes the ground, the impact softened by the thick scarf still wound tightly around my eyes.

My foot has caught on something and my thrashing does nothing to dislodge it. In my panic I realise that my ankle is being pinched at either side. There's a tapping noise on the linoleum beside me and then I sense something scratching for purchase in the bundle of fabric around my head.

I struggle and kick in vain. Before the scarves are torn away the creature makes a rasping cackle, a cry of triumph, the death rattle of a cobra.

White light pours into my eyes. I'm flailing in a white void. My limbs are remote and out of my control. The throbbing in my head almost obscures the creature's sickly clacking. Somehow I pull myself away and then I'm stumbling along the corridor, limping and bouncing from one wall to the other. Some still-alert part of my brain reminds me that this house is a mirror image of my own. I turn right, bursting through the front door without recalling opening it. The rattle behind me has become feverish.

There's no triumph in my escape. Without the scarves over my eyes I'm disoriented immediately. Not only do I not know where to run, I struggle to keep conscious of the fact that I must run and that I'm in danger.

Either I've left the rattling noise behind or it's stopped. I realise dimly that my destination, the corner shop, must be only across the road, but I become woolly and distracted. The light has become audible, somehow, a squall of white noise pulsing in time with my breathing.

I fall to the ground and roll onto my back, struggling to fill my lungs.

I surprise myself a little when I hear the word 'Catherine' from my own lips. The name echoes unnaturally, returning with a ringing, metallic tone.

My eyelids flicker open. I'm facing directly upwards. Above me, I see distinctions in the burning, pulsating light. There is not one, but many separate sources of the fierce whiteness. They're embedded in something glittering and grey that hovers inert, only metres above me. The waves of white noise become the scrapes of mechanisms. A darker patch appears up there, silhouetting a figure, spindly and insubstantial.

The white light settles upon me like snow. It's not so unbearable after all.

It heaps on my body, gathering mass, warming me at last.

Carus & Mitch

One

I'm awake and upright and clutching the blankets. A name echoes from my dream.

Mitch.

Did I shout my sister's name when I was asleep? I glance at her bed. The blankets are thrown back. It's empty.

I stand up and pull my own blanket around me against the cold. Underneath, I'm still dressed from yesterday.

"Mitch!" My voice is cracked and dry.

I burst out of the bedroom and stumble down the stairs. The bare wood creaks and splinters snag against my socks. The blanket trails behind me like a cape.

It's icily cold downstairs. The kitchen is empty and the dishes are laid out from yesterday, licked clean of crumbs.

"Mitch! This isn't funny! Come here!" In a quieter voice I add, "Please."

Sunlight glows through the streaks on the kitchen window. I remember my dream. Sunbeams dipping into water like loose coils of rope. The only noises I hear are the whistling of the wind and low murmurs from beyond the library.

It won't do for Mitch to see me upset, when I find her. I'm her big sister, so it stands to reason that I have to be the brave one. I pat the plaits in my hair. Neat enough. I push at the heavy door to the dining room.

The usual hubbub greets me. The smell of droppings makes my stomach heave. The floor is a carpet of shifting grey and orange, lit only by the sunlight coming through the door. Chickens cover every surface and fill the upturned packing crates we use as nesting boxes. A few birds shuffle around my feet, making exploratory pecks at my toes through my thick socks. One of the cockerels watches from a vantage point on top of a crate.

A long trough filled with straw is set in the centre of the table. There's a collection of freshly-laid eggs nestled in the straw. On each egg is a letter drawn with felt-tipped pen. They spell out the message, HAPPY 15 BIRD DAY CARUS.

"Surprise!"

I turn. Mitch stands partially hidden behind the door.

"It wasn't me. It was the chickens," she says, bouncing up and down. "Happy birthday Carus! I mean bird day."

I'd totally forgotten my birthday but Mitch is particular about keeping track of the date. I manage a grin and pull my little sister into an embrace. Often, lately, I've found myself surprised by her height. Surely she's taller than most seven-year-olds? That is, if there were any others to compare her to. One of these days she will look just like me, a gawky, stringy teen. What will I look like, by then?

"Thanks, Mitch."

The chickens bustle around her feet as she leans over the feeding trough to a crate tucked away at the back. It's the only one we don't remove eggs from for trading.

I try to peer into the crate too. "Anything?"

She turns with a disconsolate look on her face. "The mum chickens are just sitting there. I can't even see the eggs."

"Well, that means it's all working just right."

"They look sleepy. What if they've forgotten what to do?"

"Don't worry. They never forget. Mums just look after their kids without even thinking about it. They couldn't stop it if they tried."

There's an awkward silence and I can't think how to fill it. Mitch pulls away from the incubation crate and hugs herself with both arms. I've seen her do that several times recently and I'm not sure I know what it means. I slip my own arms around her chest from behind and we stand like that for a bit, like interlocked statues surrounded by the chickens.

I speak quietly because my mouth is right by her ear. "It's

okay. It's all going to be okay."

She doesn't say anything. Her breathing is like the swell of the wind.

I stop myself from saying anything about the marked eggs. The letters will have to be scrubbed off again before I can let them leave the house.

*

We're sitting at the kitchen table, midway through our tasks.

Mitch looks up at me through her roughly-cut fringe. Her lopsided smile means she's about to ask a difficult question.

"But what about the fish?"

I shrug. "I don't suppose there are any, anymore."

"But there are birds. I've seen them. And the chickens, they're birds too."

"What about them?"

"Well, it can't be just them on their own. And what do they eat? The wild birds, I mean."

"I don't know. Worms, perhaps. Or seven-year-old girls."

Mitch giggles but then gets all serious again. "I'd have to be standing outside before a wild bird could peck me."

She watches me with a steady gaze. Weighing up my responses. She's been doing that a lot. She's always been a talker, full of questions. But the problem is that the questions are becoming more targeted, more difficult to answer or dismiss.

I put down a chicken carcass, halfway through plucking its feathers. My head rings with a jangling sound, something half-remembered from the nighttime. "Really? We're going to have this conversation now?"

Maybe what happens next is a sign of some sort, because I'm praying for a distraction. The kitchen fills with squabbling and clucking noises. We both whirl around as a procession of chickens waddle in from the direction of the library and dining room.

"You take that side, I'll keep them away from the back door," I say.

With wide-open arms, Mitch leaps off her chair to shoo the

birds. She's giggling again.

She's hopeless. Stray chickens dart in every direction.

I crouch wide and low, blocking a bunch of them from getting back into the kitchen.

"We've lost a couple back there," I say. "I'll stay here, you round those ones up."

It takes nearly ten minutes, a few tactical withdrawals and lots of bickering before we guide the chickens back into the dining room. I kick away the stool that had been holding the sound-proofed door open and press with the weight of my body to shut it.

"Mitch? The door was wide open."

Mitch looks wistful. "I think I might have forgotten to shut it, when I was feeding them."

I don't say anything to that.

"I think they needed a bit more room too. One of them gave me a sort of look."

"Mitch, the phrase is "cooped up" for a reason. It's a coop. They can't have any more space and they did *not* give you a look."

We return to the kitchen and I carry on plucking the chicken carcass. My sister watches with a sullen expression.

After a minute of tense silence she says, "I still don't see why we can't let them out into the rest of the house. They're nice."

"Because of the noise."

"They're not noisy, most of the time."

"And what about when they are?"

"Can we uncover the windows in there, at least? The cloth is all stinky. We could give the chickens a view just for a bit."

"The dining room's right at the front of the house. So no. And it took ages to cover the windows in the first place."

Mitch mutters something under her breath.

"What was that?" My teeth are gritted.

"Shouldn't have bothered, that's all."

Count to ten, Carus.

I stand and face the window above the sink. In the small back yard, the few flowers in pots are the only bright colours against the grey concrete flagstones and the dull orange of the fence.

"You're just looking for an argument. You know exactly what the blackout coverings are for. And the door padding and the wood panels. We're not going to go over this again. Can you imagine how much the sound would travel to the outside if we let the chickens roam around?"

"No. I can't." Her voice is hushed. She's about to enter one of her serious sulks, I can tell.

"The rules aren't there just for the sake of it. I'm not making them up just to annoy you. We're doing what Mum tells us to do." My hands clench. "Told."

Mitch stares at the half-plucked chicken, which has rolled onto its side.

"Anyway, are you going to help me?" I say, trying to change the tone of the conversation. "Jom's due any minute, and we still haven't collected the eggs."

"Oh yes, right away," Mitch says, brightening. "If your boyfriend *Jom* needs them."

"Shut up."

"What is it you like best about Jom? His dark eyes? Or that he's so tall?"

"Stop it."

Mitch pulls a note from the pinboard above the kitchen table. It's filled with neat, rounded handwriting. "Dear C," she reads in a breathy voice, "I hope you are well and content. Perhaps the flowers grown from these seeds will brighten up your yard. Yours, J."

"Go and get the eggs."

I finish plucking the chicken while Mitch takes the empty basket into the dining room. She's repeating, "Yours, J" in singsong tones. By the time she comes back with the eggs, I've trussed the chicken and wrapped it tightly in paper.

"I wish we could keep them to ourselves," Mitch says, staring at it. "When they die, I mean. It's weird giving them away."

I give her a sideways look. "That's the rules. And you like all the tins of food in return, don't you?" I glance at the back door. "He'll be here any moment."

I start to unpack the eggs but then drop down again into the seat.

Mitch is at my side, holding me upright.

"I'm just dizzy, that's all." I say, pushing her away. "Not enough sleep."

*

Outside in the yard, I put the eggs and trussed chicken into the trading box and secure the latch. I have to step backwards carefully in order to leave the narrow area where the box is jammed between the inner and outer gates. It's not a perfect setup but it works. Using my body to block the view from the house, I give the outer gate a light push. There's no give at all. Jom's reliable and always secures it once he's completed the trade.

I rebolt the inner gate and step back. The inner gate should really be properly secured. If only I had a spare padlock. The deep-orange fence borders the two sides of the yard not blocked by the house and red-brick garage. The fence and gates are made of thick wooden panels and are so tall that they hide the sun until it's fully risen.

Mitch hovers at the back door, still keeping both feet on the step. She knows the rules. I usher her back into the house.

"Just another minute?" she says, bracing both arms against the door frame. "It's lovely out here."

It's true. The air is warm, now that the sunlight has reached into this part of the yard. The whispers of the wind echo from the steep, protective hillside behind the house.

I shake my head.

Reluctantly, Mitch goes back inside and waits at the foot of the staircase. As I pull the back door shut I'm startled by the sound of the outer yard gate opening. I check my watch. Jom's right on time. The problem isn't him; it's that we're getting slower.

Mitch obviously hasn't heard a thing. She doesn't feel any of the pressure that I feel. It's my responsibility that we fill the trading box on time each day. Everything is my responsibility.

I spread my arms in an attempt to block her view from the kitchen window. "All right, Mitch. Time to make yourself useful. Where do we start?"

"First things first, start upstairs!" Mitch says, like it's a nursery rhyme.

We go upstairs to the bedroom we share. Working together, we make each bed in turn. Mitch gets tangled in the sheets and I laugh, surprising myself.

"All done?" I ask.

Mitch glances around at the room and nods.

"What's next, then?"

She wrinkles her nose. "Bathroom?"

"But today is...?"

"Your birthday."

"Yes, but it's also a..."

"A Thursday." Mitch's eyes brighten. "So we don't have to do the bathroom today?"

"You tell me."

She taps alternate fingertips of her left hand in turn. "Saturday, Monday, Wednesday, Friday—nope, no stinky bathroom today."

"Right. Good. So what next?"

"Windows and corridor."

There are three doors on the upstairs landing: our bedroom, the tiny bathroom and Mum's room. There used to be a passageway, too, opposite the top of the staircase. Mitch stands close to the wooden panelling that barricades the corridor and places her palms flat on it. She pumps rapidly with both hands. The struts wobble but hold fast.

She ducks into the bathroom and comes back carrying a small plastic stool. On her way past, she glances up at the gold locket that hangs from a nail on the wall between the doors to Mum's bedroom and our own. It's understandable that she's curious. Soon she'll be tall enough to just reach up and touch it. But she'd better not. When we hung it up we agreed that it wasn't to play with. Hanging it out here on the landing was the only way I could make Mitch agree to leave Mum's bedroom untouched.

Balancing on the stool, she checks the panelling all over, a more thorough inspection. Her hands move swiftly over its surface as she searches for defects. She's better, more patient at this task than I am.

"All good," she says, hopping down.

"So we're done?"

She gives an exaggerated nod. "Yep, all finished."

I cross the landing to the single window at the top of the staircase. It's the only one that faces out from the front of the house, or would do if it wasn't covered. Reaching up, I flick at the corner of the thick fabric stretched across the frame.

"What about this?" I pull the fabric taut and fix it back in place.

"Oh, that," Mitch says, "It's only a little bit."

Is she trying to provoke me? "It matters. It really matters."

Mitch's expression is somewhere between upset and indignant. She cocks her head and says, "Shouldn't we check the other windows?" She nods at the wooden panels barricading the rooms beyond.

I stifle a shudder. "No. This barricade's the best one we've made yet. We're not going to take it down again just to get to the other rooms. And we checked the blinds on all those windows again and again before we put the barricade up."

"But they might have—"

"I said no!"

Count to ten.

"Better to have the rooms blocked off entirely now."

Mitch scowls and kicks at the skirting board. "It's stupid, living in such a big house and being stuck in a couple of rooms at the back."

Maybe it is. I can barely remember the front rooms. Our bedroom and even Mum's bedroom are tiny compared to those ones, but our rooms face the hillside at the rear of the house, so they're safer. We can leave the windows uncovered. Mitch would be even less happy if we had to stumble around in the dark.

"I know what you're like," I say, even though it's stupid to try and reason with her. "If I let you into the front of the house you'd race straight to the windows."

"So?"

"If your head pops up at a window, or if a light appears, someone could easily see you. They'd know that we're here."

"So?"

So? So what? I honestly have no idea. For a moment I imagine the house from the point of view of somebody outside. What would it look like, to them? A reminder of the olden times? Or a treasure chest filled with loot and lives?

"We promised that we'd stay hidden, that's all. We promised Mum and we're not about to break our promise."

Mitch closes her eyes, swaying her head from side to side as if she's dreaming. "I just like hearing the sound from outside. You can hear it from the back door, but only a bit." She purses her lips and makes a sighing, whooshing sound. "If this window was open, we'd hear it right now."

She makes the sound again and spins away across the landing with her arms swinging loosely at her sides.

"Stop being such a weirdo," I say.

"You're a weirdo."

"Hey, come on. We've done the corridor now."

"So now we say good morning to Mum."

"Yep."

Mitch quietens down. She looks at the gold locket hanging from its nail.

"Hi, Mum."

Two

With Mitch getting taller, the library seems to shrink every day. The top of her head grazes the underside of the staircase, and she's boxed in by the winged headrest of her armchair. Sometimes I imagine her having a sudden growth spurt and getting jammed in that little spot for good.

She glances up from her book and I look back down at mine. I haven't read a word in more than half an hour. I'm only reading it, or pretending to, because it's a book for adults, and I'm the adult, aren't I? The book's supposed to be an adventure, full of spies and secret microfilms. But it's hard to identify with people who spend their time racing around from country to country, meeting exotic people and getting into death-defying scrapes. There can't be much of that going on these days. Or much of anything.

The book's heavy in my hands. I lower it onto my lap and watch Mitch instead. My headache's back again, worse than this morning.

Mitch's tongue pokes out of the corner of her mouth when she reads. "What's an electric Ian?" she says without looking up.

"Electrician. It's someone who makes sure your lights are working, and your fridge, all that stuff."

Mitch glances at the oil lamp.

"Not that kind of light."

She's silent, still looking at the smeared glass around the flame.

"I've told you before about electricity," I say, "It's what made the oven hot and the freezer icy cold. Remember?"

She nods slowly, but I ca—n tell she doesn't remember. She holds up the book. *People Who Help Us*. It's far too young for her, but she likes the photos. The title seems ridiculous. Who are the *People Who Help Us*, now? Other than Jom, there are only the people who scratch and scrape at our windows from time to time. If you can even call them people. Mitch has never even heard them, thanks to all my hard work and tricks to distract her. Well done me.

Mitch looks forlorn. "There are pages missing."

As she fans the book, cracking the spine, I can see the torn stubs. I'm pretty sure they weren't missing when I rooted the book out from the cupboard last week.

I frown. "What have you done with them?"

"Wasn't me."

"Promise?"

"Promise. Anyway, I like it all the same. What's a post office?"

"Well, an office is a building where people go to work—"

"Like cleaning and chores?"

"All sorts. Writing things down, mainly. But a post office is different. It's not really an office at all. It's a shop where you take stuff that you want to give to somebody somewhere else. And they deliver it for you."

"Why don't people just give people stuff themselves?"

"Because they're busy."

"What if they're not busy?"

"Then it might be too far."

Mitch absorbs this information. She's probably struggling to imagine a distance great enough that you couldn't just hand a parcel over.

I lean forward to take the book from her hands. Is it too confusing for her? Maybe I shouldn't have let her read it. I flick through the pages. There are more than half a dozen pages missing. Something catches my eye as I rifle through. There's a picture drawn in felt-tipped pen on the inside of the back cover. It's a man wearing a dark coat, maybe a business suit, and a bowler hat. His tall body is bent forward as if he's leaning into the wind. In his pink hand is a basket, like Little Red Riding Hood's.

"Did you draw this?"

She cranes her neck to see, and nods.

"Who is it?"

"Can't you tell?" She pretends to be offended. It's a good drawing, it really is.

"A postman?"

She shakes her head.

"A farmer?"

"You should know! It's your *lover*, Jom!"

I look at the drawing again. Funny, I've always pictured him wearing a green jacket, for some reason.

Mitch starts making kissing noises.

I sigh.

"Do you think the eggs have hatched yet?" she says.

I make a go-and-find-out face.

She bounds across the kitchen. Squeals of delight come from the dining room.

*

Mitch's enthusiasm for the newly-hatched chicks is infectious. It's almost enough to make me view the yellow balls of fluff as pets rather than as our livelihood.

Mainly, I feel relief. I can't bear to think what would happen if the cockerel failed to produce more chickens. No more eggs, no more trading, no more tins of food from Jom.

Her legs are tucked up beneath her and the four chicks are lined up on her thigh, angled so they can't fall off. She's been near-silent for almost an hour, just cooing and chuckling to herself and to the chicks. The only other noise is the rain beginning to rattle against the window.

I've got Mitch to look after. But perhaps she needs to watch over something, too.

"Carus? Tell me the story again?"

"It's nearly time for dinner."

"I'm not hungry."

"I—" No other excuses come to mind.

I sigh and settle myself into my seat. Mitch grins, knowing she's won. The four chicks are cradled in her little hands.

"Now... how does it start?" I say, teasing it out. Telling the story brings out something theatrical in me.

"Oxford!" Mitch pronounces it more like "Ox Fod."

"That's right. So. Once upon a time we all lived in Oxford. You, me and Mum. And—"

"But where is Oxford?" she says.

That's a new interruption. She watches me carefully as I think through my options.

I frown, hesitate, then stand on tiptoes on my chair to fetch the big atlas from the highest bookshelf. My legs ache as I take the book's weight. Was I always this weak? I scold myself silently for deciding to show her the atlas. Nothing good will come of this. But I'm tired of saying no.

Mitch leans forward as I flick through the pages.

"Don't forget your new friends," I say, pointing.

She gasps and sits back again to give the chicks room. There's real concern on her face. She's growing up.

"So," I say, propping up the open atlas on my knees and turning it outwards to face her, "This is England. No, just this lumpy bit at the bottom is England. The other lumps are different countries, where people spoke different languages."

From her wrinkled nose I can see that she's struggling with that idea.

"What's all the blue?" she says. She prefers dealing with tangible things.

"Sea. Water." My throat feels dry.

"Water's see-through."

I shrug, partly to shake off a strange feeling that's crept over me. "Anyway, across the sea—and you'd need a, um, boat to go across—there are more countries. There are millions of countries in the world, and the world's round like a ball." I know it's sort of cruel, just throwing out facts like that. I expect her to worry about all that water on a round ball, whether it'll fall off, but she seems happy enough.

"Not anymore," she says, meaning the millions of countries.

"No, not anymore. Anyway, Oxford's just…" It takes me a moment to locate it. "Here."

Her eyes move around the map. "And where's *here* here?"

I hesitate before pointing a finger up at the top of the uppermost lump of Britain. I forget what that bit's called, but it hardly matters. "We're right here," I say.

"I wonder if Oxford has a post office," Mitch says, addressing the chicks. She looks up again. "Do the story, then."

I open my mouth but she interrupts. "You take too long. I know it. Let me tell it."

I shrug and settle back into my chair.

"Once upon a time we all lived in Oxford. You, me and Mum." Mitch speaks steadily in a sing-song voice as if it's a hymn, not a story.

"Mum was a teacher. Teaching children, like you teach me about chickens and yoga and heating food up. Mum taught children how to write stories and use imaginations to make up things that weren't really true."

I frown. Does Mitch think that 'imaginations' are some sort of tool or technology from the olden days?

"But that's not the same as lying," she continues. "Making up stories is how grownups tell other grownups about the world, without upsetting everyone by going around telling the truth all the time.

"We had a dad, too. But you hardly remember him and I never met him at all. He was always tired, but he smiled a lot. He got tireder and tireder until he fell over and one day he just left. But that was okay."

My skin prickles. Is that how I described it to her? "He just left"? At the funeral I was made to wear tight black shoes. I was furious and made a scene.

Mitch takes a breath. "Oxford was a city. That means the houses were pointy, and there were lots of people who'd bump into each other when they turned corners without looking where they were going. Our house wasn't all that pointy but it was beside a river. You and Mum used to swim in the river every day, and it was sunny all the time. I never swam because first I wasn't there and then I was too small."

While she's speaking I try and pick out the truth from the collection of images. It's not as easy as I'd like.

"Mum was good at making up stories. On her arm she had a brown mark from where she couldn't rub off a splotch of ink. She got tired, too, sometimes. People bumped into other people so much, and she dropped her shopping. There were cracks in the pavements and they were going to get bigger, so big that the people coming around corners might just drop into the cracks and never bump into each other at all. So we all went away in a car." The way she says it, the word sounds like something fantastical, like a magic carpet. "You fell asleep because it took ages, and I was still little and I cried all the way. We were going to our uncle's house. This house. To get away from the cracks in the pavement. What was his name?"

"Whose name?"

"Our uncle."

"Oh, it was—" For a second I thought I knew it. "I can't remember. He'd already gone away before we arrived."

"Okay. And it was raining when we got here. And..." Her voice tails off.

"It was really heavy rain," I say, "And Mum couldn't turn on the lights, even though that was when there was electricity and everything should've just worked."

Mitch folds her arms across her chest and one of the chicks slips further into her lap. "Who's telling this story?" she says.

"Sorry. Carry on."

"Never mind. I'm finished." She turns her attention back to the chicks, cooing softly.

I envy her ability to become distracted so easily. No thought or idea or fear grips her for long.

I remember that rainy night when we arrived, me with my red coat over my head and Mum dashing ahead with baby Mitch held under her hunched body. While Mum searched for the fuse box, I ran laps around the house, including the front rooms. It was a big house, back then. It's so small now, even though there's only the two of us. The walls are closing in.

*

I'm upstairs and Mitch is downstairs when a bad feeling prickles up from my toes and along my spine. I'm surprised to be up here. My hand is cupping Mum's locket where it hangs on the wall of the landing. When I pull my hand away the locket jangles faintly.

Rain from outside hammers at the windows just like my heart is hammering in my chest. I trip halfway down the staircase and tumble into the library, the air leaving my lungs. Mitch is no longer dozing in her armchair where I left her. In my hurry, I knock books from the shelves and onto the rug and finally come to a stop, panting, against the kitchen table.

The back door is open. A puddle is collecting in the slot that once held a doormat.

Mitch is outside, kneeling in the yard in front of the shuttered, padlocked door to the garage. We've never used it, even when Mum was here. There's nothing inside.

Wet blotches mark her shoulders. There's a drier patch on the concrete beneath her. Maybe she hasn't even noticed the rain.

She turns sharply. Mum would have said that her face was a picture of guilt.

I'm winded from my fall. Even if I wasn't, I'm not sure I'd have been able to speak at that moment.

Mitch's raised right hand drops to her side. The padlock, still clamped shut, clangs against the metal shutters of the garage.

We're both motionless for a while, maybe only seconds, her kneeling in the yard and me leaning on the kitchen table.

"I was just—" Mitch begins.

"Get inside!" The words barely make it out.

"Okay. But—"

I burst into motion, pushing against the table to propel myself out of the building. I grab her from the armpits, swinging her little body up and off the ground. Rainwater sprays from her shoulders. She wails, probably more from the indignity than pain. But even if I'd hurt her I wouldn't have moved any slower. I half push, half throw her into the kitchen and now it's her leaning on the table, only for a moment though, before she slumps to the floor. Her legs are curled underneath her body. Her back rises and falls with ragged sobs. Water gathers in rings around her.

I'm still outside among the stabbing raindrops. My breathing slows a little. I put out a hand to steady myself against the metal shutters of the garage, which rattle under my palm. Crusted flakes of ancient white paint dig into my skin. I glance down. The heavy padlock securing the door gleams silver, without any of the dullness of rust. I bend down to touch it but then my head floods with pain.

As I pull the house door closed the sound of the wind becomes something else. Whatever it is, is coughing and creeping, just beyond the gates, around the corner where I can't see.

*

"I'm serious. Not another word."

Mitch mumbles something as she climbs the stairs ahead of me.

I'm not able to hide my frustration. "What did you just say?"

"You're not Mum, you know."

I don't know what to say to that.

She must know she's hit a nerve. I hover on the landing beside Mum's hanging locket while Mitch brushes her teeth and climbs into bed without saying a word. The only time she meets my eye it's with a furtive, fearful glance. She buries herself under the blankets so that only a tuft of coppery hair is visible.

I go back downstairs but it's still light and nothing quite makes sense without Mitch. I try reading in the library but not for long. Eventually I end up in the kitchen, just staring out into the darkness of the yard.

I give in. She's scared and confused, but she's also cold from being out in the rain. From my special hidden supply I fetch a jar of cocoa and then I heat water in a saucepan on the gas hob to make a passable hot chocolate.

Still in bed, Mitch accepts it and drinks the lot in a few gulps. Perhaps it counts as a truce.

I slip into my own bed and lie awake.

Three

I'm gripping the blanket so tightly that my nails dig through, making marks on my palms. My legs ache as if I've been walking for days.

Mitch has overslept but looks sort of angelic, so I leave her be. I check on the chickens, collect the eggs, and package them up to put them into the trading box.

I think a rebellious thought. I could wait for Jom while Mitch is out of the way. I picture him in his green jacket, or maybe a black business suit and bowler hat, leaning into the wind. Would it be too badly against the rules, just to call hello over the tall gates? I've never so much as written him a note, even though he's put a few into the trading box along with the tins of food. What if Jom thought I fancied him, like Mitch says I do? What if I scared him away? Nothing's worth risking that. Without the food he brings, we'd only have the eggs and then they'd run out if we had nothing to feed the chickens. Just the thought of it makes me feel hollow and hungry.

I take a mug of hot water and honey to Mitch in bed. She shuffles herself into a seated position. Her eyes are puffy. At first I'm afraid that the unsteady look she gives means she hasn't forgiven me for being so rough yesterday. But then she beams.

"Carus!" It's as if she's only just recognised me.

"Who else were you expecting?"

Her face clouds. For a second she looks upset. I hand her the mug of hot honey.

A wave of guilt floods my body. I've no idea why. I could almost cry right there and then, but the feeling passes.

Mitch looks up at me through her fringe. There's no lopsided smile. "Shouldn't I be doing something?"

"Should you?"

"I was supposed to get up." The corners of her mouth twitch. "The chicks!"

"The chicks are fine. They'll be glad to see you. And I've already taken out the eggs."

"Oh. That's right, yes."

"Are you all right?" I place my hand flat against her forehead. "You don't feel ill?"

Her eyes are glassy. "No. It's just a bit..." She passes a flattened hand in front of her face. Then she looks at me as if I were the one talking and she's waiting for me to finish.

"Let's get you downstairs," I say.

She's weak. I have to support her all the way down the stairs and her free hand fumbles on the banister. I heave her onto one of the kitchen chairs and she sits placidly while I fuss around her. She eats crackers and scrambled eggs in silence.

I sit across the table from her, not eating, just watching. The wave of guilt spreads through me again. Part of it must be that, secretly, I'm grateful that she's not asking difficult questions.

"Are you sure you're not ill?" I say.

When Mitch looks up her head lolls heavily.

"I love you, Carus," she says.

*

In the afternoon Mitch snoozes in her armchair, a deeper sleep than normal. I'm tired too, and my ears are ringing, but I force myself to go out to the yard. The eggs I put in the trading box have been replaced by a scuffed tin of baked beans, two packets of crackers and a small sack of chicken feed.

Baked beans are Mitch's favourite. She'll be so pleased. Even though I'm outside and don't feel safe, I smile.

*

We spend the rest of the afternoon and evening in the kitchen, where we can stretch out a bit. The room we call the library was once just a corridor and only has space for the rug, a single bookcase, and the two armchairs jammed under the staircase. The good thing about the kitchen is that I can keep an eye on the yard. Later, we'll retreat to the safety of the bedroom where I'll wait in the dark for Mitch's breathing to change. It's only when she's asleep that I can be sure she'll stay quiet.

The large, round-cornered table fills most of the room. The end where we eat is kept clear and clean. The other end, where we're sitting now, is mostly covered with piles of Mitch's books. There are bundles of cloth, too. I found them in the bedroom at the front of the house years ago, before we blocked up the corridor. Mitch's clothes get snagged and torn all the time and I do my best to fix them. Her trousers are made more of unmatched patches than they are of the original corduroy.

If I concentrate hard, I can sort of remember the kitchen as it was when Mum was still here. Not very clearly, though—that was more than five years ago, after all. When we arrived here I wasn't much older than Mitch is now. That's a weird thought.

I remember the heat from the oven when Mum baked cakes. The fridge made a humming noise. Mitch still calls it "fridge" even though nowadays it's really just a cupboard like any of the others. The old names for things fill her with excitement. Is that okay, or unhealthy? Should I stop her from being so curious about things that don't matter anymore? It's all broken, after all. Everything is, inside and out.

Mitch splays her dog-eared issue of Reader's Digest upside-down on the table. She gets up and stands before the sink. My body tenses as she places both hands onto the window, peering out. A fog halo spreads around her fingers. It must be getting cold outside, as well as dark. Are we near autumn?

"What *is* air, anyway?" she says, as if we're halfway through a conversation on the subject. She does that a lot, forgetting what she's said out loud and what's just in her head.

I put down the blanket I'm mending, glad of an excuse to look away from the spiderweb of botched stitches. "It's a gas. You breathe it in and then breathe out something else. I forget what."

"It's important, isn't it? Like food and water."

I nod, even though she still has her back to me.

"Sometimes I can see bits coming off the flowers," she continues, "Floating in the air. Is air made from bits of flower?"

"It's made of lots of things."

She turns. "Like what?"

I try to remember lessons at school. "Oxygen, that's what your body uses to stay alive. And there's the bits of flowers and other things, but really, really tiny." I pause. "And then, um, neon and carbon."

Mitch plays with a loose thread trailing from the blanket, her mind already wandering. "But how come the air's okay to breathe?"

"I don't know."

"And the water? How come water still comes from the taps?"

I stiffen again. "I don't know. But we're just lucky it does."

"Does it come from rain?"

I remember hearing something about reservoirs, once. But then my mind gets crowded with other images, all mixed up. The sea, remembered from early childhood. Vast, powerful, thundering clods of water thumping down again and again. Lakes and rivers, too, like the one where Mum used to watch me swim from where she stood nervously on the bank. Her long straight hair almost covering her face as if she was the one who was soaking wet, not me.

"Yes," I say, trying to keep my tone level, "from rain."

She looks out of the window again. I stare at her back, willing her to turn around and settle down with her book. The fog halos have grown bigger than her hands.

When she finally does turn, she's smiling her lopsided smile.

"What about people?"

"What about them?"

"Are there still people? Out there?"

I shudder. I can imagine the rattling coughs as if they're here in the kitchen, creeping and hiding.

"You know there aren't."

"But what about—"

"No. Mitch, just... no."

Mitch half-turns. She's looking at the noticeboard on the wall behind the table. Jom's note, the one she thinks is so funny, is pinned to the bottom-right corner.

"Leave it, Mitch."

Four

For the second night running, it takes a mug of hot chocolate to make Mitch to go to bed early. She pushes it away at first but I make sure that she drinks it. Once I hear her fluttering, whispering snores, I leave the room to prowl the house, checking and rechecking the barricades. At some point I go to bed, but keep rising and then resettling, until I lose track of the difference between standing or lying down, walking or sleepwalking. In the quiet dark, each step I take produces a jangling sound. I don't know why.

I must fall asleep properly at some point, because then I see things that only happen in dreams. I struggle to keep my head above the surface of the water. Some kind of animal—a horse?—nudges against my cheek and I can't tell if it's trying to help or push me under. My skin itches where it touches me. Its muzzle feels scaly like a fish.

I pull my head up to breathe. My throat is raw, the coughing fierce.

Mitch's body makes a neat hillock in her bed. Once I found

a baby sparrow on our Oxford doorstep, panting with its legs curled like cherry stems. We took it in and fed it until it could fly away.

The sound of the chickens echoes dully up the staircase from the dining room. Light streams through the uncovered window.

What time is it?

I jump out of bed, rubbing my eyes. My skin is clammy and cold. I look at my watch. I have to hold it at an angle to see the clock hands beneath the part of the glass that's been fogged up ever since it got submerged once. It's past ten o'clock.

"Mitch!" I yell, jostling her in her cocoon of blankets. "Did you get the eggs out in time?"

She doesn't make any sound but just lolls into my arms. White flecks mark the corners of her mouth. I push her away and her body rocks to stillness as I burst out of the room.

We've never failed to place the eggs in the trading box before Jom's visit. Never.

I sweep through the library and heave open the padded door to the dining room. The chickens squawk in alarm at the sudden interruption. In each of the nest boxes is a brace of eggs laid that morning.

Despair wells up inside me. And something else, too. Anger. Real anger.

I check my watch again. It's only twenty past ten. Perhaps Jom might have been held up, just a little? Maybe he's outside still, checking the trading box right at this moment. I could call to him through the fence, make him hold on for just another minute.

First things first. I grab the wicker basket from behind the door, then scrabble to collect the eggs. In my hurry I crack a couple of them. No matter—better to supply some than none at all.

I dash through the kitchen. I imagine the scene to come. Me scolding, trying to sound like Mum. Mitch defensive at first, then cowering, then helpless with tears. It's not fair. I have to be the one making the rules all the time. When will Mitch finally grow up?

But there's no time.

The yard is peaceful. Shifting discs of sunlight slip across the flagstones, filtered through the trees on the hillside. I stand beside the fence, holding back, listening. There's no sound. I pull back the heavy bolt of the inner gate and step through. The outer gate is the same height as the inner one, far taller than I am. It's closed tight, held in place by the U-shaped latch hooked over the top of the fencepost. I turn in the narrow space to face the wooden trading box. I lift its hinged lid.

At first I can't believe that there's nothing inside. I stand gawping at the empty space.

What had I expected? We didn't provide the eggs, so why would any tinned food have been left for us?

But I can't accept that there's no hope. There's a faint chance that Jom's been delayed. Carefully, I place the basket of eggs into the box.

I'm standing before the almost-bare cupboard when Mitch comes padding into the kitchen. Her eyes are even more puffy than yesterday.

"I feel funny," she says.

My hands shake. "You overslept."

Mitch rubs her face. Her fingernails make dark blotches on her cheek. "My mouth feels weird."

I guide her to a chair and give her a glass of water. At least we still have that, we won't die of thirst. I realise that my own mouth is painfully dry, so when she doesn't reach for the glass I drink it all and then refill it. The water sits on the table halfway between us. It's calm and still.

I cook and serve a couple of eggs, sunny-side up. There's a single can of tinned peaches in the corner cupboard. I push it all the way to the back, for an emergency. Mitch eats the eggs slowly as if she has to concentrate to chew. Eventually, she pushes the plate away.

"You have to eat," I say.

She shakes her head. "I don't like it. I like baked beans and crackers."

"There aren't any. We didn't make the trade this morning."

For the first time, she meets my eye. Her cheeks look sort of misshapen.

"It's okay," I say, "It wasn't your fault."

But from her look I can tell that she knows. It was her fault. We're going to go hungry, and it's all her fault.

*

We eat a hardboiled egg each for lunch. Afterwards, Mitch is sheepish and slow and almost useless at completing her chores. I don't mind doing her tasks instead, though. It's nice to have her quiet for a change.

After lunch Mitch curls up on the library rug like a cat. I read my book, tickling her every so often with my bare toes.

I tell her the story of us. I'm not sure she even notices it, apart from being soothed by the rise and fall of my voice. Sitting like this, in the centre of the house, away from the windows and with none of Mitch's surprises, I realise that I'm happy.

By late afternoon Mitch is alert enough to complain about being hungry. She's probably never noticed before how hand-to-mouth we live. Without Jom's daily delivery of tinned food and crackers, we have almost nothing. If she's ever left alone, she needs to understand that.

The rest of the day passes in a fog. On Tuesday the eggs are still there in the trading box, untouched by Jom. Is he punishing us? Or has he abandoned us totally?

Just getting through the day is tough. Mitch refuses her breakfast eggs and I can barely stomach mine.

My head throbs constantly. It's like my nightmares are echoing around in there.

*

I must have dozed off. I'm in the kitchen sitting in my chair, and the air's getting chilly.

I don't feel at all rested. My feet ache. My ears are ringing with the same jangling sound I remember from the nighttime. My headache is worse than ever, too. No matter how much I sleep, it never goes away these days. If I let on to Mitch just how much it hurt, she'd be terrified for me.

I'm suddenly wide awake. Where is Mitch, anyway? But a peek around the doorway steadies my heart rate. She's still curled on the rug like a newborn baby. The posture looks defensive, but she's smiling.

I hear a noise. It's not quite the jangling sound from my dreams, but it's close. It's coming from outside. A rustle, a click of metal.

I leap up from my seat. My hands fumble with the handle of the back door.

"Jom!" I shout as I burst into the yard, "Jom, is that you?"

It feels natural to call out to him. Isn't Jom my best and only friend? But I mustn't scare him away. I run to the gate but I'm not brave enough to open it. My whole body presses against the wooden panels. The concrete flagstones are cold through my socks.

"Jom?" I say again, quieter.

There's no sound from the other side. I unbolt the inner gate and open it just a fraction. Nothing. But I feel a hum in the air. He's been here. I stand between the two fences and press my ear against the outer gate. I can only hear the wind.

The trading box is held shut with a metal peg, just as I left it. My hand hesitates just above the latch.

Please, Jom. Won't you help us?

Tears fill my eyes as I lift the lid.

Sunlight glints from the metal tins, making my eyes water even more. Three unlabelled tins, two packets of crackers, a sachet of seeds. There's a folded piece of paper, too. A note. I unfold it to see familiar, rounded handwriting.

Don't you dare forget again. J x

Five

"Whistle while you work, do-da-do-do-do-do-dooo!"

Mitch has never been able to whistle. She's only ever heard the song from me and I haven't sung it in years. Maybe she doesn't even know what whistling is.

Her head disappears again under the sink. When she emerges she grimaces at the thick layer of grime on the cloth in her hand. I know we've neglected our chores recently, but I could have sworn I'd cleaned the bathroom yesterday when Mitch was still asleep. I definitely remember being upstairs on the landing.

"You've perked up." I'm hovering at the doorway. As pleased as I am that she's doing her daily tasks, I'm anxious to get on with the important job of checking the security.

Mitch switches to a different tune. "I like coffee, I like tea, I like Carus, I like me."

She works her way around the edge of the bath, spraying and wiping with diluted bleach. When she finishes, her face is streaked with muck. That's the problem with Mitch. She's good at chores but always ends up transferring all the dirt to herself.

"Come on," I say, "That's enough for now."

She fetches the stool and plonks it before the barricade on the landing. She stands on one leg to reach high up, feeling her way. Those darting hands, checking for chinks and cracks. Safe hands.

I stand with my back to Mum's bedroom door. Is it dirty in there, too? Should I have made cleaning Mum's room part of the chores? I look at the gold locket hanging on its nail beside the door. After quickly making sure that Mitch is still occupied in her task, I reach up to curl my fingers around the locket. It's warmer than I expect. My touch produces a low jangling sound even though I'm being careful not to jostle it. I snatch my hand away just as Mitch turns around.

"Fine, fine, fine," Mitch sings as she checks the lower part of the barricade. She shifts the stool to the window, but not before stealing a look at the gold locket herself.

Her world is stranger than mine. At least I have memories of outside. For her, there has only ever been these few dark rooms. Outside has always been just the yard with its drooping flowers and tall fence. Everything beyond that point are just stories, either mine or from books. The photo encyclopedia she loves so much is as fictional as any storybook.

I lean back against the door and my eyes close. Mum would

have known how to keep things running properly. How to keep both of us on track. Mitch has been happy enough most of the time, despite everything. But what about me? Sometimes it feels like I fell away into the cracks, like the people in Oxford and everywhere else. When England broke, Mum dragged us out here in the middle of nowhere. She didn't quite lock us up and throw away the key, but she might as well have.

Mitch's singing has stopped. My eyes open.

She's balanced on tiptoes. At first I think that she's just checking the blinds, but her fingers are holding the fabric away from the wooden frame so she can peep through the gap. She's looking outside. Over her shoulder, through the narrow slit, I can see down into the garden at the front of the house.

There's a strange brown smudge out there on the ground, a dark oblong surrounded by green.

"Get away!" I scream, launching myself across the landing.

In my rush I kick the stool from under her. When she falls, I only half-catch her. She yelps as her body pivots around my outstretched arms, her legs flipping upward. Her head hits the carpeted floor with a dull thud and I scramble to stop her from bouncing towards the staircase.

She curls into a ball with her arms wrapped around her head. Her fingers tremble.

"You can't do that!" I shout. Spit flies from my mouth with each word.

Mitch just moans.

"You know you mustn't!" I say, no quieter.

He voice comes muffled from inside her cocoon. "I'm sorry."

*

At first I'm paranoid that Mitch has really hurt herself, that I've given her brain damage. But I soon realise that her sulkiness has less to do with the accident and far more to do with me in general. She curls up on the rug in the library, her body making a curved wall around the four yellow chicks that dart from side to side.

I nudge her with my foot. "Hey, weirdo. Time for dinner."

She doesn't say anything but just pulls her head further in. Her little fingers brush each chick's fuzz in turn.

"Jom brought us sweetcorn," I say.

"I don't like sweetcorn." Her voice is thick.

"That's not true. You loved it last time. You said they were like tiny, little suns."

"I like baked beans."

Count to ten.

I take a breath before answering. "I know. But Jom obviously didn't have any baked beans this time. Just sweet corn. And we should be grateful for that. If we'd—"

Mitch sits up sharply. Her eyes are narrowed and dark. "If we'd what?"

"If we'd made the trade every day, without missing any, maybe we could ask him for what we want."

"That wasn't my fault," she says.

"Nothing ever is." I didn't mean to say that. "Look, that's not fair on you. But Jom—"

"You mean your boyfriend."

"No. He's just a person who helps us."

"Helps *you*."

"Stop it. Please? Just stop it."

The sound of the wind outside cuts out for a moment. I sense that Mitch is sizing me up. When she speaks, her voice is calm and level.

"Jom hates us."

A shiver runs through my whole body. "What?"

"I said, Jom hates us. He wants us to die."

I crouch down but Mitch backs away so that I end up perched awkwardly several feet away from her. "Don't say that. Jom's kind. He brings us food."

Mitch studies the chicks for a while before speaking.

"Why?"

My throat is dry. "Why what?"

"Why does Jom bring us food?"

"Because we trade with him!" I'm aware that my voice is rising in pitch. "Because of the chickens, the eggs."

She wrinkles her nose. "But he has all that food in tins. Why does he care about eggs?"

Still crouching, I have to steady myself with my hands. My headache's started up again and my throat is sore. I open my mouth to speak, but the dryness stops any words coming out.

Mitch scoops the chicks into her hands and stands up. From my crouched position, she looks absurdly tall.

"Who is he?" she says.

"He's just Jom," I manage to reply.

"But who else is out there?"

I shake my head. How could I possibly know? The world is broken. There can be nobody outside.

Mitch is still watching me carefully. "Did he know Mum, before she disappeared?"

My eyes sting. I feel tears trickle down each cheek. "I don't know. I suppose he must have. I don't know."

There's silence for a minute or so. We're fixed in position like statues either side of the doorway. Finally, Mitch turns and pushes open the dining room door. When she comes out again, the chicks are gone. I'm still kneeling on the rug and I'm not sure if I'm crying or not.

She stares at me again. Now her eyes are fiery, not sad.

My head hurts so much that I can't speak. It's hard even to look up at her.

Abruptly, Mitch screams. It's a shriek that comes all the way from her belly, ragged and knife-sharp at the same time. I want to clap my hands over my ears, but I'm so tired.

"I hate it!" she yells. "Everything!" She waves an arm to indicate the whole house, or at least the part of it that we live in. "How can *you* stand it?"

"We don't have a choice," I say. My voice is tinny and weak.

"Why? You keep saying that. But you never tell me why! What's going on out there? What's outside? I'm not a baby anymore!"

I just end up shaking my head. My mind's full of stories that don't fit together. The broken ground, the rising water, the broken people. The shouts, the screams. They were awful, just like Mitch's scream. People were gathered around me, around

Mum, leaning over us. I beat them away until they left us alone. How can I explain it to Mitch?

"We just have to stay here," I say, even though I know it's not enough. "We have to stay safe."

"Why? What's the point, Carus? If staying safe means just hiding in the dark?"

"Because..."

"What?"

"Because we promised Mum."

Mitch grows taller and taller while I shrink down so that I'm almost swallowed up by the fur of the rug. Which of us is the older sister? Who looks after who?

Mitch's voice is slow, careful, heavy. "Mum's dead."

There's another ragged scream and it takes me a few seconds before I realise that it's coming from me. Mitch looks horrified. At the edges of my vision, I can see my hands but I can't tell what they're doing. My head hurts. It hurts so much.

Mitch's mouth twitches. Then she turns and dashes up the stairs, two at a time. I hear a door slam and then thud thud thud.

*

"Mitch?"

My left hand rests against the wall, cupping Mum's locket hanging from its nail. My other hand is pressed flat against our bedroom door.

"Mitch? I'm sorry. I'm okay now."

There's no sound from inside.

"We don't need to do any more chores today. If you come out we can just sit and read."

"I'm not coming out." Mitch's voice is muffled. She must be hiding under her blanket.

"You'll get hungry."

She doesn't answer. Gently, I try the door handle. It doesn't budge. Mitch must have pushed something up against the door, jamming it. She's too stubborn to come out any time soon. She'll stay locked in there. A prison within a prison. A box within a box.

I grit my teeth. I squeeze the fingers of my left hand around Mum's locket on the wall making it jangle faintly. Is there something loose inside?

What would you do now, Mum? Was I ever like this when I was her age?

I push the locket and it swings like a pendulum, chiming with each arc. Time is passing. I'm losing my grip.

I slide down to the floor with my back against the bedroom door. I can tell by the changing colour of the staircase wall that it must be getting dark outside.

"You have to let me in," I say, and instantly regret it. It's that sort of bossiness that keeps messing things up.

There's a hammering in my head and it won't go away.

"Mitch," I say again. "I'm tired. Please, let me come in. I just want to sleep."

There's still no sound from within our bedroom. I push down the rising panic. It's okay. She's just fallen asleep. Mitch can sleep anywhere, in any circumstances.

But I really am tired. I go downstairs, while I can still see in the growing gloom, and fetch the gas lamp from the kitchen. Upstairs, I hover on the landing, facing the locket and the door to Mum's bedroom. I stand like that for a couple of minutes, waiting for my heartbeat to slow down. I mouth a silent apology to Mum, then push open her door.

The air's different in here. Dusty, but somehow untainted. It's as if all the badness that has built up in the house since Mum left hasn't got this far. The room is holding its breath, just like I am now.

I place the lamp on the bedside table beside a copy of *Gulliver's Travels*. The spine of the book has cracked. It sits upside-down where Mum left it, as if she might come back at any moment to pick up where she left off.

The lamplight casts a flickering glow on the walls of the small room, doubling off the oval mirror and the part of the window that's not curtained. I stand and look in the mirror and a girl looks back. Her hair is wild on one side and her cheeks look puffy. Her freckles have come out, despite not getting much exposure to sunlight. She looks tired and lost. I neaten my hair a little but the girl doesn't seem to care.

Do I look like Mum? If only we had a photo so I could compare. The freckles are hers, I'm almost certain. I try to picture her, but in my mind's eye she's constantly in motion, her features contorted.

Next to the mirror is a narrow wardrobe. It's filthy. I imagine a layer of grime sealing it shut like parcel tape. It lets out a little cough of dust as I tug the handle and the door groans. I tense up. Would Mitch have heard that next door?

There's only one item of clothing hanging inside. There wasn't much to start with, and in the early days I looted all the useful items, wearing them, wearing them out. Now most of Mum's jumpers and jeans are only useful as supplies of fabric to repair our other clothes.

My fingers trail the length of the single hanging dress. It's impossibly soft, as if somebody's blowing air against my hand. By lamplight the dress looks black but I know that it's indigo. It's covered in white silhouettes of birds. Sparrows, perhaps.

I feel like a naughty kid. How would Mitch react if she knew I was here? Didn't we make a solemn pledge?

I'm breaking promises all over the place today.

I close the wardrobe door, producing a cloud of dust that makes me sneeze. Carefully, I settle myself onto Mum's bed. It feels terribly wrong to be here, but my legs ache so much and the bed's softer than my own. I only just remember to turn off the lamp before sleep pulls me under.

Six

The water and the wind swirl around me, spinning me on the spot and I can't really breathe even though I'm gasping and crying out.

My eyes are open. The light from the gap in the curtains is solid, like a pole jammed into water. I grasp at it and pull myself up and out. So now I'm awake but where am I and where's—

"Mitch?"

It takes me a few seconds to realise I'm not in my bedroom and there's only one bed in here. Mum's bed. And Mum's not here either. Everyone's gone.

"Mitch!"

I swing my heavy legs over the side of the bed and cry out again, this time without forming words. Searing white pain springs through my right foot. I look down. The base of the oil lamp is lying on the floor beside the bed. The glass cover is splintered on the carpet in ugly shards. Did I knock it off the bedside table in my sleep? Wincing, I twist my foot to see one of the shards sticking out of my heel. I gag without bringing anything up.

A dull sound echoes from somewhere, like distant thunder.

Mitch.

The shard comes out of my foot whole, but I'm in such a rush that I rip a gash in my index finger as I pull it out. I push myself off the bed to avoid the smashed glass and burst out onto the landing.

There's something glinting on the floor. Mum's locket. It must have fallen in the night when—when what? The chain is looped into two entwined circles. The locket itself is split in two. I'd never noticed before that it opens on a tiny hinge. I scoop it up and pull the chain over my head instead of hanging it on its nail.

"Mitch! Where are you?"

I hardly notice the pain in my foot as I stumble downstairs. The cold of the kitchen floor wakes me up from my half-sleep.

The back door is open again.

Mitch is in the yard, standing in front of the garage. It's exactly the same spot where I caught her the other day.

Except there's a difference. When she turns to look at me, she's smiling.

I sway on the spot for a few seconds, horrified despite Mitch's expression. I stumble outside on heavy legs.

She's holding the heavy silver padlock in her hand. The metal shutter of the garage has been pushed all the way up on its runners. Light streams into the small brick building. I shield my eyes to see inside.

"There's more than I've ever seen all in one place," Mitch says.

And she's right. Hundreds of silver cylinders reflect the sunlight. The tins of food are stacked against one wall and in clusters on the concrete floor. Biscuits, too, and paper packets and sacks of chicken feed. As much food as Jom's ever brought to us, all here in our back yard.

Mitch takes a step into the garage but I grip her shoulder.

"It's out of bounds," I say.

She looks at me as if I'm mad.

I ignore her and take the padlock from her hand. There's a key still in it. It's tiny, with a faded sticker showing a cartoony, yellow seahorse, dots representing its scaly muzzle. The key and the picture are familiar, but I can't quite place them.

Mitch meets my gaze blankly as I twist out the key. Instead of putting it in a pocket where I might lose it, I place it inside the open locket hanging around my neck. The locket snaps shut with a jangle.

"Don't you want to see all the food?" Mitch says.

I don't, but I can't say so. We both enter the garage but I hang back a little.

"It stinks in here," Mitch says.

It's a rich stench like sulphur. I wonder if the smell has penetrated the tins and packets.

Most of the tins are unlabelled but Mitch calls out the ones that still have packaging. "Peaches, kidney beans, minestrone soup." She pronounces the last one "mine strown". She pats the towers of tins lightly in a happy dance.

I watch, helpless, from the doorway. It's only when Mitch turns her attention to something dark at the back of the garage that I remember how to move. Whatever it is, it's wide and square and it's covered with a thick blanket.

I dart in front of Mitch, standing between her and it. Garden tools lean against the wall to one side, a spade and a fork.

"Leave it alone," I say, trying not to show the dread that I suddenly feel.

Mitch still looks alarmed though, so I keep my voice calm and level to say, "It's not ours, that's all. Come on, let's bring the food in. We deserve to celebrate."

*

It's certainly a feast. Mitch acts like a queen at the head of a banquet table. I don't mind playing the part of the serving staff, bringing her new food to taste. I know that, even now, we should eke out our supply carefully. But how could I explain that to Mitch? She probably can't imagine living long enough to eat her way through all those tins.

"I like *that* one," she says through a mouthful of food, pointing with her spoon at a tin of custard. Rather than pouring it over fruit from one of the other tins, she's been scooping cold spoonfuls into her mouth. "But I don't like *those* ones. They taste like eyes."

I frown. "They're lychees. And how would you know what eyes taste like?"

The spoon waves to dismiss my comment. Mitch grins toothily and a trickle of juice drips down her chin. "Aren't you going to eat any more?"

"I'm full."

I'm not, though. There's a hollowness in the pit of my stomach, but I can't tell whether it's hunger or something else. I lean back in my chair and watch her. She drags the six open tins towards her and hums as she peers into each one.

A thought is gnawing at me. "Where did you get the key to the garage?"

"I found it."

"Where did you find it?"

She pauses mid-chew. "Dunno. Just found it."

I place my hand on my shirt to feel the bump of the locket underneath. The seahorse key jangles faintly within, like it always does. "It was dangerous, opening the garage door."

"I wanted to see what was inside." As if that makes it okay.

"Don't ever do it again."

Mitch shrugs and then nods.

"I'm serious. You said the same last time. *Never* go outside again without me. I want you to promise."

She keeps on munching. Perhaps she's trying to ignore me into leaving her alone.

"Mitch. Promise me."

Her chewing increases in volume, her mouth half open. I know what she's thinking. Finding the food has proved that she was right to be curious.

It'll only get worse.

There's only one way to stop her.

"Promise!" I shout, even though I know it's pointless. "Say it! Promise!"

Mitch's eyes widen in fright and I realise I'm standing up, having kicked away my chair. Wind from somewhere swirls around me, licking at my hair.

"You're scaring me." When she puts down her spoon, her hands are shaking.

"Good. It's good that you're scared. You don't know what's out there, Mitch."

Now she's standing too, but only to back away from me as I approach.

"What *is* out there?" she shouts, "Why don't you just tell me?"

My head throbs with pain. Suddenly I feel tired all over, my body and my mind.

"Go to bed," I say.

Immediately, she does as I say. She doesn't block the bedroom door this time, but when I arrive with a cup of hot chocolate as an apology, she watches me warily. I stand over her as she drinks, then I make her another.

Seven

Mitch's yells wake me in the night. I patrol the house, followed by jangling sounds that lead me back to her. I hold her hair back as she retches into a bucket. I think of Mum constantly. What would she think of me? I was supposed to care for Mitch, and look at her now.

I'm doing my best.

*

In the morning Mitch is weak and isn't able to get out of bed. I bring her food and drinks—cold ones when she's overheating and hot ones when her skin is icy cold.

Between visits to our bedroom, I pace around the house aimlessly. Everything's secure and safe. There are no noises from outside that I can hear. Jom's delivery doesn't appear in the trading box, but it hardly matters now that we've got the food from the garage. If he's left us too, so much the better.

I leave the bedroom door open. Mitch's moans echo around the house.

Finally it grows dark again. She mutters in her sleep. Light, rattling coughs escape from her body. The waves of sound lap at my face and over my head.

*

The next day she's no better. I have to push food between her lips. She barely looks at me. In the evening I make hot chocolate but she swats the mug away weakly. Bubbles form at the corners of her mouth.

I did this.

I don't know what to do, Mum. Something's gone wrong. We're safe in here, but that's not good enough anymore.

Eight

"Mitch!"

The only sound is from the wind outside. Mitch's blanket is thrown back. The bed's empty. On the floor a dark stain spills from the mug lying on its side.

I take the stairs two at a time. The locket jangles around my neck in time with my breathing.

The bathroom, library and kitchen are empty. The chickens in the dining room are silent, as if they understand that something's wrong.

Back upstairs, I check under both beds before returning to the landing. There's only one room left.

"This isn't fair," I say as I push at the door to Mum's bedroom. But she's not here either. There's a layer of dust over everything, including the shards of shattered glass still littering the carpet.

I check and recheck. My headache returns and hurts more than ever. By the time I search each room for the third time I have to concentrate hard to remember what I'm looking for. I find myself tapping at the barricades rather than hunting for Mitch.

I shouldn't be this calm. In the kitchen I make myself a breakfast of crackers and kidney beans with pineapple chunks to follow. When did I last eat? Once I've finished I sweep up the crumbs and rearrange the chairs around the table because one's missing. I clean the stain from the mug in the bedroom. There are sickly white globules stuck to the bottom of the mug. Up close, they stink. I dab my finger in and taste one, but it's vile and makes me feel ill.

I did this.

I have to do all of Mitch's chores for her. I'm not as good as she is at checking the barricades, so it takes me twice as long. But at least I'm satisfied that we're safe.

We?

The safe feeling wears off. I pass through the house like a phantom. I check and recheck the barricades and blinds.

What's happening? Why haven't I gone after her?

Because safety first.

Just because.

*

If I'm going outside, Mum, you're coming with me.

I'm in her room again, tiptoeing around the glass splinters. The locket still hangs around my neck but that's not going to be enough. My hands tremble as I take the blue bird dress from its wardrobe hanger. I pull it on over my clothes. It sits oddly with my jumper rumpled underneath, but I feel stronger right away.

We go downstairs, me and Mum's dress. On the kitchen window above the sink are the ghosts of a small pair of hands surrounded by a greasy halo.

A couple of unwashed chicken-feed pots have fallen from their stacked tower in the yard. Mitch must have knocked them over when she left the house. Does that mean she's still weak? Perhaps she hasn't gone far. I unbolt the inner gate and try to cling onto this small hope.

The missing kitchen chair fills the small gap between the inner and outer gate. Out of habit, I check the trading box but there's nothing inside. The latch on the outer gate is raised up. I push at the gate. It opens.

Bright, direct light bathes my face. The warmth is incredible.

"Is anyone there?" My voice disappears into the open air. Who am I talking to? I shudder as I realise that I don't expect it to be Mitch.

I have to concentrate hard to force myself forward. The outer gateway slides past as if it's moving rather than me.

Now I'm creeping slowly around the corner of the house. I feel off-balance, being outside the house, outside the places I've known for years and years. Standing in an open space makes me feel disoriented, as if I'm floating or maybe sinking. The sound of the wind, only faint from the back yard, is now a roar. Between swoops there's another noise, like somebody drawing breath. But the air against my skin is still and calm.

My eyes adjust to the brightness. There's a wide driveway ahead of me, running alongside the house. It's speckled with weeds that push up from between the cracks of the flagstones. A rusted saloon car sits on two warped concrete tracks tipped up at odd angles, revealing gaps filled with moss. At the end of the driveway two stone gateposts mark the edge of the property, grand enough to suggest that there must be no neighbours. I remember the sense of vast openness that night when we arrived and on the morning of Mum's accident. Beyond the stone posts, a narrow road slips away out of sight.

There are no threats, no shadowy figures, no beasts waiting to pounce. I feel a strange sense of disappointment, mixed with relief.

The view beyond the gateposts makes my heart race. Miles away, at the foot of the hill on which the house stands, waves sweep against a pebbled shore. Spray bursts up as each wave breaks. Each swell corresponds to the sigh that echoes from the hillside behind the house. Not wind, then. Water, all along.

The air hums and groans and pants but I can't breathe all that well.

There's something out there in the water. Small and dark and sharp-ended.

Is it a boat?

No, that can't be right. There are no people to go out in boats.

The water seems to come closer, or maybe I slip towards it. Now that I look more carefully, that's not a boat at all. In fact, there's something terribly wrong out there, something I didn't notice at first.

The water is a muddy reddish-brown. Starting from the horizon, from the object that I thought was a boat, a dark red smudge grows and grows. Soon the spray against the shore is a crimson mist.

My throat constricts as if there's red water in there, too, choking me.

I'm gripping the hem of the bird dress with both hands. Mum wants to help me, but she's scared of the water. Her hands stretch out, trying to reach me. I force my head to turn away and she relaxes a little. I shield one side of my face so that I don't have to see the red water any more.

The area to my right is overgrown with tall grass. It must once have been a garden, but now it's spotted with ugly, thorny bushes. Close to where I'm standing, some of the stalks of grass are broken and trampled.

Is there something in there, flattening the grass?

No.

Oh, please no.

My legs won't move. My throat clogs. I dig my fingernails into my palms to wake myself up, but instead of sitting up in bed I'm still here looking at a black space filled with whatever it is.

I edge forward slowly to the point where the grassy barricade is broken. It's dense and dark in there. I push away the grass with both hands.

Is that—

There's something at my feet, too dark to make out. I swipe at the grass, nicking my hands on the thorns of the bushes. Light from over my shoulder penetrates the gloom.

No.

It's on the ground, lying prone. Lifeless, small. I see limbs and hair.

Please don't let it be.

I'm doing my best.

At least, I did.

The wind picks up. Water sprays from all directions, spinning me around and pulling me under.

My eyes are stinging. It hurts to look.

Suddenly I realise that the thing in the grass isn't lying down, but *squatting*.

It bursts up out of the darkness. I stumble backwards onto the concrete but the thing claws at my face and my hair's snagged and I'm shouting until my throat aches.

Nine

The thing chases me as I clamber along the driveway back to the yard. Its nails jab at my shoulder blades and its wet hair whips my skin. Spittle from its mouth hits the back of my neck and trickles down my back beneath my clothes.

She's not going to let me get away.

Not she. It.

By the time I reach the outer gate I'm on all fours, pulling myself forward with my hands because the thing's got my heavy legs. I pull and pull against its grip and I think I might be shouting or screaming or something. I wrench free, drag myself through the gate and slam it shut. I'm panting, exhausted, with my sodden back against the wood, but there's no time for resting. The sigh of the wind and waves has become a high-pitched squeal that rings in my ears along with the jangling from the key in the locket around my neck.

Instead of ending up inside the house I'm in front of the garage. The chain has become painfully tight around my neck. I fumble with the locket. The seahorse key is tiny and my huge fingers struggle to fit it into the padlock.

Once I've pulled up the metal shutter I stand there swaying like a sleepwalker. Why am I here?

I go inside. It reeks in here. With more than half of the food tins now in the house, the garage is almost empty. The wide rug-covered object still crouches against the back wall. I'm not going near that thing.

Beside it are the garden tools. Weapons. I hold my hand over my mouth against the stench as I grab the spade. My vision blurs again as I leave the garage. I look at the kitchen door as I pass. It's safe in there. Why can't I just go inside?

I kick at the outer gate because my hands are too shaky to turn the handle.

I can't see the thing anymore.

Perhaps it's retreated back into the tall grass. I'm stronger now. I know where I'm going. I approach the same spot as before and push the grass aside.

There.

She's crouching in the same dark place as before, all hair and limbs.

"Mitch?"

Her pose is like a baby animal's. For a moment, I almost feel sorry for her. I bend down to brush away the white bubbles that have dried on her cheek.

I did this.

"It's okay," I say. "It's all going to be okay."

Dead though she is, she doesn't like that. When she leaps up, she takes me by surprise even though I should have been prepared. She spins me around, shaking me until my teeth rattle. I struggle to swing the spade.

Her hair tangles into the tall grass. She doesn't make a sound—how could she?—but I'm shouting for both of us.

As terrifying as it all is, I feel desperately tired. My body's a heavy weight, sinking into the soft ground.

It's almost a relief when she lifts me off the ground. She heaves me around so that I don't have to use my own energy or think for myself. She drags me further into the garden, through the undergrowth. We reach an area where there aren't any thorn bushes and the grass is totally flattened down in the places where it's not a muddy smudge.

I relax my muscles, letting her jab at me, hurling me from place to place while I swing the spade with weaker and weaker thrusts.

My eyes blink slower and slower until they're closed more than they're open.

Ten

She must have let me go.

Is she still out there?

No. Not like she was.

I'm in the kitchen. My back's against a table leg. The spade rests against my thigh, but my muddy hands are still gripping the handle. Both the spade and my shoes are thick with clotted soil.

I fought her off.

Didn't I?

I'm so tired. My shoulder blades ache against the carved wood of the table leg.

I look up at the kitchen window. The handprints are still there, only just visible. Beside them, somebody's written Mitch's name, her real name, in neat, round letters. I frown and look at Jom's note pinned to the cork noticeboard above the table. It's the same handwriting.

I crawl into the library and into the centre of the rug.

I deserve a rest.

Eleven

When I wake up I'm not sad any more.

I'm angry.

Mitch did this. She was lazy and slow. She forgot to trade with Jom. She asked questions and she ran away, and now I'm alone and I prefer it.

I pass through the house like a phantom, a bad one. I throw plates onto the floor in the kitchen and pull a cupboard door off its hinges. I rip pages from books in the library. I pull the blankets from Mitch's bed and hurl them down the stairs.

Even Mum's room isn't safe. I crack the mirror with a fist.

Now I'm standing on the upstairs landing. My head's lowered but I'm looking up, like a cat about to pounce. I'm in front of the barricade that blocks the way to the front of the house.

It's so dark in here.

Darkness doesn't feel all that safe anymore.

So what's it all for, without Mitch?

With a yell I launch myself at the barricade. It feels good just thumping it with my fists and forearms. It doesn't give way at first—it's a good barricade, the best we ever built—but eventually I claw away one of the panels. I smash again and again at the remaining slats, shielding my eyes from splinters with my other hand.

I turn my attention to the covered-up window, using a freed slat to jab at the blinds and wooden panels and fabric covering.

"Mitch!" I shout at the window and the world outside. "Mitch!"

A splintering sound tells me that I've smashed the glass. Light skewers the ripped blinds and the darkness.

I stand panting and retching. Dust particles spin around me in a lattice of light.

"Be calm."

At first I don't even register the voice, like it's just a thought in my head.

"You have to stay safe."

I wheel around. Both bedroom doors are closed. There's nothing behind me.

But the voice is telling the truth, all the same.

I pass through the house. I pretend I'm a friendly ghost like Mum is. I sweep up the mess and fix the cupboard door. The barricades will need closer attention, later. For now, I pin one of the blankets from Mitch's bed over the corridor barricade and another up against the window. The wind and the waves trickle through the smashed glass but at least I can't see them.

*

I'm sitting in the kitchen, concentrating on being angry at Mitch.

"She was selfish," I say. "She wouldn't let me look after her."

Mum sits silently in her chair, the one that Mitch used to sit in. She doesn't speak all that much. Her skin is pale, almost blue, and her hair hangs lank and sticks to her face. I'd tidy it up if only she'd let me get close to her. But maybe it's best to leave her alone. Mum's the one who has to look after me, now that she's back. Isn't that how it should be?

"It wasn't my fault," I say, and take Mum's steady gaze to mean that she agrees.

Her face ripples as though she's looking at me from underwater. Or maybe I'm the one underwater and she's the one trying to reach for me to pull me out. But Mum's afraid of water, isn't she, so why did she bring me out onto the bay in a boat in the first place?

That wasn't my fault.

For the first time I see the dark stain on Mum's head, almost hidden by her hair. She was dead from that before she hit the water, probably. She never did reach out to me once she was down there under the surface, while I was scrambling back into the boat. Her outstretched hands just trailed after her as she sank into the gloom. When I pulled her out her fingers were still curled into claws.

I sigh. A whole meal is laid out before me, but I've barely eaten anything. There are crumbs on the plate, but only because I've mashed up the crackers in my hands.

I watch Mum for a while before I say, tentatively, "I hate Mitch."

Mum just smiles. Yes, I'm right. Mitch was stupid and hateful and wrong all along.

I push the chair away and head into the library.

Mum pads after me.

I don't tell her off for the water she drips onto the rug. That's not my job any more. If she wants to drip, she can drip, and then she can clear it up.

Twelve

I wish Mum would help with all the extra chores, but she just wants to watch. I'm holding nails in my mouth, like the handyman in the photo encyclopedia. I hammer the nails in, careful to avoid my fingers.

It's a good idea to board over the kitchen windows. Was it me or Mum who thought of it? It doesn't matter. The sunlight's getting brighter and brighter each day, and we should keep it out and stay even safer than before. Now that we don't rely on Jom there's no reason to go out into the yard.

Thinking of the yard reminds me that not all of the food is in the house. I jump down from the chair I'm standing on and push open the back door, which is tricky because the boards already stop it from opening fully.

The wind catches at my hair, and the sun's itchy. I stay calm by reminding myself that this is the last time I'll have to go outside. I take the seahorse key from Mum's locket which she lets me wear still. I unlock the padlock and pull up the metal shutters to the garage.

The smell's worse than ever.

I carry the remaining tins into the house, piled into my arms five or six at a time. In the kitchen I pat each of the towers in turn, like it's a dance. Then I go back to the garage even though I've moved all the food.

I take a few steps towards the wide, low, blanketed thing at the back of the building. The smell is richer and rottener here, and I gag. But then I take a few more steps towards it. I'm so very brave, these days. Even so, I reach it before I'm quite ready. My hand pulls away the blanket even though I didn't tell it to.

It's a box. A heavy leather and brass chest. I expect another padlock or at least some obstacle, but the latch is already hanging open. My fingers fit the curve of the metal strip. It's a familiar sensation, as familiar as any of the daily chores. That thought makes my head swim so I lift the lid.

My eyes water. The stench is overwhelming.

At first I think the chest is full of little animal skulls. There are so many of them that they stop being individual objects and more like crests on a whitish-beige sea.

Eggs. All of the eggs meant for Jom.

I lift one and its shell breaks between my fingers. It burps a yellow stench.

I don't understand. I can't bear the smell.

But there's something else in there, too. It's buried underneath the skull-like eggs and the pages ripped from books and the few grey, greasy packages containing our trussed chickens.

All this feels more familiar all the time. Just a part of the normal routine. Check Mitch is asleep. Collect the locket and key from the nail. Open the garage. Dump the eggs. Collect a tin or two for the trading box. Maybe write a note, too. Elegant. Self-contained. But the reasons nag at me and the smell really is foul. I take a deep breath and push through the shells that crackle under my hands.

I find a smaller box. A box within a box.

It's only made of cardboard and egg yolk has stained its warped walls. I retreat away from the big chest and place this new box on the concrete floor.

I pull out a gold-coloured cup stuck to a heavy base. A trophy.

Best Backhand '08.

Next is a photo. At first I think the young girl is Mitch. I gasp when I realise it's me. Beside me is Mum. Her hair's curly and not wet. She's smiling, but not at the camera. At me. There's a man too, but I don't know him. He's wearing a green wax jacket and his beard makes him seem kind. I fold the photo and slip it into my pocket.

There's only one other thing in the cardboard box. I lift out the folded piece of paper, which has soaked up egg yolk to become crunchy and brittle. It's hard to read the writing so I go outside even though I hate how bright it is.

The note says:

Hi Janet & co,
Hope journey was decent. You must be exhausted. Sorry can't welcome you but called away sooner than expected. Help yourself to anything you find & stay as long as you like.
Carrie, pls keep the chickens fed and happy. Michelle, we will meet one day, promise!
Love, Uncle J x

I stare at it for a while without thinking too much about the words.

At the top of the note there's small, printed text. I have to scrape at the paper with a fingernail to reveal it. I can read the words *John Kavanagh* and then a phone number.

The wind swirls around me. It takes the note that's held only lightly between my fingers and nips it away from me. The paper does a somersault and then sails over the gate and out of the yard.

It doesn't matter. It didn't mean anything anyway.

I'm cold even though it's sunny.

Best get indoors.

*

"Whistle while you work, do-da-do-do-do-do-dooo!"

Keeping busy is good.

Once the kitchen window and door are securely covered with thick boards, I head back upstairs with my hammer swinging from a belt buckle.

Mum's already on the landing. That's good. She must be checking the barricades. Four eyes are better than two.

"Do you see any gaps, Mum?"

She's pressed up close to the window as if she's looking outside, even though it's covered. She must have been there for a while. There's a puddle of water on the carpet forming a halo around her. Mum's more see-through than usual today. She moves out of the way to let me pass.

"Thanks, Mum. I'll take it from here."

The new barricade blocking the corridor to the front of the house is better than ever. It's three planks deep at its thinnest point. Nothing's getting through there. Not light, or people, or anything.

But now I can see what Mum was looking at. The window covering is a shoddy job because I was in a hurry when I put it up.

"Sorry, Mum," I say, even though I know she won't tell me off.

I hop onto the stool to fiddle with the fixings. Part of one board has come away entirely. I'm just about to push it back into place when an impulse makes me prise it away from the frame.

I look through the gap. Outside I can see the garden at the front of the house. To the left, almost totally obscuring the grey concrete of the driveway, is the dense grassy area where Mitch had crouched, or lain, or whatever. I'm very brave and I keep looking.

I sense Mum at my shoulder, looking down into the garden too. Drips of water tickle my neck.

I stand on tiptoes, following the direction of her gaze to a space directly below the window. The grass is still flattened down as if somebody's been tramping around out there.

There's a muddy brown smudge down on the ground. In fact, there are two of them. Two thin heaps of soil, side by side. The longer one has begun to sink into the ground and grass and weeds are pushing through. The smaller one is freshly dug. At the head of each one is a cross made from two bound twigs. I look down at my hands, remembering how the twigs snagged at my fingers.

As soon as I look away, the heaps of soil don't seem all that important any more.

I reach into my pocket, pushing past the folded photo, searching for another nail. I must have used the last one downstairs. I pull the nail from the wall beside Mum's bedroom door where the locket used to hang.

I hammer the last board into place.

Commentary on stories

O Cul-de-Sac!

Previously unpublished.

I wrote my first notes on this story in July 2014, after visiting friends who lived in a large, new house in a cul-de-sac set apart from a larger housing estate. I found the concept of houses and families being in such close proximity—all gathered around a turning circle that acted as a peculiar point of focus, all windows angled toward one another—fascinating. I was keen to address the changes in lifestyle I'd experienced after the birth of my first child in September 2013, so I knew that the family that moved into the house in my story would include a newborn baby, the couple consolidating their change in circumstances with a move from the city to the countryside.

My initial story notes and a draft of the first 700-or-so words featured a husband and wife who treated one another with suspicion following a breakdown of communication caused by sleeplessness and the culture shock of becoming parents. The couple would be preoccupied with the past and the future. (*Chloe stroked Becky's cheek as she watched an older Becky, outside, crawling and then, tentatively, walking. Months from now, maybe a year.*) The mother would be intimidated by the neighbours, with whom she had little in common. (*As Chloe shuffled to face each house in turn, light snuck above the rooftops but holding Becky meant that she couldn't shield her eyes. She saw silhouettes in all of the windows.*)

A snippet on the *Answer Me This* podcast a couple of years later provided a potent jumping-off point. A listener wrote in with a moral quandary: she had moved into a new area and a neighbour insisted on washing her car, even though she had refused the offer. Should she pay the neighbour, or ignore the strange intrusion? For some reason, this situation sparked all sorts of new ideas, including circumstances that might lead the young mother to feel more paranoid and more isolated. I removed the husband, introduced an older woman and made the move to the countryside due to necessity and the new mother's fear of the consequences of being discovered. I chose the name Carly before making the connection with the goddess Kali, the 'divine mother' and destroyer.

I can't remember when I became certain that the story would be narrated by a sentient house, who would also be the central character. All I remember is that the first line (*O neighbours! If only we might speak!*) rolled around in my head for an awfully long time before I started writing.

As is usually the way for longer pieces, I let the idea sit and accumulate details. I wrote 'O Cul-de-Sac!' over a three-day period in August 2017, then produced two more drafts over the next handful of days.

Read/Write Head

First published in Garbled Transmissions, 2013.

I gathered steam for a while before I began writing short stories, collecting one-line ideas in a notepad. One such idea was *What would it be like if you could defragment your own mind in the same way as your computer?* The appeal is obvious—a sort of colonic irrigation for the mind, leaving you clean and clear, but like most genre authors I was more interested in the downsides. I think I may have been reading Daniel Dennett and Douglas Hofstadter's book, *The Mind's I*, around this time, and was mulling over the idea that a person, or a persona, is a sum of their experiences and memories—and surely mannerisms are a result of the connections between those memories, those shortcuts that we label 'inspiration'? So how would it be to sever all those fragile connections and start afresh? Not good, is my thinking.

Eqalussuaq

First published in Not One of Us #58, 2017. Selected by Ellen Datlow for The Best Horror of the Year Volume Ten, 2018.

I've been fascinated by sound recordists and foley editors for a long time. In particular, I'm a fan of Chris Watson, who was a member of Cabaret Voltaire and The Hafler Trio, and who now produces the most wonderful ambient/field recordings for Touch Records as well as working as a sound recordist on nature documentaries, including the David Attenborough documentary series, *Frozen Planet*.

This story went through more iterations than most. First titled 'An Empty Vessel' and then 'Surface Noise', it featured a disastrous trip to the South Pole to gather recordings of creaking icebergs—that is, I cribbed directly from Chris Watson, who achieved the incredible iceberg sound footage for Frozen Planet. A chance invitation to write a story for a shark-themed anthology prompted a rewrite to include the Greenland Shark and necessitated a shift from the South to the North Pole. Though the story was accepted, the anthology fell through, but I left the new elements of the story intact and it was soon picked up by *Not One of Us*.

Finding Waltzer-Three
First published in Interzone #255, 2014.
I keep a log of all the writing time I spend on each of my projects (see the commentary on 'By the Numbers' for more about my preoccupation with data). Here's a sobering thought: 'Finding Waltzer-Three' was written in the midst of the first draft of my first published novel, *You Don't Belong Here*, which would eventually require 252 hours of my life to take to its final state—whereas this short story required only three and a half hours to draft and edit, and was promptly accepted for publication in *Interzone*. My first novella had been picked up at this stage (though not yet released), but having a story appear in *Interzone* was my first significant publishing milestone. The story was directly inspired by a haunting, almost static scene from the terrific Czech SF film *Ikarie XB-1* (Jindřich Polák, 1963).

St Erth
First published in Into the Woods, Hic Dragones, 2017.

This is one of my favourite stories I've written, and I'm far less certain of its origins than I am of other stories. I remember that some of the details preceded it (there's a note from 2013 in my 'Ideas' Word file that says *One child shows another a dark stain on a wall where some kid supposedly beat his own brains out, for unknown reasons.*) I read J. G. Ballard's *Concrete Island* in 2014, and I'm guessing that was a factor in the eventual tone of the story, which I wrote the following year. My wife and I did once holiday with friends in Cornwall—we didn't camp in the town of St Erth, though it was during a Google Maps scouring of the surrounding area that I hit upon the title of the story.

Tunnel Vision
First published in Kitchen Sink Gothic, Parallel Universe Publications, 2015.
This is one of the rare stories I've written that is based almost entirely on personal experience. At primary school, aged ten, I really did suffer from tunnel vision, which crept in during afternoon lessons. In the bathroom I considered praying to a God I already didn't believe existed. I thought that it was a done deal that I was dying, to such an extent that it wasn't worth telling anybody. I even went to my after-school swimming session, barely able to see more than a palm-sized patch in the centre of my normal field of vision.

Days later I made a correlation between the tunnel vision and a banging of heads with a friend while playing tig in the school playground. It would be a couple of decades before I mentioned the story to anybody else, having held onto a sort of shame for the bathroom prayer in particular.

The Eyes Have It
First published in The Third Spectral Book of Horror Stories, Spectral Press, 2016.
I often think I'd have liked to have trained as an optician. There's something about such a specific area of expertise that

appeals to me, and I find eyes fascinating in a technical as well as an emotional sense. This story idea was another very early one (April 2012), with the initial story note: *An optician begins to see something when he stares deep into the eyes of his patients. Something lurking there?* It's an idea I'm certain I'll return to at some point in a longer piece.

The Forge
Previously unpublished.
The origin of this story was an idea I noted down in January 2015: *Telling convincing lies by actually making yourself believe them (by changing your own brain patterns?)* Early plot outlines involved a serial identity thief and, later, an assassin, but I eventually settled on a love rival trying to win back an ex-partner by making himself more like the 'new man'. Again, I suspect I'll return to this idea in the future.

All I Can See Are Sad Eyes
First published in The Literary Hatchet #13, 2015.
I suppose this is thematically similar to 'The Forge'. At some point in 2014 I made this note: *In a crowd, a man notices a woman. She's interesting, but he's attached and that's that. She appears again and again. He approaches her, she doesn't recognise him. She keeps reappearing, and he becomes obsessed and paranoid. Who is she? Why does she ignore him? He contacts the police, but what can he report? His life unravels.*

I suppose the interesting part, for me, was 'His life unravels'. Why would that be? I relished the idea of a personal catastrophe prompted by almost nothing.

Winter in the Vivarium
First published in Winter Tales (Fox Spirit), 2016.
This was written in response to a call for submissions for the Fox Spirit anthology *Winter Tales*, edited by Margrét Helgadóttir. My

brainstorm for themed story ideas in June 2015 went as follows:

Explorers digging through ice to discover C21st town

People using VR to experience summer

People playing a snowbound VR game called 'Winter'

Captain Oates sacrifice played on larger scale—e.g. to save city

Ice sculptures appear—cf Anthony Gormley statues

Center Parcs societies—heated tropical towns in snowscape

All good ideas, I feel, and obviously the fifth and sixth were both incorporated into 'Winter in the Vivarium'. The inspiration for the dome was specifically the 'subtropical swimming paradise' at Center Parcs in Woburn Forest in Bedfordshire, which I visited around Christmas in 2014 with my wife's family. Snow had covered the outdoor swimming areas and made a bizarre contrast with the goggle-shaped window that acted as a portal into the dazzling, foliage-filled dome. The snow statues and their sudden manifestations are explicitly modelled on the spindly Gormley figures that appeared on the rooftops of Oxford at some point in the early 2010s.

Lines of Fire

First published in Game Over, Snowbooks, 2015.

This was another story written for a themed anthology: *Game Over*, edited by Jonathan Green for Snowbooks. (This story acceptance would later be a factor in Snowbooks taking on my first novel, I'd have thought.) Having chosen Bomberman as the classic videogame to inspire the story, I wove in memories of a visit to a friend's house at an awkward age when he had discovered women as a source of lust and I hadn't (the 'erect nipples' conversation still makes me wince), plus the grid-based layout of a half-remembered holiday cottage complex. The story was originally titled 'Oh Sinnerman, Where You Gonna Run To?' after the Nina Simone lyric, but was sensibly changed by Jonathan Green.

'Honey spurge': Confidental report into dispersal, growth and catastrophe
Previously unpublished.
I'm not much interested in botany, but still I noted down the baffling-to-me name *Euphorbia X Pasteurii / E mellifera X E stygiana* after encountering it at the Oxford Botanic Gardens on an outing with my son, who was gleeful about the seed pods that pinged open in the heat. As he danced up and down, taunting the plant, I was quietly developing a scenario of Triffid-esque calamity—typical behaviour. I'll be honest: the concept of presenting the story as an 'executive summary' written by an civil servant was partly in order to avoid laborious botanical research.

By the Numbers
First published in Voluted Tales Vol. 14 Issue 10, 2013.
The central concept was one of those ideas hit upon in the pub, long before I tried my hand at writing fiction. I suppose I must have been using spreadsheets a lot at the time—my first job in educational publishing involved long stretches of wallowing in metadata. A little later I would become interested in quantifying how I was using my free time. In fact, it was an exercise in logging how much time I played videogames, watched TV, and so on that led to my writing my first novel. That is, after spending two weeks noting how many hours I frittered away, I felt certain that I had plenty of time to dedicate to NaNoWriMo, in which an each member of an internet community tries to produce a 50,000-word novel during the month of November (though, true to solitary form, I did it solo in February 2011). Anyway, I'd read several articles on the 'quantified self', which amounted to 'life hacks' aimed at using time productively. My first pub question was this: 'What would it be like to have all the numerical data about your own life?', and then, 'How much would you pay for it?' At the time my answers would have been respectively, 'amazing' and 'a lot'. By the time I wrote 'By the Numbers' (in June 2012) I was far less sure I'd have wanted that data, an opinion evidenced by its effect on the protagonist of the story.

The House Lights Dim

First published in Sanitarium Issue 11, 2013.

This is the first short story I ever wrote, or rather, the first I ever completed. On 26th March 2012 I booked a day off work, strolled to an event at the Oxford Literary Festival ('What's the Point of the Arts and Humanities?' with a panel featuring Alan Moore, Josie Long and Philip Pullman), then stopped off at G&D's ice cream café on Cowley Road, opened my laptop and started writing. During the previous year I'd made some notes and some abortive first sentences of what I'd initially intended to be a novel, but this time I was determined to start and finish a piece in a single sitting. The resultant tone was a little stiff and old-fashioned, and the piece was unconsciously modelled on the style and early scenes of John Wyndham's *The Day of the Triffids*, which is still one of my most fundamental influences. But I completed it and that felt amazing.

I'd end up stockpiling a few stories before starting to send them out in earnest. Gratifyingly, 'The House Lights Dim' ended up being my first published story, appearing in *Sanitarium* in July 2013. It was also made the main cover story, which did no end of good for my confidence.

Carus & Mitch

First published as a standalone novella, Omnium Gatherum, 2015.
A version of this blog post appeared on the upcoming4.me website in February 2015.

For such a short book, 'Carus & Mitch' involved a lot of work. Or rather, a lot of work ended up contributing to 'Carus & Mitch'. Or rather, I worked through an awful lot of bad ideas to find a good one.

I started writing seriously about four years ago. Like a few other writers I've met, the push from intending-to-write-something-someday' to actually-writing-something-right-now was provided by NaNoWriMo, the November writing challenge. I was impatient to get started, though, and completed my first 50,000 word draft of a novel in February 2011.

It was awful. I promise that 'Carus & Mitch' has no connection with that sorry collection of words. Nor will any other novel that could ever be considered publishable.

Undeterred, I completed another 50,000 word draft of a different novel in November 2011.

It was pretty shabby. 'Carus & Mitch' bears no relation to that novel either.

But the floodgates had opened. I wrote short stories, planned out novels and studied my favourite authors.

In November 2012 I wrote a YA novel about two young girls who lived entirely alone. When they finally left their house, adventures ensued.

It wasn't too bad, on the whole. But I revised it several times before I realised that what I'd written was actually two distinct stories. In the first story, Carus and her younger sister lived alone in a remote house, fearful of the dangers outside. In the second story, Carus had a series of episodic adventures while travelling across a destroyed Britain. The first part was creepy and bleak; the second part was a romp involving canal-boat chases, fake ghosts and rival soldiers warring over a supermarket. They didn't match up at all.

I took other writers' good advice and put the manuscript away. For a whole year, as it turned out. I had plenty of other story ideas that flowed more easily. When I reread the novel, I stopped at the point where the first part ended. I felt pretty sure that there was something interesting there.

I've always been a fan of stories structured as mysteries, with details being withheld from the reader. And I'm crazy for unreliable narrators in fiction. Having made the decision to keep Carus and her sister Mitch within their house, I wanted to raise all sorts of questions about what may be outside, without revealing it. And then I changed my mind entirely about what actually was outside the house. I began to really enjoy the thought of writing a post-apocalyptic story without any vision of the apocalypse or even its after-effects. All that the girls would know would be that there were dangers outside. The final wrinkle in this new story would be that Carus, but not Mitch, had once lived elsewhere, but at such a young age that all of her memories would be untrustworthy.

Once I had the plan straight in my mind, writing 'Carus & Mitch' was no trouble. It involved a month's work from start to finish including editing, writing no more than a couple of thousand words each day in the hour before my day job began.

It's difficult to say how much those earlier, aborted drafts fed into the final version of the book. But I do know that the process of writing 'Carus & Mitch' has been invaluable to me, in terms of identifying the aspects of a story that really appeal to me, and in terms of identifying the type of writer I'd like to be. I enjoy writing unsettling, domestic stories and I like puzzles. I'm a huge fan of John Wyndham and Shirley Jackson, and their fingerprints are all over the story, as much as my own.

I don't think I'll ever finish that YA adventure romp.

Book soundtracks

Like many writers, I work to music. For me, it's music that's barely music—drones, washes, minimal thrum or industrial groan. I'm in awe of people that can work in silence. Some people swear by writing in coffee shops, which I understand—regular hum and chatter is better than no background noise at all. The crime writer Ian Rankin often refers to albums that he considers totemic while writing, including Mogwai and Aphex Twin—they disappear into the background, a bed upon which ideas settle. My totemic albums change from project to project, though common denominators include *Biokinetics* by Porter Ricks, *Grapes from the Estate* by Oren Ambarchi, *Water Park* by Dirty Beaches and *Transverse* by Carter Tutti Void.

I've taken to using music to support my writing in another way, too, though it's also partly ceremonial. When I've completed a first draft of any project of novelette length or longer, I create a playlist that, for want of a better term, I call a soundtrack. It's generally unrelated to the music I've been playing while writing. Instead, the playlist is an attempt to pin down the tone of the story—or, more often, the tone I'll be aiming for during rewrites. Some of the track choices may be literal—named songs often crop up in my stories—and others are more about capturing a particular mood. I'm as much a film-lover as a book- and music-lover, so I'm unabashed about imagining the playlist as the soundtrack of the 'film of the book'.

I'm the worst kind of nerd, the type that is a stickler for rules, however arbitrary. Here are my guidelines for creating a book soundtrack:

1. The first and last tracks ought to work as an accompaniment to the story's 'opening and closing credits'.
2. The playlist should include both diagetic (i.e. in-world) and non-diagetic (i.e. conventional overlaid soundtrack) music.
3. Broadly, the tracks should reflect the mindset of the central

character(s).

4. The ordering of the tracks should reflect the changing mood or plot events.

5. Despite Rule 4, the playlist should be listenable in its own right, without sounding jarring. Unless jarring sounds good.

Rule #3 is an important one. My stories are mostly first-person or close third-person POV, so I need to have a pretty good idea what makes my main characters tick. The soundtrack usually turns out to be useful in this respect.

'O Cul-de-Sac!' and 'Carus & Mitch' have many similarities: they both feature female characters almost exclusively, they're confined to single interior locations, they're preoccupied with a fear of what may be outside. Their soundtracks are correspondingly similar, too.

'O Cul-de-Sac!'

My Love, My Love – Julia Holter
Opening credits. Julia Holter singing Karen Dalton's lost lyrics is as heartbreaking as you'd expect until the oboe or an organ comes in and is that a train? and it builds and builds and now there's feedback and birdsong and maybe someone making a cup of tea and that was bloody beautiful.

(There Ought to Be) A Moonlight Savings Time – Buddy Campbell and His Orchestra
I often have this kind of 20s tune in mind during benign scenes in which characters potter around. Imagine this track sung by the house as it gazes up at the night sky, revelling in its new occupants.

By Whom And Why Am I Previously Unreleased? – Fire! with Jim O'Rourke
The juddering picks up from the sense of unrest at the end of 'My Love, My Love' and, to my mind, it is the sound within the walls of an uneasy house.

Secret Love – Doris Day

The house is female, I think, and if it could speak it might sound a little like Doris Day. The lyrics are simultaneously lovely and terrifying, which is very much the tone I was aiming for with the story itself.

Peace – Oliver Coates

Another interpretation, this time of Micachu / Mica Levi's composition, a sleepy cello piece that contains an undercurrent of dread. Let's say it conveys the house's growing realisation about the dynamic of its new family.

Beast – Aldous Harding

While the male vocalists in this soundtrack represent non-diagetic music, all of the female singers represent the voice of the house. If the house would speak like Doris Day when content, Aldous Harding's wavering melodies introduce notes of hysteria as it learns more about its resident family.

Doctor, Lawyer, Indian Chief – Hoagy Carmichael

Final scene and closing credits. Another gorgeous tune with uncomfortable undertones, not least because of its outdated racial stereotypes. Carly sings this song herself in the story, and in an early draft the lyric about changing home address threw the house into blind panic.

Listen to the soundtrack to 'O Cul-de-Sac!' on Spotify at spoti.fi/2FWemM6

'Carus & Mitch'

Générique (Thème de Myriam) – Pierre Henry

Opening credits. An uncharacteristically swooning piece from the pioneer of musique concrète. And that rumbling, gut-punch of an ending! Visualise a high exterior shot of the house, tracking smoothly closer and closer, the wind blowing leaves around. The increasing suspicion that just beyond the frame of the 'screen' might be ruin, ruin, ruin.

Happy Birthday to Love – Tommy Dorsey
An introduction to the superficially peaceful world of Carus and Mitch. Mitch presents her birthday gift and the girls waltz together around the room, chickens clucking at their heels.

A House Safe For Tigers (choir) – Lee Hazlewood
·I find this choral track from Lee Hazlewood's soundtrack to Torbjörn Axelman's film endlessly replayable. The lyrics sum up Carus's maternal attitude towards Mitch—that is, her hope that Mitch will 'never need to die' and 'never learn to cry'. The switch from 'safe for tigers' in the title to 'safe from tigers' in the lyrics introduces a lovely ambiguity—is the threat inside or outside the house?

Lichter 3 – The Notwist
The Notwist have produced some terrific indie-pop albums, but I've often used their instrumental *Lichter* EP as a background to writing. This track is inserted here for pacing, and to reflect the relative contentment of Carus's and Mitch's strange life.

Whistle While You Work – Artie Shaw & His New Music
Mitch sings this while cleaning, of course, though she struggles with the whistling section in the original version from Disney's *Snow White and the Seven Dwarfs*. She has never seen this, or any, film.

Autumn – Heslington Primary School
This 'song' (from Trunk Records' superb *Classroom Projects* compilation of tracks from educational LPs for schools) represents Mitch's peculiar education, and her increasing disorientation.

The Sad Panther – Colleen
Disorientation is the name of the game here. Music boxes played backwards? That'll do nicely.

Poppies (live) – Buffy Sainte-Marie
I find this track incredibly eerie—particularly the final minute in which it degrades into stuttering, staccato snippets of melody. The references in the lyrics to dreams and caution might easily have been expressed by Carus.

The Piano Drop – Tim Hecker
I listened to Tim Hecker a lot while writing, and this track from *Ravedeath, 1972* has long been my favourite. It continues the juddering ending of 'Poppies', expanding it into something more cosmic, with odd moments of warmth. It's the soundtrack to Carus being in denial.

Aurinkotuuleen – Paavoharju
The Fonal Records compilation *Summer and Smiles of Finland* is another album that often provides a background to my writing. Like the Hecker track, this conveys warmth whilst also sounding utterly broken. At this point in the story, Carus is suffering panic attacks.

Loch Raven – Animal Collective
While Animal Collective have become more of an outright pop outfit in recent years, their 2005 album *Feels* is often quiet and haunting. I love the sparse drumbeat and the delirious tinnitus-ring in this track. Also, *Feels* was the soundtrack to a car journey I made in California a decade or so ago, travelling the length of a vast lake that provided an important image for the end of the story.

Saturday Sun – Nick Drake
End credits. Carus hammers nails into the final board across the window, blocking out the sunlight for good.

Listen to the soundtrack to 'Carus & Mitch' on Spotify at spoti.fi/2DuB4fS